# A Flame Worth the Candle

Arthur Kevin Rein

OPEN
BOOKS

Published by Open Books

Published by Open Books

Copyright © 2023 by Arthur Kevin Rein

Interior design by Siva Ram Maganti

Cover image © Studio Peace shutterstock.com/g/ArtemZakharov

*For Barb*

# Prologue

I'm not ready to write this book. I should wait for the hand of time to steady mine, to heal the wounds that still weep. Then I remember that, in a sense, I have already waited. I speak of events that happened eight years ago, in 2013, a time I have already written about. But that was different, a tale of high times and innocence when compared to what came after. In the months between I've discovered a new truth: the loves we cannot have are the ones that never die. There is a danger in a statement so simple because sometimes words have two meanings, and the intoxicated mind will always opt for the one most comfortably at hand.

My life is on hold now. I'm in the middle of a year-long, self-imposed break—a fact that is itself part of the story I'm trying so hard to avoid. The pen has betrayed me, luring me to places I'm loathe to remember, much less enter. I know of what I speak. Timing is a cruel master. Had I been sitting in a different chair, it wouldn't have mattered. Put me on a different rotation, on another floor, away from that awful place and I'd have never known. And she wouldn't have felt compelled to give up her life for mine.

# CHAPTER ONE

# The Ghost Returns

I was looking at a ghost. I don't mean that in the literal sense, of course, although he was on the gaunt side of thin and the cast of his skin close enough to pale to make me wonder where he'd spent the summer. No, it was because Diane, his younger daughter and by all accounts a highly reliable source, had told me this man was dead. Yet, here he was, drinking a Sharp's near beer in Noquebay Tavern in the middle of August. Stranger still he should have found his way to our resort on the north shore of Red Wolf Lake in Northern Wisconsin. Then it was clear. He was looking for her, for Diane. He was there with two others, and they had told him where to find her. He should have been around fifty years old, but he looked older by a decade, his face like an old road, a dead end of fissures and potholes. He pulled out a cigarette.

"Sorry, no smoking." Another part of bartending I wouldn't miss, cigarette smoke.

"You're shittin' me. I can't smoke in a bar? Since when?"

"2010. Three years now."

"You haven't met Sammy Robel. He's the tobacco cop around here."

The snide remark came from Steve Manticore. This was the first time I'd seen him since our near-death match in a row boat a month earlier. During the fight, we'd fallen into Red Wolf Lake. I could swim; he never learned. Then his motionless body began its slow descent. Diane was there. She sent me after him, and I fished him out.

Sitting on the other side of the ghost was his son, Ben Warren. The middle of three children, he was the only one of Carter and Ethyl Warren's kids, so far as I could see, who didn't win the genetic lottery. Both of the girls were pretty, Diane especially so. Jean had married into the powerful Manticore family, then disappeared six years ago. Diane and I had spent the first half of the summer chasing the identity of a body at the bottom of the lake thinking it was Jean. Ben was never involved in any of that. In fact, even though I'd been dating his sister for a month, this was the first time I'd gotten a good look at him. His eyes were recessed under a prominent, sinister brow. He was only in his twenties, but already he had a good start on a beer paunch. Diane had told me he wasn't married, but steady with the same girl for five years. He worked at the ski factory in Walnut Creek for non-union wages and benefits and thought he had the world by the ass. "We can go home and drink, Dad," Ben said. "Wait for her there."

Carter Warren shook his head and put the smoke away. "Guess I been away too long. These headaches are killers. A beer and a smoke usually help."

Steve pointed at the Sharp's. "Ain't no alcohol in that one. And Carter, you're not the first to get a headache from this bartender. You got any Advil?"

"Nah, left them in the car." He pointed at Ethyl Warren's old Chrysler, the one Diane often drove, so I had to believe this really was her old man.

We had a bottle of ibuprofen on the back shelf. I spilled a couple of pills into my hand and put them on the bar. "Here you go. Maybe help that limp of yours too." He looked the type that had seen a lot of pain: thick skinned, thick jointed especially in the wrists where, on the left he wore a wristwatch with the face on the inside of the forearm, a habit I'd somehow associated with a short temper and a bad disposition. Much like Steve, he was thin and muscular at the same time. Their clothes were different, of course. Steve wore his usual: tight jeans and a tight t-shirt. Carter looked as though he had purchased everything a size too large.

He downed the medicine with a swig of Sharp's and nodded a thank you. "You must be this Sam Robel I been hearing about." I told him I was. "Your dad runs the place for how long now?"

"This is our first summer." He asked how business had been. I gave him the usual upbeat response, though that wasn't true. Our first year in business had been a trial by fire. We'd been up and down at best, but Dad wouldn't want me talking family business in the bar to a stranger.

Carter got off the barstool and stretched a kink out of his right hip. "I shoulda been better to this body. No, and that's the truth. When did you say Diane supposed to be back?"

"Any time now." I wiped down the under-bar and shelved some glasses. "Should I call her? She'll want to know her father's waiting for her."

"Oh, I'm sure you're wrong. No, don't call. I need surprise on my side."

Steve sniffed then laughed derisively. "Still can't see the forest for the trees, Robel."

Steve looked a mess. His eyes were bloodshot and his nose was running. "You allergic to something, Manticore? Maybe you've been too much in the woods."

His eyes passed coldly across my face. "Mind your own business."

Another customer called for something down the bar. As I walked away I wondered what Steve was doing with a former convict. Carter Warren had already told me he'd been home to see his wife, Ethyl, for the first time in ten years. Sure, she'd visited him while he was doing twenty years in the Wisconsin Prison System for accidentally killing a man while robbing his home. Released early, he said, for good behavior, but still on probation.

My father walked in the tavern from the short hallway that came from our kitchen in the central part of the lodge. It was a Friday afternoon, too early for the evening rush. Besides Carter and Steve, a couple from Cabin #1 had brought their two kids up to play the pinball machines. Dad came behind the bar and asked how I was doing. An inch taller than me, he was still fit in

3

his forties, and wore glasses similar to mine.

I said, "Everything's good. Coolers are full. Ah, Dad, this is Carter Warren, Diane's father."

Dad hid his surprise well. In the time Diane and I had been dating, she'd become good friends with my parents. Not only that, she'd had many meals with our family, shared the work in the bar and around the resort, and went on trips to town to pick up supplies when needed; which is where she was at this particular time. Therefore, Dad was under the same impression as me, that Carter was dead. The situation was awkward.

I said, "He's waiting for Diane. She should be here any second." Just then she appeared out front, driving our SUV into the resort.

"Does Diane know you're here, Carter?" Dad asked.

"No. Haven't seen her in ten years."

Dad lowered his brow. "She'll be coming in the back door in a minute. Maybe it'd be better for you to come back in the kitchen."

"Well," Carter growled. "I don't wanna—"

"No problem." Dad put his hand on Carter's shoulder. "Bring your beer. Diane is like family. We love her. Great girl you got there."

Carter slipped off the barstool and grabbed his Sharp's. "I guess. I wouldn't know too much 'bout that."

Ben stayed put, but Steve made a move to get his beer and follow along.

I said, "Not you, Steve. We'll be back."

By then, Dad had Carter halfway down the hall. "Well, I do know her. She's something else." Dad handed him off to me and went back to the bar.

Carter's sallow complexion gained a couple shades of color. He asked to make a stop in the restroom which was right there. While I waited for him, I heard Diane come in the back door with the groceries and other supplies from town. Carter emerged, his dark brown hair rearranged but not combed, his shirt tucked.

"Okay, let's go," he said.

I hesitated. "Ten years she hasn't seen you." I opened my hands. "She never came to visit?"

"Never. All the others did, but not Diane." He looked down.

4

"She's a tough one. I've written letters, askin' her to come and see me, but never got a reply." There was the first sign of softening in Carter's leathery face. "I'm not above askin.' She's my youngest and all, but I ain't gonna beg."

Diane had a stubborn streak, and now I could see where it came from. Somehow, that also reminded me of her irreverence, which I loved so much. She was a social rebel, drinking and smoking from her mid-teens. I tell myself now, that was more of Carter's DNA showing through. At the same time, she was refined at the dinner table. When she ate with us, the only person at the table who didn't learn anything about manners was my mother. Diane could swear like a longshoreman and had no pity for the sexually prudish, but harm an animal or play the bully to a soft-hearted soul and you'd feel her burn.

I worried how she would react to Carter walking in on her. I was about to find out.

I opened the door to the kitchen. Carter and I entered. Mom was just in front of us, at the kitchen table unpacking groceries. Her daytime attire was shorts and a blouse, tennis shoes and anklets. I didn't see Diane. Her voice came from the open pantry to my immediate right. "Liz, where do you want the extra sugar?" She came into the kitchen holding a five-pound bag in her right hand like a shotput. She saw me and smiled. She had eyes, dark, almond-shaped and glistening, that charmed me so easily I sometimes had to look away to remember what I was thinking. In the last couple of weeks, she'd toned down her clothes; probably my mother's influence. She still wore the short shorts, because her legs demanded nothing less, or more. But her blouses and make-up only went on the wild side when we went out, which was rarely. Her gaze went immediately to Carter.

She gasped. The bag of sugar dropped and exploded on the floor with a thud. Her eyes narrowed. She grabbed hold of my arm. In a shaky voice, she asked, "Why? How? How did he get here?"

Mom could read Diane's reaction as well as me. "Sam, who is this?"

"Get rid of him, Liz." Diane's anger was palpable. "He's no

5

good. He should be in prison. He must've escaped. Call 911."

"Was in prison." I put my hand on Diane's as she squeezed my arm. "Released on good behavior."

Diane laughed in a way that seemed painful.

"That's right." Carter was now on my left, facing Diane. "And I know it's a surprise Diane, but I'm out fair and square. I'm glad to see you."

"Well, I'm not happy to see you."

"Diane, now, have some respect. We're in this lady's house and I'm still your father."

"I haven't had a father for ten years." Diane let go my right arm. "You can't just walk in like this. It might work with Ethyl but it won't work with me."

Carter inched forward. "I already talked to your mom. Going there now. Thought we could ride together. She's makin' a special homecoming supper. She wants everyone to be there—your brother, you and me. Just like old times."

"Old times! Old times? What about Jean?" Diane asked. "How can it be 'old times' without her? She's still missing, or don't you care? Don't they let you read the papers in Waupun Prison? Six years now. Sam and I spent the whole summer trying to track her down. The body at the bottom of the lake wasn't her." She stopped for a moment and scrutinized her father. "Are you shaking your head? What's that supposed to mean? Don't believe me? Or the story? Well, it's all true. So, no, it won't be like 'old times' and no I won't be going home with you."

Carter took a half step toward Diane. "But you're being—"

"You have your answer, Mr. Warren," said my mother. "We'll give Diane a ride when, and if, she needs one."

Carter halted, nodded, and thought for a moment. He took the last swig from his bottle of near beer and set it on the table. "Guess I done what I can." He turned and went back down the hall.

Mom shut the door. I turned to Diane. Tears welled in her liquid, brown eyes. I pulled her to me. She sobbed into my shoulder. "You wanna sit down?" I asked. She gave a little shake of her head.

Mom drew a glass of water and gave it to Diane. Then we stood a minute longer until she had control of her breathing. We sat down at the kitchen table. Diane apologized for "bringing round my family's dirty laundry." Then apologized again. Once Mom and I got her over her anguish and embarrassment, she was able to tell us more about Carter:

"This doesn't make any sense. I honestly didn't expect to see him so soon. The last I heard, he wouldn't be up for parole for another four years. By then, I'd be long gone, and Sam," she waved her tear-soaked tissue at me, "you'd be at school, and everyone else I lied to wouldn't know or care."

"Do you feel safe going home tonight?" Mom asked. "Because if you don't—"

"No, I'll be fine. It's where I live. Not going to let him walk in and knock me out of my house. He thinks prison was tough." Jaw set, brow lowered, Diane looked away.

Until that very second, I'd been locked in. But that determined *I'll beat the shit out of that convict* look of hers just struck me as funny. I stifled a laugh.

Mom's shoulders sagged.

Diane side-eyed me. "What? You don't think I mean it?"

"No, not at all. I know you do, every word. It's just that you're all of five foot seven, one hundred fifteen pounds and he's, well..."

"I know. I know." She had to purse her lips away from a smile too, so I didn't feel so bad.

"I wouldn't want to be him tonight, that's for sure."

"Good answer," Diane said.

Mom said, "If things go south, you can always come here."

"Thank you." Diane smiled. "I have my aunt and uncle down in #5 too."

"Wes and Fanny! That's right," I said. "They were talking about winterizing that cabin anyway, making it year-round. They wouldn't mind a sublet. And you *are* their favorite niece."

A few minutes later, I was driving Diane home. She was mostly quiet, mentally preparing I'd imagined for the meal and the evening before her. There was something about her father's reappearance that stuck in my brain all afternoon. I wanted to ask her about it before we arrived. She'd told a lie because she was ashamed of the skeletons in the family closet. Fine. She'd said it to me back in the day when we were friends, nothing more. I didn't deserve to know everything back then. No problem. But once we started dating, even then she didn't trust me with the real story. That hurt. That smoldered like the slow sting of a second-degree sunburn at two in the morning.

"I just don't see why you didn't tell me," I said. We were less than a half-mile from her place.

"I didn't think it was important."

"Not important." I paused. "You sacrificed five pounds of sugar to not important." I slowed to turn into the driveway.

She flushed. "Listen, I can't talk about this now. I've got enough in my brain already."

I pulled to a stop. She gathered her things. It was then I noticed her father and brother, Carter and Ben, sitting in green and white lawn chairs on the backyard grass, Carter with his Sharp's and Ben with his PBR in hand. Diane got out, walked to the front of the car, and stopped. Both men stood up. The original plan was a simple drop off, but this looked like an ambush. I got out of the car, but did it slowly as if it'd been planned all along. I didn't want to look like some kind of hero to the rescue. These guys wouldn't have an appreciation for that. I said hi to them. I have never been any kind of actor, and they weren't buying what I was selling. Neither offered me anything to drink.

Carter tipped his bottle in my direction. "Wasn't sure my lovely daughter was going to show. Much appreciated, Sam, you driving her back. You wouldn't think a father gone ten years now, home for the first time'd have to worry 'bout such things but... well, there you go."

Diane crossed her arms. "I was asked to come. Here I am. And... I *live* here."

I shut the door to the car.

Ben shifted his hips. "Don't recall an invitation for you, Sam."

Staying for dinner was the last thing on my mind. I only wanted to be sure Diane got in the house safely, or, if she wanted, could leave with me. "She's got a couple of my CDs. I'm here to pick them up."

Diane caught the ruse right away. "Come on, Sam. They're in my room."

We walked past Carter and Ben, their bottles steady, their gaze following as we entered the back-porch door and headed for the second-floor steps. Ethyl was in the kitchen, presumably making supper. Someone was singing "I Just Called to Say I Love You" by Stevie Wonder. It had to be a cover because it was a female voice. Then I realized it was acapella. I stopped on the second step and said, "Diane!"

She was in front of me. She looked back and asked what was the matter.

"Who's singing?"

"That's Ethyl. Surprising, hey? I haven't heard that in years. Come on."

We got to the top of the steps, and I said. "She's got a pretty voice. You never told me."

"Carter did too, before the cigarettes ruined him. Why? Do you sing?"

"I wish. But I know a good voice when I hear it."

Diane rummaged around her room in search of a CD she could give me to make the story plausible. I said, "Were you and your dad always this way, you know, the cats and dogs thing?"

She sat down heavily on her bed. "I guess not. They tell me I had him wrapped around my finger when I was little. I don't remember. What I know is that he missed both of my Christmas concerts, fourth and fifth grade. I sang a solo both times. He never showed. I was heartbroken. Turned out he was with the boys, couldn't get away. I never sang again."

"No chorus. No Glee Club? No singing in the shower when you're all alone?"

"Maybe you'll find out... someday."

"And you're all right staying here?"

"I'll be fine. I can handle this group. Carter talks tough but only acts it outside the house."

"Diane, he might not be the same. He's been in prison for ten years," I said.

But she would not be persuaded. She slapped the CD in my hand and we went back downstairs. The family was seated around the table.

Carter asked, "Got what you came for, son?"

I wasn't his son, but wasn't going to make a point of it just then. Somehow that phrase always triggered me unless it was said by my father. I held up the CD. "Yes, sir."

"Then be on your way," Carter said. "This is the supper hour around here."

Ethyl straightened. "Carter, there's no need to snap at Sam like that. He's been a great help to me these last weeks."

"So has the garbage man," Carter retorted. "And we don't have him for dinner either."

"Real classy, Carter," Diane said. "You've come a long way."

# CHAPTER TWO

# Sunday Driver

Diane called Sunday morning. I paid close attention to the sound of her voice, listened for sounds of strain or duress, asked her yes and no questions about how she was doing just in case someone was listening. Everything checked out, so far as I could tell.

The first evening meal with Carter was pretty quiet from Diane's point of view in that Ben and Carter did most of the talking. They spoke mostly of hunting and trapping. I could almost hear Diane's eyes rolling in their sockets. Ethyl sat by, grinning like a cat, happy to ignore the question they should have been asking, *why oh why, dear father, did they let you out of prison so soon?*

"But no one wanted any part of that," Diane said. "I'm sorry this blew up our whole weekend. We're having more family over today. Think you can come over tomorrow night? I'll give you all the gossip then."

We set a time. I sighed and ended the call. August wasn't the height of summer. There was, in fact, always a sense of desperation tinging the air, that whatever had been left undone better get to it, for time was growing short. Diane and I didn't feel this urgency in the same way. She was looking for work. I was going back to school and staying home. Where she would end up was anyone's guess. The job market in Walnut Creek was trash for anyone with a head on their shoulders and more than an ounce of ambition. She had one excellent offer, an office position at a road construction company that offered good hours, pay, and benefits with an opportunity for advancement. The only problem was the job was in Green Bay at Van Zandt Construction with her aunt and uncle, over an hour away. For obvious reasons, I didn't want her to go. Eight years have gone by, and even now, the memory of Fanny Van Zandt, her husband Wes, and cabin #5 remains one of the brightest of the summer. But damn them both for offering her that job.

The resort was not quite as busy as in July, but we still had pretty girls coming to vacation every week. The difference was that I was dating now, and Diane was hotter than any of the new girls. So, even though that August weekend had been all kinds of the wrong excitement, it was a hell shot better than the weekend before, which had been drab by comparison.

---

If there was a great equalizer on the resort, at least where my two brothers Kevin, almost fifteen, and Joe, still waiting on sweet sixteen, were concerned, it was the garbage truck. Kevin had sat too many times on the backend of the 1972 Ford F-100 pickup. Smelled enough rotten eggs and baby diapers to last him a life-time. Seen more than he ever wanted of banana peels and tomato sauce and mashed potatoes all in the same container. He wasn't going to let Joe and me do all the driving, not on the garbage route, anyway. By August it was either teach him to handle the three-speed on the column, the gas and clutch, and the manual steering, or lose one-third of our crew. It was a no-brainer. With a shrug and a nod, the three of us headed to the training oval—the gravel road that ran through the partially-finished campgrounds about four hundred feet behind the lodge.

I hadn't always been the oldest. James Jr. had me by over three years, but joined the Army out of high school and died in Afghanistan a year before we moved to Noquebay Resort. The two events were *not* independent of each other, especially for me. In grieving his loss, I'd gotten stuck. I was angry at James for leaving me, and moving north hadn't helped, not even a little. Without Diane I'd still be stuck in that quagmire. At about the time we started dating, I finally came to grips with the loss of my older brother. He didn't come north with us, but his dog tags did. And in mid-July Diane and I put them to rest in the deepest part of Red Wolf Lake, an area called Finnegan's Hole right in front of Noquebay.

The garbage truck was a pale-blue relic that burned oil and had a hole in the muffler. Joe drove us down Lake Road, turned right into the campgrounds, and stopped at a straight part of the gravel road, a good place for Kevin to start the lesson before entering the oval obstacle course. Joe shut off the engine. Kevin got behind the wheel. I stayed in the box and talked to Kevin through the open back window.

The posts for the underground electric had yet to be installed, so the major obstructions were trees. They hadn't all been removed, and some of those remaining were near to the access road. If I was crazy enough to stand on the running boards and Kevin's depth perception was off by sixteen inches or more, those trees could have easily clipped me clean off the truck and knocked me cold. That's why I stayed in the back.

Kevin knew all the basics—how to shift the manual transmission, where the various gears were on the shift pattern. The toughest part for every beginner was always coordination between gas and clutch. There was no way to learn the feel of a clutch pedal. Every vehicle was different. Like all beginners, he revved the engine, let the clutch out too slow, and then popped it. We lurched forward like a scared rabbit. He took his foot off the gas, and we stalled. Happened every time.

Kevin wasn't going to make the same mistake twice. After a quick restart, he revved the throttle but not as much, let out the clutch with a little more grace, the transmission engaged. We jerked ahead. The engine lugged, almost a stall, then alive, then a stall, our heads snapping.

I looked ahead. "Clutch! Kevin, stop!"

He veered off line and into a tree.

"Whoa!" Joe cried.

*Thud.* "Shit! Did I hit it?" Kevin asked.

"Hold on." I jumped out of the box, went to the front, and eyed the bumper. The trunk had put a nice crease on the chrome, dead center. "Not too bad. Just back it up."

"Not too much gas," Joe said.

Kevin did pretty well with the throttle but the truck wanted to move forward when he let out the clutch. "You're in second gear," Joe said. "Move it over." On the H-shaped shift tree, reverse was right next to second gear. It was easy to get the two mixed up.

He found reverse on his second try and moved the truck pretty well, the give-and-take between the pedals his best yet, probably because he wasn't thinking about it so much.

"Great," I said, standing next to the driver's door. "Now do it that way when you're in first. Then just keep going all the way around. Pick me up when you get back here."

It took him a little less than a minute to make the circuit back to me. I spun my arm like a windmill. "Keep going."

Joe yelled out the window, "Second gear, coming up."

On the next straight away, he shifted, lugged the engine again, but it didn't stall, and he made it all the way around. I put up my hands for the stop sign. "All right. Now make like there are garbage cans out there every other tree, whatever. Stop and go."

Kevin scratched his head. "Oh-kay, here goes." He spun the right, rear tire, fishtailed, and sprayed me with stones.

"Hey!" I yelled.

He didn't let up on the gas quickly enough. The rear end of the truck kept swinging wide on the curve and the box side-swiped a poplar tree. The truck screeched to a halt. Joe was out of the cab in a second, checking the damage. "Well, there's bark on the truck and some really nice racing stripes." He looked closer at the tree. "And baby blue on the tree. Guess that's fair."

Kevin came around to take a look, his brow furrowed. "Ah, crap. I'm a dead man."

"I don't think so," I said. "We're all gonna put our mark on this thing before we're done. I ran over a garbage can the other day. Joe already put a dent in the door, and Dad didn't say a thing."

Kevin looked at Joe. "Oh yeah," Joe nodded. "The baseball. But that wasn't from driving."

Kevin completed the stop-and-go loop, then another. They came back to me and Joe said, "Hop in. We're going down the road so he can back into the garbage pickup spot."

Kevin exited the campgrounds, took a right down Lake Road, then a left into the disposal drop area. The waste company came once a week to pick up garbage from Noquebay Resort from here. The biggest problem were the wildlife scavengers continually trying to get into the large steel bins. Kevin pulled in and took a quick left, backed up to the bins, then pulled out without a problem. On the way back to the resort, he got the transmission to third gear, then downshifted to second as he coasted between the lodge and pool, and parked behind the garage.

# Chapter Three

## Trust

Monday morning. I was sent into town to pick up a few things at the hardware store. There, I had the bad luck of running into Steve Manticore, who was walking out as I was walking in. His oldest brother, Mitchell, was right behind. Taller than Steve by a couple inches, older by two decades, and heavier by twice the twenty-pound bag of charcoal he carried, Mitchell grinned like a gargoyle as if proud of the arrest bracelet lugging around his ankle. It didn't slow him a bit; he walked by, telling his half-brother to keep it short.

Steve greeted me with his typical greasy sneer, not a surprise because I had so much to do with the dismantling of his stepfather's farming and construction empire. Even though his animus for Willard Manticore Sr. was well known, the family fortunes were still closely connected to those of Steve, whether he liked it or not.

He said, "What the hell you doin' here, Robel? I saw the football team walking to practice not thirty minutes ago."

I didn't take the bait. "I hear business out at the farm is really bad. All the cops crawling around the place. Maybe they can pitch in, bale some hay." I noticed he had purchased some hardware that we were using out at the resort on the mobile home park. I pointed at the bag in his hand. "Those connectors are for trailers. Must be worse out there than I thought. You moving out of the house, turning into trailer trash?"

Steve's sneer turned into a smile, or his version of one. "Still the smart ass. You don't know shit. The old man is smarter 'a them cops any day. Not that you'll ever know what I'm talking about."

"I already know. Remember?" I turned to go in the store. "It's been real."

"What's the matter? Diane still got you on the leash?" Steve tugged on his shirt and laughed.

"That's right. I'm going in to pick up a light switch and eighty pounds of salt for a date."

He looked down his nose. "Sounds about your speed. I used to think she was too much for a pussy like you. Maybe I was wrong. Could be it's her calling. Saving a lost cause like you." He'd said it over his shoulder as he walked out the automatic doors.

———————

That night I drove to Diane's house. She lived with her mother, and now her father, in a worn out, two-story salt box. A gravel road led to a back door that was the only true entrance to the home. The front door sat suspended two feet above a patchy lawn, no steps or sidewalk, never used. A pale-yellow barn sat in the backyard, glum in its retirement, the roofline frowning into the ground, inside the stanchions and pens long gone. Windows clouded and always closed, the interior had the slightest scent of grain dust and hay mow.

The best thing about the house was the screened-in back porch that had an old couch about the size of a love seat. From here, Diane and I sat and looked out through the screens at the barn, the woods to the left, and the cornfield to the right. Up to that day, the only other soul in the house was Ethyl, who watched television in the front room, the volume on so low I often wondered if she could hear the shows at all. More likely, she was eavesdropping on her daughter, who didn't often bring boyfriends home. But then again most of her dates had money enough to take her out, and I didn't. I remember wishing Ethyl would skip her legendary afternoon nap, go to bed earlier, and leave us alone. Now, she even had a reason. Her husband was home and tired out early. It was dark, about eight-thirty, when he said good night and went upstairs to bed. I had no such hope for Ethyl, so we kept on talking.

I'd been wondering for two days how the welcome home meal went, and all the meals since, for that matter. Diane and I started out sitting face to face, the best way for storytelling, each of us with a knee cocked up on the couch and one foot on the floor. I was busting with curiosity.

Diane said the dinner started off as awkward and uncomfortable as humanly possible. Her mother, never very good at social conversation, tried to keep the tone light, as if this were not the "return of a family convict who had fucked up the lives of everyone at the table." Diane went along with it anyway, hoping to keep the meal as short and painless as possible. Ben was of a mind to let bygones be bygones. "As usual," Diane said. "That left me the odd one out."

Diane brought up her sister's name, Jean Warren Manticore, and that the meal couldn't be a true family reunion without her. Diane and I hadn't talked about her sister, had barely mentioned her name, since we received the news four weeks earlier that the body found in Red Wolf Lake was not Jean. The dental records didn't match. I asked her again, what she wanted to do next about finding her?

Though Diane had nothing new to support her opinion, she now thought her sister was still alive and living on the run. I reminded her there may be another body at the bottom of Finnegan's Hole, and because the lake was so deep the divers may have missed it. I slid closer and put my arm around Diane's shoulders. This was always a delicately emotional subject. Jean was twelve years old when Diane was born. "From the day I was brought home, Jean treated me like I was her own daughter," was something Diane had said numerous times. I learned early on never to challenge any of this history in Diane's presence or the penalty would be dire: go straight to the gates of hell, lose the rest of your turns, do not collect $200. When Carter left ten years ago, Jean's presence in Diane's life became even more important. Ethyl went into an emotional slide that landed her in a place of days spent in bed, sleepless nights, and endless rumination. Who then to raise Diane but Jean, which she did, and very well. Diane remembered every detail. Every. Single. One. So yes, she owed it to her sister to do whatever she could to bring her home again, whether she be dead or alive.

"It sounds like the dinner went as well as you could expect," I said. "No one died or ended up in the hospital."

Diane huffed a laugh. She leaned back into my arm. I snuggled my lips and nose into her hair and breathed in the smell of her shampoo. She said, "But get a load of this." She looked up without moving her head. "He asked me to forgive him. Can you believe that? First day home. Ten years down the drain and—" she snapped her fingers—"just like that, wipe the slate clean."

I nodded. "That is surprising."

"Right?"

"Not just the question but that he'd have the guts to ask, you know, right off the bat like that. He had to know how you'd react. I mean, ten years and no visits. What *did* you say?"

"For a second, I just sat there. I was blank." She threw her hands. "Can you believe that? Me, and nothing to say?"

"No, I can't."

She jammed me with her shoulder. "Okay, you don't have to agree so fast."

"You must have said something though, eventually."

"We were having peach cobbler and ice cream, and I had a brain freeze going on, so I told Mom the dessert was really good and she said thank you but everybody was quiet… you know. Because they all knew there was something else coming and they were waiting, and so was I. And I'm thinking 'No fucking way, no way he's getting off that easy.' I take a breath and say, 'I can't answer that.' Which is true, I can't. Then I told him, 'You're home not even a day. I don't know you. Are you still drinking? I don't know. Are you going back to robbing cabins? I don't know.' Then he puts his hand up like he's going to interrupt or argue or whatever and I say, 'No! I'm not done. Are you getting a job to support Mom? And what about the guy you shot? Ever think about his family?

Answer those questions, then I'll answer yours.'"

"Holy shit," I said. "I'd say your brain thawed out, like the Fourth of July. Was that the end of the meal?"

Diane shrugged. "Pretty much. But then Ben says 'he did his time, that counts for something.'" She said the State of Wisconsin might be satisfied, but she wasn't. I shook my head and thought to myself my father would call Diane one tough sonofabitch, in the nicest way possible.

As much as I liked the back porch, it was attached to a house that transmitted sounds like an echo chamber. We couldn't get away with anything out there. As far as our romance was concerned, we'd outgrown the whole setup.

I asked, "So the barn, no one uses it anymore?"

"Nope."

"Not even the hay mow?"

"Well, yeah. My brother stores boats and shit up there over the winter and some other stuff. Antique farm machinery mostly."

"Empty now." I looked at her and raised my eyebrows. She startled a bit and drew away. "I mean, no one goes up there during the summer. Why would they? It's probably hot. No windows."

"Probably," she replied slowly, still watching.

"But you could always crack a door. Hay mows have doors. Yours has three by the way. So whadda ya think? You, me, a blanket and an empty hay mow."

"I have been thinking about it, not down to the last detail like you." She squeezed my upper arm. "But… it's too soon, Sam. I'm not ready. You know what I'm saying?"

I looked down. We were sitting very close, my right arm around her. I scratched at something with my left finger. "Yeah, I do," I said, but really, I had only a vague idea of what she was talking about. She'd only had surgery a month ago. Her last boyfriend, Max, had said goodbye under duress two weeks before that and immediately left town.

"Okay," I said. "Dad says I'm not over losing Max either."

"Oh, it's not that." She moved her hips away a bit and faced me. "It's about losing the baby. I still think about that." She straightened a little and paused for a while. "If it wasn't for that buckle you fished out of the lake and everything after, would you have ever asked me on a date?" She tilted her head. "Seriously?"

There was no playing dumb here, not for me. I knew what she was talking about, and she knew that I knew. Almost a year earlier, on the first day of history class, a long-haired bundle of dark curls with incredible legs sat down next to me. Her name was Diane and I was so distracted I didn't take a single note for a week. Through the year, we talked more and more, but I always had the notion she was out of my league. And we didn't have the same circle of friends. That all changed when, in May, I fished a piece of cloth out of Finnegan's Hole. The cloth looked like a buckle Diane's sister had been wearing before she disappeared. "Asked you out? How do I know? Maybe."

"That's a no." She shoved me on the chest, then snuggled back under my arm. "Are you over Erin?"

The conversation was getting too heavy for my tastes. Now she was bringing up the name of a girl I'd known for five days in June. Erin was from Chicago, a summer romance for sure, and someone who'd helped us retrieve the belt buckle from the Manticores. But she was gone, had been gone for two months, and was now hundreds of miles away. "Yeah I'm over her, no doubt."

"Ah, huh, really. Did you and Erin?"

"Did Erin and I what?"

"You know, do it."

"Wait a minute. I never asked you anything like that," I said.

"You didn't have to." She shuffled her shoulders. "Doesn't matter, I already know."

I said that was impossible. I'd never told anyone about Erin, and I knew Erin hadn't said anything either. Diane said Max had told her.

"He never heard anything about sex with Erin from me," I said.

"No, but he knew about the condom you got from Nic Vedder the very same night."

The skin on my neck tingled. I bluffed a shrug. "Just because a guy has a condom don't mean nothing. Some guys have the same one in their wallets for years."

"Yeah, okay, show me."

*Oh shit*, I thought. "Show you what?"

"Ah ha! You don't have it."

"Yes, I do." I lied.

She paused, then made a sudden grab for my back pocket. Her hands were quick and surprisingly strong. Before I could find my ass with both hands, she had the wallet. Then I tried to pry it from her grasp. The wrestling was in full throat when Ethyl's voice came from the kitchen:

"What are you two fighting about?"

"Sam's wallet," Diane said. "He says he has a rubber in it and I say he don't."

"Diane!" I croaked and then laughed.

"Oh, for god's sake." Ethyl waved us off. "If you're not going to tell me the truth, just say so. I'm going to bed." She went up the steps, then paused. "And don't break that couch. It came from your grandmother."

I admitted there was no condom in my wallet. We sat down next to each other again.

"But you just asked me to rip one off in the hay mow. You think I want to get pregnant again?"

"No, of course not."

"Well…"

"I figured I didn't have to since, you know, you're on the pill."

She turned under my arm. "I never told you that."

"I saw them in your purse, so I—"

"Oh!" She pulled away. "I see what's going on. You thought 'She's on the pill, so she's up for sex.'"

"Was that wrong?" I asked.

Her shoulders slouched. "Not all together. But!" She grabbed my shirt. "I'm on them to regulate my period. That's how I got in trouble last time."

Her logic was sound, I see that now, but the focus on the "last time" triggered me. Maybe because I was still trying to figure out why she'd brought up the issue of the buckle. What difference did it make if it brought us together or not? A veiled comparison to Max probably, that's what I thought, because he never needed any excuse to ask any girl on a date. So, there I was, with a girl I adored but who would confide in me only so far as our *friendship* would allow. I wanted more than that, much more. At the same time, I was feeling the presence of Max, a rival with whom I couldn't compete because he wasn't there.

I said, "Well maybe if you'd tell me some of this stuff, then I wouldn't have to figure it out on my own."

She leaned away. "So now I should tell you my health history?"

"No. But if we're at least talking about sex and you're on the pill maybe it's something you should tell me."

"I just did."

I snapped, "No, you didn't."

Silence.

I should've kept my mouth shut but, "Like this business with Carter."

She crossed her arms. "What's *he* got to do with this?"

"You weren't the only one got ambushed two days ago. When he showed up in the bar and told me his name, I stood there like some kind of dumbass because my girlfriend told me he was dead."

"To me, he was."

"That's not the point," I said. "You couldn't... You didn't..." I could barely bring myself to say the words. "I was the only one who stayed with you through this whole thing, looking for your sister, the Manticores, the news reports, the whole nine yards. And still you couldn't tell me the truth."

She pulled away and sat on the edge of the couch. "So now you know. Are you happy? Because I'm not. Would you be proud of that story? Well, I'm not. And you know what? Just based on the last forty-eight hours with him back in the house, I don't see me hanging around. That job in Green Bay is looking better and better every minute. In fact, I'm taking it."

"Wow." A knot twisted in my throat. "You had no problem telling me that piece of news."

Footsteps halfway down the stairs stopped us. Ethyl, in her bedclothes, asked, "What's all the shouting down here?"

"Nothing Mom," Diane said. "It's over. Go back to bed."

More silence.

"It's over?" I asked. It sounded like a decision, a proclamation when she said it. "Were you saying that to her or me?"

She dropped her head and put her fingers in her hair. "There's too much going on right now. I've got to, we've got to slow everything down."

"Right. The whole month's been a whirlwind." My heart cringed. I got up. "I'm going. I feel like an extra here." I got up, and making no gesture to kiss her, I turned toward the door. "When the wind stops blowing, let me know."

"Sam." She looked up but she didn't stand. Even in the dim light, her dark, almost black eyes shined with what, the first intimation of a tear?

I turned briefly but couldn't pause to find out. The burn in my own eyes was making it hard to see my way to the car.

# CHAPTER FOUR

# Gold in the Garbage

Garbage. Refuse. That's what my life had turned into, and as if to confirm my mood, it was Tuesday and so trash pickup day on the resort. I remember feeling worse getting out of bed than I did when I tried to go to sleep, and that was saying a lot because I felt like crap when I got home from Diane's house. Bed became a place for end-of-the-world scenarios, and why not? I'd just broken up with my first real girlfriend, a person who could never be equaled in this or any other lifetime. I woke with a headache and a queasy stomach, the perfect combo for a garbage run.

Garbage didn't go away during vacations; it did, in fact, grow in a gelatinous goo that bred in an incubator of endless heat and moisture, fed by cabin parties, the inevitable by-product of humans on holiday. Twice a week the crew assembled—my brothers Kevin and Joe, and myself—and made the rounds, twelve stops in all including the lodge and two fish cleaning shacks.

By the end of June, we'd found some gold in the garbage. Our first discovery was that *Playboy* was popular reading material for men away from home and usually discarded prior to the end of the week. We kept a sharp eye out for the serviceable copies and shoved them under the front seat of the F-100 for safe keeping. The second surprise was what Dad called the "Tom Sawyer Effect." When resort kids saw us driving the truck and tooling around the resort on the running boards, they thought it was so cool, they wanted to join us. At first, we brushed them away like so many flies, but then thought better of it and struck a deal. They could ride, but to pay their way the new riders had to collect trash at each stop. They loved it! We couldn't keep them off the truck. We became supervisors and dropped the tailgate to make room so the working class could ride.

We were into mid-August so we had the routine down pat; except it was Kevin's first drive. Further, we were down a bit on the Tom Sawyer crew. That made Joe and me the garbage grunts. We stood on the running boards, hopped off at each stop, threw the bags into the box, then moved on. What smelled worse it was hard to say: me and my brothers, doused right down to the heels in bug spray, or the trash, wet and putrid, surrounded by a halo of primordial heat, each can a gob of animal, vegetable, and God knew what, breaking down in a germ-infested free-for-all. This was especially bad when the renters hadn't followed instructions, bags were used improperly, or not at all, and we ended up packing the cloying waste ourselves.

Most of the job was behind us. My head still throbbed, my stomach continued to toss, but no worse than at the beginning of the route. Kevin stopped the truck between #4 and #5, the cabins farthest west on the resort. Out on the pier, I could see Fanny up and about, fresh as newly washed laundry even after an evening of bar hopping. She rarely wore skirts anymore, but the bloodlines between her and Diane were obvious enough in the way they walked and I imagined that, in her day, Fanny had worn her share of high heels. The Van Zandts had their own dock right out front.

Fanny walked from pier to truck and said, "Kevin, look at you, in the driver's seat. 'Bout time those other two did some of the heavy lifting, bless their souls." She winked at him in a way that said "watch this," then looked across the hood. "Oh Sam, don't leave. Got something to show you."

All at once, my stomach was folding on itself again.

She walked around the front of the truck and watched as I tied up the bag from the trash can for #4. "Well, look at that." Her southern draw was in bloom that day. "Plumb full of beer bottles, returnables, no less. I know my neighbors, brandy old-fashions all day long. Never saw them with a beer, not one." She looked me in the eye, her dark eyes knowing but giving nothing away. "And if they're gonna drink beer, it certainly isn't gonna be Pabst." Palm up, she pointed. "Odd, don't you think? My niece wouldn't have anything to do with this? Or you? I mean, bury the evidence in the garbage can next door? Oldest trick in the book."

Suddenly the bag weighed a ton. My throat burned like acid. Truth was, I had been at a beer party in her cabin a couple times, but not the one from last week. I was working in the bar all night and missed it completely, but I doubted my objections would carry any weight with Fanny right then. "Ah, Diane? I don't... No, not me." I sent the bag over the side and into the box, bottles clucking like chickens in a hen house. A couple cabin kids walked up with the bags from #3 and #2 and threw them on the truck, then took their places on the tailgate.

"No, I'm sure not." Fanny turned toward the cabin. "Hold on, I've got one more thing for the dump." She grabbed something off the table just inside the door. I saw it and immediately my legs turned to Jell-O. She held up a small, portable speaker, the one I'd left at the earlier party. "Found this sitting in the kitchen a few weeks ago. Keep forgetting to ask. Belong to anyone you know?"

I grunted something and shrugged.

"No, Sam," Joe said. "That looks like yours. It's been lost for weeks."

"Who asked you?" I said.

"I'll take that as a no," Fanny said. "Throw it out then. Diane said it's not hers and I don't know how to use it." Ever so slowly she turned the speaker over and handed it to me, not bothering to point at my name, etched on the bottom. She smiled and walked away. "By the way, three aspirin, two Rolaids, and a cup of coffee."

"What?" I asked.

"Fanny's morning after tonic. Looks like you could use it."

Kevin and Joe laughed, and so did the two kids on the tailgate.

A U-turn sent us back toward the lodge and a wide square of lawn, home to the fish cleaning shack, the most-feared patch of land on all of Noquebay's thirty acres. While in college, I studied

Dante's Inferno and the nine circles of Hell and was genuinely surprised the fish shack was not mentioned. "Double Wrap Fish Remains in Newspaper" said the sign. It didn't matter. On cool days, the odor surrounding the shack would leave the air permanently deformed; on bad days, it was enough to melt brain tissue. We treated fish entrails like radioactive waste: double bagged, double ties, backmost part of the truck.

The collection point for our garbage service was a quarter mile down the road. The garbage scow turned left onto a two-rut trail and stopped. The roar of the muffler signaled our arrival for a huge black bear and her two cubs, who were trying to destroy one of the metal bins. We'd obviously surprised them, because mama bear turned on us right away.

"Holy crap!" I yelled at the boys on the tailgate. "Come here, right now. Get in the cab."

Joe opened the passenger door. The boys jumped in the cab and smothered Joe, leaving no room for me. "Move over, you two, move over," I said. The bear was about fifty feet away. If she got angry, she could cover that distance in seconds and dispose of me even quicker. She lowered her head and made a move in our direction. Terrified, one of the boys slammed the door shut. Joe shoved one of them onto the floor. Kevin pulled the other boy onto his lap. The bear broke into a sprint. Kevin revved the engine. The muffler bellowed. If it slowed the bear, I didn't see it. I dove head first through the open window. Kevin grabbed me by the shoulders and yanked my legs into the cab. I heard a thud against the door. Joe cranked frantically on the window. A second later a huge paw struck the glass pane. Everyone shuttered at the sound of cracking glass. We were never able to lower that window again. Swinging its head back and forth, the bear stood on its back legs sniffing about. Inside the truck, we frantically scrambled to get everyone legs down and heads up again. Faces pressed against every available square inch of glass, we watched mama bear circle the truck, prowling, searching for another way into the cab. The windows steamed from the heavy breathing and tracking her became almost impossible. Then suddenly, she gave up the quest and went back to her cubs.

Ten minutes later, the bears had vacated the premises. The five of us had disentangled our bodies and freed ourselves from the cab. "We definitely got to get some bear spray," Joe said.

"And a .44 magnum," Kevin added. "Just in case."

Finally, Kevin backed up into position near the bins. We jumped into the box and with all the precision of an exploding bag of popcorn, tossed and pushed the load into the gaping, metal mouths of the steal bins.

Suddenly, I noticed Joe had disappeared. I asked Kevin where he was. He pointed to the passenger's seat in the cab. The bears all but forgotten, Joe had harvested a new *Playboy*. He couldn't wait to see Miss April. Kevin went back in the driver's seat. I jumped over the side of the box and onto the ground, which was a mistake. I felt a little dizzy and regretted the coffee-only breakfast.

"Wow. Which cabin did this come from?" I asked.

"Number 2," Joe said. "Look, the cover's perfect."

"And so is Miss April," I added. I stepped in something wet and mushy. The world went sideways. I slipped, bent over, and lost my breakfast.

"Oh, nice," Kevin said. "What's wrong with you?"

Joe swatted deer flies off the magazine. "*Playboy* a little too much for you?"

"Hey, let's go," said one of the resort boys.

"Yeah, in a minute," Kevin answered. "Maybe it was breakfast. Was the milk sour?"

"Sour?" Joe laughed. "Yeah, after it hit the beer."

I looked up, sweat stinging my eyes. "What are you talking about?"

"You were at Diane's last night. Everyone knows you drink when you're over there."

"Yeah, that's what we do." I shut the door, climbed on the running board, and said, "Let's go."

Kevin started the engine and drove down the road, flies and mosquitos swarming in our wake.

---

My father's recipe for recovery from most ailments, be it mental or physical, was a bit different than Fanny's. It consisted of a wheelbarrow, two shovels, two rakes, and one pile of dirt. Admittedly, you got this treatment whether you were screwed up by the whims of a female or not, just ask Joe and Kevin. But in my case, sweating it out had its advantages when all I wanted to do was take my mind off of *her*. We'd rotate the jobs, fifteen minutes per shift. I started out on wheelbarrow, filling and hauling.

I looked across the Narrows of Red Wolf Lake and thought of the old man, Willard Manticore Sr., now on house arrest because his health was too poor to keep him in jail. His oldest son, Mitchell, was out on two million dollars bail, his passport confiscated, charged with interstate transportation of stolen goods and a dozen other counts. His formerly sprawling Square M Construction company was on the rocks, and so was the old man's farm and ranching business, but you couldn't tell that from looking at the place. Except for less traffic around the headquarters of Square M, everything looked the same. And it pissed me off. I wanted to see falling columns of stone, heaving ground, burning buildings—a Biblical disaster.

The topsoil was for the "Noquebay Mobile Home Park." Construction had stopped for over two months because the old man had tried to squeeze my parents out of business by illegally using his influence on the board of directors at the local bank. We came within days of being foreclosed and thrown out on the street. Now, on a warm August day, we were back at it, putting down lawns for the lots that would someday be the pad for a new mobile home.

Joe called, "Time!" He grabbed the cooler for a drink of water, then handed it to me along with his shovel. I poured half my allotment over my head and half in my mouth. I passed the jug to Kevin then sat down on the dirt.

Joe looked at me. "You sure are quiet today."

I shrugged and used the tail of my shirt to wipe sweat off my face. "Pissed about the Manticores, maybe."

Kevin set down the jug. "Why? They're in it up to their elbows. That's what Dad said."

"That's what everybody says." I spit on the ground. "We busted their irrigation system too late. Their crops are going to be just fine." I stomped on a clump of topsoil.

"Yeah, but who's running it?" Joe asked. "Junior was doing the ranch and farming, and no one has seen him for weeks. You don't think Steve is doing it? Or Mrs. Manticore?"

"Steve is a sandwich short of a picnic," I said. "It's probably still the same guys, even though they're supposed to be hands-off of everything. I just saw Mitch in town the other day."

"Thought he wasn't supposed to leave the house," Kevin said.

"Yeah, well, they got the sheriff watching," I said. "Manticore sends his deputies a new set of blinders every week."

An hour later, we'd rotated through the positions and I was back on shovel again, though not to Joe's satisfaction. "Hey, Sam, you're daydreaming again. Speed it up."

"That ain't it," Kevin said. "They broke up last night."

"Thanks jabber mouth. How did you find out?" I asked.

Kevin wheeled by with a load. "Heard you on the phone this morning."

"If you broke up," Joe said, "why are you on the phone with her?"

"Who said it was Diane?"

I'd been talking to Sarah Crimmins, a former girlfriend of Max's and a good friend of mine from Red Wolf High School. She had a friendly ear.

———————

Noquebay Lodge was built back in the day when building codes were only suggestions, and in the Northwoods of Wisconsin, rarely followed. Shaped like a barn right down to the peaked, metal roof, there was no insulation in the walls or on any of the electrical lines. No self-respecting Northwoods resort could be without a tavern, and ours was at the front of the Lodge. Business hours had shrunk recently with the demand. During the week, we opened at six p.m. and usually closed by ten p.m. I was wiping down the bar when Dad walked in around an hour after opening. The place was empty.

"Hey, another busy night," he said.

"You know the story, Dad. Word gets out. When I'm on duty, they stay away."

"I'm sure that's a coincidence, Sam." He checked the beer coolers. "Heard you had a rough one last night."

I shot to attention. "How did you…" I put up my hand. "Never mind, I already know. Yeah, it wasn't pretty. We lasted a whole five weeks."

"Give her some time. It's been a hell of a summer for her. For both of you. Think about it. The body in the lake. Then it's not her sister. The miscarriage. Her dad just shows up out of thin air. It's a lot to work through."

"Yeah, I suppose," I said.

"How'd she handle all the body in the lake business? Was that a relief or just something more to worry about?"

"We talked about it. It was bad in a way because she saw her mother going right back to her depression. Now that Carter's home, who knows what'll happen."

The bell above the front door rang. Nic Vedder walked in and gave us a salute. He was the only son of Phillip Vedder, owner of the private cabin just beyond Noquebay and right next to cabin #5. For the second time in four days, I was dumbstruck to see a customer in the bar, this time for a different reason. Last I heard, Nic had enlisted in the Army.

He said, "Hey boys, how goes it?" His goatee was growing back, which I presumed he'd shaved in boot camp.

"Nic, what the hell!" I said. "The Army throw you out—already?"

Dad said, "Yeah, can't be furlough, can it?"

Nic pulled up a stool and sat down. "They wouldn't take me. I flunked the test. Turns out, I have dyslexia." The Army hadn't had enough time to change him. He wore the same clothes, cut off sleeves showed off his tanned, muscular arms. His shorts were so long I often teased him they looked like the Capri pants that women wear.

"No shit," I said. "No wonder you couldn't pull a grade in school."

"Ya think? They said my IQ is actually above average. Can you believe that?"

"Well…" I tilted my head.

"Okay. Don't answer," said Nic. "Just give me a cola."

I got him a drink and told him about the repercussions of the belt buckle incident and the body in the lake. Nic said he'd been following the story through his dad. He hadn't heard of Carter Warren's return from prison. Turned out, Nic and his family had been coming to the lake for decades, so he knew about Carter all along, even the twenty-year sentence, so he was surprised to hear about his early release too. I asked Nic what he thought about Jean Warren Manticore, since her disappearance six years ago was once again a cold case.

Nic said, "If she's hiding, she's done a damn good job of it. Changed her name, maybe even changed her looks. How would you ever find her? Only people can do that are the mob and the FBI, and they don't always get a hit either." I asked him about it because Diane and I had a disagreement, had almost fought over it.

"Proves my point," Dad said. "You and Diane don't talk about the usual stuff. That's some heavy shit right there. I'll be back in thirty. Call if you need something." He walked out the front door.

"And that stuff didn't even come up last night," I said. "We were too busy breaking up."

"You broke up. So, what was it? She don't like the music you play? She don't like rockin' the cradle? What?"

I turned away. "Well, you haven't lost a step."

Nic took a drink. "I'm kidding. You don't have to tell me a thing. Just thought since Max is gone, you might need a wall to bounce—"

"Well, his name came up."

Nic arched an eyebrow. He knew a lot more about Max and me than what was printed in the newspaper or put online. Before Max disappeared, the three of us had spent hours together skiing and wakeboarding. He said, "And not for the first time, I'll bet."

"How did you know?"

"It's obvious. You're in a rebound relationship. *Capisce?*" I told him I had only a vague idea of what it was, because I'd never had one. He chuckled. "You're in one right now, and let me tell you, it's hard enough when one of you is on the rebound, but both." He looked down at his feet. "Look out below."

I argued I was over Erin well enough. She'd left almost two months ago, and anyway, we'd only lasted a few days so it really didn't count.

"Wait a minute. Wait a minute." Nic pointed the can of soda at me. "Is this the same girl I saw you with out on our swim raft back in June?"

"Yeah," I droned.

"And later that very afternoon you were in my kitchen asking to,"—he put up finger quotes—"borrow a condom."

"You know it is."

"Hey, don't try and bullshit a bullshitter. You don't forget a girl like that."

He finally accepted my explanation of where I was at with Erin, but went on to say it wasn't her he was referring to anyway.

"I haven't dated anyone else," I said. "So, who's to rebound from?"

"Max!" Nic sat back to let it sink in. "Besides your family, who have you been closer to this last year than Max?"

"And you think I'm on a rebound? From a guy! I didn't date him, for god's sake."

"Don't matter. Diane's on the rebound too."

"From the same person?"

"From the same person," Nic echoed. "I gotta say, quite a situation you got there."

"Yeah. Lucky me."

"Jealous feelings on both sides. Really complicated crap, I'd think."

"You don't know the half of it. One day I'm jealous of Diane. The next day I'm jealous of Max—"

"And he's not even here!" added Nic. "She's going through the same thing. Guaranteed."

"Diane? No. I don't see it."

"Guaranteed! Pretty warped, man. How long were you dating?"

"Over a month. And we have some outrageous history together. The paint heist. We dumped the Manticore's own barn paint into their irrigation system. You remember. They ended up with acres and acres of pink corn. That was us!"

"Exactly," Nic said, chuckling at the thought. "So why do you worry about some other guy looking over your shoulder? Nothing gonna turn off a girl faster than that. Get some cajones, man."

I was glad the Army hadn't taken Nic, but they could've performed a little b.s. extraction before they let him go, just as a public service. I flushed at his last remark, and the cool air blowing through the screens wasn't helping. "What are you talking about? The crap I did this summer to root out the Manticores, breaking and entering, all that shit. Like I said, you know the story."

Nic showed me his palms. "Hey! No doubt. Top shelf stuff. Now use that confidence when you're with the ladies, and you're golden."

"Doesn't matter anymore. Carter's only been home for a few days and she can't stand it. She's moving to Green Bay. Fanny and Wes have offered her a job, even a place to stay until she finds one of her own."

Nic lifted his head and squinted, as if thinking on something. "I don't see a long-distance romance working with her. Got to keep her here somehow. The old man, you say." He tilted his chin a bit. "She tell you why she's so hell bent on leaving?"

"Oh yeah," I said. "She thinks he's a total fuck-up, selfish, did stupid shit and the whole family suffered. Now he comes home and everyone has given him a pass except her. Then he asks Diane to forgive him, which shocked the hell out of me, 'cuz a guy like Carter, you don't expect that. Anyway, she told him no fuckin' way. Show me something first, then we'll talk."

"Gotta love her. She's kinda bad ass." Nic laughed. "Anyway, there's your answer. She's got to forgive her father. Then you might have a shot at keeping her... for a while."

"For a while?"

"Yeah. Throw me a bag of chips. Thanks." He tore open the bag. "What do you think? Your everlasting summer is going to go on forever? That was June. Helicopters flying over Red Wolf, you and Erin and Max and Diane cruising the lake after sundown—that world is gone, dude. You've already been cut in half. It's like a divorce."

"What? Diane and me?"

The chips crunched. "No, no, no. The four of you down to two. I'm waxing philosophical here with my above-average IQ. Try to keep up. That world is gone. Maybe she's mourning. Maybe you should too."

I crossed one leg behind the other, straightened my arms, and propped my hands against the edge of the bar. "Can't understand why the Army didn't take you. You'd be perfect for counterintelligence."

# Chapter Five

# Return of the Stranger

For two days I had neither seen nor heard from Diane. I hadn't called her either, the first time that had happened since her surgery a month earlier. I don't recall if we'd said it straight out, but maybe we needed a break. Some things don't need to be recited chapter and verse. It had rained a little in the morning so my brothers and I didn't get back to work on the top soil until after lunch. We put in over two hours, working under cloudy skies on a warm and humid day. The breeze came up and blew the dust around so by the end of the afternoon I was covered with sweat and dirt.

I picked up a towel in the house and headed for the pool wondering if I'd see the two girls from #3. The Bartlett family was renting that week and Janet had brought along a friend named Ashley Bottoms. I didn't know much about either of them, only that they appeared to be about my age, and though Janet was blond and the taller of the two, Ashley was prettier and had an ass befitting her name. Two months earlier, I would've been spending half of my free time making up the details of some random meeting between me and the two girls, the other half trying to make it happen. But not then. The real reason I wanted a dip in the pool was not to see if the girls were there, but to cool off. If they or anyone else saw me streaked in dust and sweat, so what? What did I care. If they were there, fine, but I wasn't going to pursue either one. I didn't have it in me to get back in the chase. Besides, both of them were too much of what was called 'on brand.' Everything they wore, from their sunglasses to their shoes, had a designer tattooed on it somewhere. Erin had some of that going on, but she had it under control. A little bit of that went a long way. And when I saw Joe and Kevin taking an interest in the girls, I was relieved.

———————

The next day, more silence between Diane and me. No phone calls, not even a text. None from me to her either, so there was that as well. The sadness of losing her was setting in. I was sick of everything, the resort, my clothes, my brothers and sister, even the summer. I was to the point that going back to school for my senior year looked inviting, and that had never happened at any point of my life. I was like a worker bee without a queen. Why collect pollen if there was no honey to be made. Why cut the grass or collect the garbage? Everything seemed pointless.

Right after lunch, I found myself pushing a hand mower back and forth on the peninsula, a finger of land that extended from Noquebay proper toward a small island about a quarter mile beyond the tip. The shoreline had become a minor problem here, or rather a certain very aggressive plant called the knotweed was the problem, which had to be cut regularly or it would have taken over the entire resort. There were piers jutting off the peninsula and a parking area at its base. A car pulled into one of the spots. I turned and headed toward the tip of the point. I was halfway into a good sweat when I heard someone say:

"It's just going to grow back, you know."

Even over the sound of the mower, the voice struck a chord in my ear. I let go the throttle. The mower died. I froze.

"Your mom said I'd find you here."

Now everything stopped. The mower, yes, but the wind died too, and for a second, there were no waves lapping on the shore and no swallows flying through the air. I was sure of the voice. Of course, I knew it, probably always would, like the song of one bird for another, forever imprinted. I pried my fingers from the mower handle, turned, and looked at the girl from the Vedder swimming raft, who'd so entertained Nic as he spied on us through the binoculars, and had entranced me two months earlier. The short, blond hair was the same, her eyes still as blue, and that smile, the radiant smile she now tried to hide.

"Hello, Sam."

"Erin. Wow…" Now my heart was in a sweat. I was thinking too fast, thinking the worst. I had indeed begged a condom off Nic. It had broken. I worried she'd gotten pregnant. Now she was here to tell me.

"I know. What am I doing here? Right? I could have called or a dozen other things." She stood three steps away. I wanted so much to close the distance to nothing, but because she had broken it off, it was up to her to make the first move. My clothes were a mess—sweat-stained shirt, old tennis shoes, cut-offs—the usual fare for me but nothing she hadn't seen before. I smirked and flashed my open palms at her. She took two quick steps and we hugged. I smelled perfume on her neck, the same one I'd noticed the night we met. It was a good hug, and it surprised me. Not, somehow, like the squeeze of a woman about to drop the daddy label on me.

We parted. "What a surprise." I combed my disheveled hair with my hand, embarrassed to be standing next to this girl who glowed like honey in the sunshine. "You'll never know how much I needed that."

"Me too." She looked about. "Is there somewhere we can go… to sit. I have to talk to you." I didn't like the sound of that. Maybe my optimism was premature. My mind went immediately to the grassy ledge at the end of the peninsula where, weeks earlier, we'd watched the moon and the Milky Way. But that was a singular moment, that location too thick with memories. To go back there again would put too much at risk.

There was a two-person bench at the end of a nearby dock. I pointed. She nodded. The short walk was uncomfortable and silent. Boats and pontoons lined the T-shaped pier. The breeze was light and the sun kind enough, peeking from behind the occasional cloud. A few seagulls kept watch, two in the water, one perched on a dock pole. We sat. The bench allowed for six inches between us, an important distance, one that wouldn't have been there eight weeks ago.

"Don't take this the wrong way," I said, my heart beating my ribs silly. "But you're the last person I expected to come out of that car. Are you by yourself?"

"Yes. I asked to rent from your folks, by the way. I'm in #11."

*Not #10. Good,* I thought.

"Yeah, #10 was open but I thought, no, not a good idea." She grinned broadly.

I laughed. "So now you're reading my mind. What other super power do I have to worry about?" I looked over my shoulder. "Whose car are you driving?"

"Mine. It's a 2009 Corolla. Got it for my birthday."

"Hmm. The plumbing business must be going well for your dad."

"It's going." She looked down and grabbed the edge of the bench. "Sam, I know Max is gone. I've been following the story up here on the Internet. Are you still in touch with Diane?"

"We *were* dating." I squinted, as if from the sun. "Until three days ago. We broke up."

"Oh, I'm sorry." She bit her lower lip. "Maybe you'll get back together."

A quick shake of the head. "Diane has never been one to go back." Erin appeared confused. I said, "Once she breaks up, there's always someone else she's moving on to."

"Oh, I see."

"What about you? How are you and John doing?"

She glanced at me quickly, and I thought I saw a glimmer of gratitude in her eyes. I surprised her, I think. It was the first time I had referred to her boyfriend by his proper name. She said, "That's where the story begins, and a big reason I'm here. There are two, no three important things I have to tell you about John."

I had no idea where this was going. I motioned with my hands for her to go ahead.

"The first thing, he's four years older than me. My parents absolutely lost their shit when they found out we were dating, but weren't totally surprised. You were the first guy I was ever with that's the same age as me."

This took me off guard, but it shouldn't have; all the clues had been there. Her approach to everything, from how she interacted with her parents to the way she set me up, was a step ahead of anything I'd seen before. She arrived at Noquebay a complete stranger to everyone here, and within days she had me inviting her on a night-raid scheme Max and I had cooked up. In the years since, a lot of people have come and gone at the resort, and she is the only one I can honestly say could have pulled it off. It smacked of big city hubris, or someone who'd seen and done a few things more than me, or both. It was both. Especially where sex was concerned. "You must drive them totally crazy, your parents, I mean."

"Oh, I do." Her feet swung freely. "But I tell them, 'hey, my grades are good, I'm an all-conference swimmer, I don't do drugs, I'm not reckless. Count your blessings.'"

Not reckless? She'd come with us on the midnight break-in of the Manticore property, so that sounded like a stretch. In fact, the sight of her bikini-clad ass sliding under the bay doors of the boathouse that night was something forever burned in my brain. She was the only one of us slim enough to fit below the doors, so she'd saved us from failure. Just to pay her back, while we snorkeled to get a look at the underwater pump siphon, I let her get too close. The pump turned on suddenly and I damn near lost her. But her parents never heard about any of that, so the rest—the grades, the swimming—sounded legit. "Okay, John is four years older. I can't wait for the other two things."

Her feet were quiet now. "I'm not sure how to tell you the rest." She shifted on the bench. "John and I broke up, I don't know, one or two weeks ago. Third,—"

"Wait, wait, wait." I turned toward her. "Just to be clear. You're single? Unattached?"

"Of course."

Her little confession had me bolted to the bench. All at once, a dozen possibilities were dancing through my head like so many unattended children at a wedding reception. Did she drive three hundred miles to tell me she broke up with her boyfriend? How long did she intend to stay? I didn't know what to say or ask. And I couldn't deny the timing: a pregnancy would certainly split them apart if he wasn't the father. Suddenly that was back on the table.

"Sure, right." Was all I could think of. "You were saying there's something else?"

"The last thing. And before I tell you, you gotta know, I only found out a month ago, in July."

*Here it comes*, I thought. *Her first missed period.* I wasn't ready, but we might as well get it over with. My mouth too dry to speak, I shrugged an okay.

Her red fingernails tapped the edge of the bench. "John's family, and so John too, have connections with some kind of think tank company."

Now I was lost. "Think tank. What the hell is that?"

"Yeah, right, I know," she said. "It's his brother, actually. He works for this company. They do work for the government. It's all very hush-hush stuff. He, his brother, can never talk about it. He's got a security clearance of some kind. A nice guy but sort of a geek, and I think he has a crush on me, maybe just because I talk to him."

"Yeah," I said sarcastically. "It's because he wants to talk to you."

"No! He's a nice guy. Anyway, I got to asking him about what he does, and he let slip a couple things…"

There was more to the story, much more, and as she went on I got closer and closer to the edge of my seat. When she finished, I said, "This is unbelievable. We have to find Diane and tell her."

Erin said, "Give her a call."

"I will. The only question is whether she'll answer." I paused. "You know, I thought, for a second you'd come to tell me you were pregnant."

"Pregnant!" The seagulls scattered. Her eyes went wide. She grabbed my arm and suppressed a laugh by pressing her lips against my shoulder. Her mouth there sent a jolt of heat though me. She'd done the same thing when, right after our first and only night together, I'd asked a silly question. How dangerously easy it would've been to fall back into June, and start all over again.

Diane did answer my call, with a very soft, almost shy, "Sam, how are you?" To hear her say my name again took my breath for a moment. I had enough sense to ask how she was, which elicited something generic in response. When I told her what the call was about, that Erin had returned, and we should talk right away, her tone changed dramatically. She was not at home, but could meet us there in about an hour.

The drive to Diane's place was ten minutes, so during the time left I changed into fresh clothes then walked back to #11 and helped Erin get settled. Because she was only seventeen, she needed permission from her parents to stay at Noquebay alone. In fact, the name on the register and the credit card were her parents' and not Erin's. She'd checked in before coming out to see me on the peninsula.

I thought it would be uncomfortable being alone with her in the cabin again. It wasn't, and at that moment I didn't know if that was good or bad. As long as there was work, we were safe. Moving her luggage, putting groceries in the refrigerator, and opening the windows—working with her reminded me of our stint together as bartenders in Noquebay Tavern. Our second date had started out that way. She still moved about the room with the graceful athleticism she'd gained from competitive swimming, and which drew me to her in the first place. The work didn't take very long, or not long enough, and we were left with more than twenty minutes to kill before we had to leave.

I opened a couple of diet colas and we sat down on the couch. I raised my can. So did she. We tapped to the summer of '13 and drank. I said, "You drove a long way all by yourself. You didn't have to. But I'll tell you, Diane is going to, well, I don't know how she'll react. I don't know much at all." My hand lying lazily between us, I leaned back and rested my head on the back of the couch.

She took my hand. "Oh Sam, breaking up is such a drag, isn't it?"

I gave her hand a squeeze. "The one in July was no picnic either."

She leaned in and kissed me, put down the soda, and put her hand on my chest. And once more I was helpless in her arms. We fit together perfectly, like two finely milled pieces of wood fashioned by a master carpenter. No glue required. Her legs coiled about mine. Without conscious thought, our arms became a gyroscopic tangle, as did our tongues. Yours is mine, and mine is ours. She'd tripped some kind of internal clock, but was time running forward or backward? I couldn't tell, the numbers were a blur.

# Chapter Six

# A Summons to Memphis

When I turned Erin's Corolla off Wasko Road onto the gravel driveway of the Warren home, we were only five minutes late. Diane greeted us by the back door of the screen porch. There did not appear to be anyone else at home. We walked toward her. She looked at Erin. "So, it really is you." Then at me. "Hello, Sam." Her tone was guarded, almost formal, unusual for her.

I nodded. Diane was in dark slacks and a very nice white, button blouse; something of a contrast to the shorts and shirts Erin and I were wearing. Diane's long, dark hair was back in some kind of ponytail and she was wearing less makeup than usual. I said, "You look good, like you've been to an interview or something."

Her mouth twitched in a noncommittal way. She spoke to Erin. "This must be pretty big stuff to bring you all this way."

I answered for her. "It is, Diane. It is." I pointed. "Can we sit on the porch?"

Diane waved us in. The furniture was wicker, and dated at that, both the couch, on which Erin and I sat, and the chair that Diane selected directly across from us. Before sitting, she lowered the shades by half to dim the late afternoon sun still streaming through the screens. The aroma from recently cut alfalfa on a nearby field wafted by. She offered us something to drink. We declined. Finally, she sat and said, "I can't imagine what this is about."

Even though the couch was rather small, I was not sitting close to Erin. I looked at her and suggested she start with what she told me about John and his family.

"John who?" asked Diane.

"John Moscatelli. I was dating him most of the summer."

"Before or after Sam?" Diane asked.

"Both." Erin sat forward, elbows on her knees. "We broke up a few weeks ago. But that's not why I'm here. It's more about his brother. He's working for an intelligence organization that does work for the federal government."

Diane's eyes went wide. "You're working with spies now? What the hell."

"I know," Erin said. "It sounds a lot more glamorous than it is. Over the months I was dating John I got to know his brother, Chet, pretty well. Like I told Sam, he's a shy sort of guy, no girlfriend that I ever saw, married to his job. I showed enough interest in his work." She looked meaningfully at Diane. "You know how it goes."

Diane sat back, and I saw the first smile of the day. "I think I do. But what's this to do with me?" The fingers of her left hand lightly drummed the armrest, the nails—the were pink with white crescents that day—clicking on the wicker. It was a new habit, these tapping nails. I'd harassed her into giving up the cigarettes, and when finally she did, this nervous little tic was born.

Erin put her hands together. "Before I broke up with John, I knew they figured out the body from the lake wasn't Jean, your sister. Sam had told me in one of his texts that no one was sure if she was dead or alive and living somewhere; so I thought I'd ask Chet to do me a favor. John made a stink about it. But, like, he owed me. I'd dumped Sam for him, didn't I?" She made it sound so matter-of-fact, it put me back in my seat.

"Hey!" I said. "I'm sitting right here."

Erin sat straight and put her hand on my forearm. "Sorry, Sam. I didn't mean it like that. It's just the way I said it to *him*."

Suddenly distracted, Diane looked at me as if wondering. *Are Erin and you back together?* Or maybe I'd imagined it. In any case, Diane recovered quickly. "So Chet, what favor?"

Erin refocused. "After talking to Chet over and over he finally told me what he really does—he finds people, or his spy shop does.

I thought of Jean right away. I gave him her name and everything I knew and said 'bet you can't find this one,' or some such crap. Just to challenge him a little. John didn't like what I was doing, but it didn't bother Chet."

Diane crept to the edge of the chair. Her eyes grew dark. "And…"

I said, "It took a couple of weeks. They even used facial recognition but… You tell her, Erin."

"He found her. We found your sister."

Diane slid off the chair onto the floor and collapsed. Kneeling there, sitting on her feet, she put her face in her hands and said, "Oh my God." Her voice was strained, barely audible. She started shaking then cried so intensely I couldn't tell if they were tears of joy or anguish or relief or all three.

We went to her, the two of us, one on each side. I put my arm around her shoulders and rested my chin by her ear. Erin put her right hand on Diane's knee and we waited. I grabbed a box of tissues off the end table and gave her a handful.

"She's alive. She's alive, Sam," Diane said finally, sniffling. "Six fucking years. Not a letter. Not a text. Not a call." She made a fist with her left hand and beat it repeatedly into her thigh. "Why? All these years. She put me through…" The blows became harder. I grabbed her pounding arm, first with one hand, then I needed both. She twisted toward me and started swinging with both fists. She landed a couple of glancing blows. One knocked my glasses away, but none were aimed in a way to do any damage. I snatched both wrists and secured them between us.

"It's all right," I said. "We'll figure it out."

She rapped her forehead against my shoulder, then lifted her mascara-lined face to me, her eyes red, tears coursing to the corners of her mouth. "Oh Sam, I'm sorry. I'm so…"

I let go her wrists and wrapped her up. "I'm sorry too, Dee. Me too."

We needed a break, especially Diane. She left to clean up her face and change into some more comfortable clothes. I got three glasses of ice water from the kitchen. Ten minutes later we were together again, each of us had caught our breath. We sat in the same seats as before. Diane apologized to Erin for what she had just witnessed, but not to me, which I took as a compliment.

Erin asked, "Was it a good thing that I asked? I mean, I can see how much it means to you, but maybe I shouldn't have. It certainly was none of my business."

Diane put her glass of water on an end table and rubbed her palms together. "You'd think that'd be an easy answer, but it's not. I would have thought so too before today. I'm happy to hear about it, of course. Who wouldn't be? My sister, the one person in my whole family that I loved—love—the most is still alive. But I'm scared. I have this awful feeling in the pit of my stomach and I don't know why."

I moved to the edge of my seat. "I have a pretty good idea. It's a shock to hear after all this time. Who wouldn't feel that way? And there's still so much we don't know about her."

Erin said, "Maybe if I tell you a little more about what Chet told me, that'll help."

Diane nodded. "Do you know where she lives?"

"Memphis, Tennessee," Erin said. "Chet said she's very under the radar. They couldn't find a phone number on her and she's changed her name to Bethany Brooks. Never stays in the same job very long. It looks like she doesn't live at the same address for more than a few months. Not doing very well financially either, from what they can see."

Diane rubbed her forehead. "Oh my god, Sam, how far is Memphis?"

"I checked. About seven hundred miles. Twelve-hour drive. I did a Google on Bethany in Memphis and got nothing. She must be renting. She might not even have a driver's license. We'd have never found her."

Diane sucked on her lips, looked at Erin and whispered, "Thank you so much. I'll never be able to repay you."

Erin held up a palm. "No. We're even. A couple months ago, you could have kept me off that crazy, midnight mission with Sam. I'll never forget that night as long as I live."

"Neither will I." Smiling, I looked down. "I thought everything would have to be perfect for us to get away with it. Turned out, nothing went right, and we still got the buckle."

Diane said, "Max told me you got lost on the way back to the boat, Sam."

Erin said, "That's nothing. When we were under water, the pump turned on and sucked me against the grid. I almost drown."

Diane looked at me, eyes narrowed. "You never told me that."

"Never came up."

"She almost died, and you just let it slip." Diane rolled her eyes. "Max mentioned something about you two falling asleep after skinny dipping."

"It wasn't a skinny dip," I protested.

"But we did fall asleep in the beach towels," Erin said. "And we hooked up the next night anyway, so…"

"Erin!"

Diane pointed at me. "I knew it. Huh. The night the boat blew up?" We said it was. "Yeah," Diane said. "Max and me too."

Erin said to me, "You never said a word about that."

"What?"

"That Max and Diane were dating."

"Well, I'm so glad you two got together and cleared it all up."

"Also, none of my business," Diane said. "But I gotta ask. Was the snooping around you were doing with Chet the reason you and John broke up?"

"Yes, but not the way you think. He wasn't jealous of his brother in a romantic way. Oh, no, no, no. He was jealous I was spending time with him."

"How dare you!" Diane said.

"Right? And it wasn't just Chet. If I took off, say a weekend with my girlfriends to do something, he didn't like that either."

"Uh oh," Diane said. "Control freak."

I shook my head. "Even I, who knows less about women than anyone, I know that ain't gonna fly."

Diane stood and looked at me. "Call me tomorrow?"

"Yeah. Sure. Memphis. We'll figure it out." I waved Erin

toward the car.

On the drive home, I thanked Erin again for everything she'd done. Getting John and Chet to do the legwork no one else could've possibly done. She'd come a long way to deliver the information in person. It meant a lot to Diane. More than that, I got a chance to see the girl who'd been such an important part of my summer, my life, one more time. I parked the Corolla next to #11. We got out and talked across the hood, me resting my leg near the grill; she was standing next to the fender. It was after suppertime, about 6:30 p.m.

With a tightening in my throat, I tossed her the key. For once, I knew exactly what was going on between us—it was the end of the road. There wouldn't be a crash and burn. I was both glad and sad we hadn't had more time earlier, before going over to see Diane, because we both knew if we'd had an extra ten minutes we'd have ended up beyond entangled in her bedroom. That was what my throat was telling me; there was a sadness because I knew just as well as I was standing next to her, that there was so much more to this girl than what I knew, so many more places to explore, things to do. What a trip it would have been. But she was a big-city girl from Skokie, and I was three hundred miles and a world removed in more ways than one.

Plus, there was another girl, and I was crazy about her.

"You have something to eat inside?" I asked, though I knew very well. I'd help stack the refrigerator.

She pointed over her shoulder. "Yeah. Fine. Not very hungry anyway."

"Huh. Me neither." I looked down. My fingernail found a chip in the paint. "Tomorrow, your plans are—"

"Try to get some rest. Leave after breakfast in the morning."

I nodded. Blinked repeatedly. Lost for words.

"Sam, it's okay. I understand. I saw what happened. You were great, leaned right into her anger. That was something."

"Well, I couldn't get away, so I ducked."

She showed me her smile, which always made me melt. I'd remember not to joke around again. Too risky.

She said, "I'm serious. Don't minimize what you did."

"Okay. I won't."

"You two belong together, Sam. Good luck." She stepped closer and opened her arms. We embraced there for a long time, as tight as a pinecone in spring. One second for every hour we'd spent together that summer; then, many seconds more for the times that would never be.

# CHAPTER SEVEN

# Deborah Manticore

The next morning, a Friday, I was up early, put on a better-than-average shirt, and had breakfast. I'd asked Erin to stop by the tavern before leaving and you know what they say about last impressions, they don't mean a thing. Throughout the night, I thought a dozen times of how crazy it was to let a girl like Erin walk out of my life, but there was no way to make it work. Not there. Not then. I was in the kitchen reading a book when the bell on the tavern door rang. I'd already opened the door leading from kitchen to tavern so I could see her come in. She stood near the bar in blue jeans, a light sweater and sandals, her hands clasped in front of her.

I walked toward her, raised my hand, and said, "Hi. How'd you sleep?"

"Oh, all right. What about you?"

I put my hand in my back pocket. "Not so all right."

"Yeah, me neither." I thought she blushed a bit. "Have you called Diane?"

I nodded. "She's coming over later to figure something out. She wants to go to Memphis, of course, and track down Jean, or Bethany." I motioned to the bar stools for us to sit. "She acts like it's a trip to Marinette to do some shopping. She's not being real. For one thing, we got no car."

One of her eyebrows raised. "We?"

"Yeah. She wants me to go along."

"No surprise there. Who else can she count on? You said her family is a disaster. I hope you're flattered."

"Well, yeah. I guess so." I paused, wondering how much I should reveal. The argument against going involved some fairly personal stuff, but Erin had always been a sympathetic listener, she wasn't a gossip, and she lived four hours away. If her parents came back to Noquebay next summer I might see her again, but she'd be eighteen by then and her life would be her own. I said, "It takes money to travel. I'm flat busted. She might have a few bucks, and okay, I do too, enough to get me to Green Bay, maybe."

She turned a bit toward the bar. "You could take food with you. Your real problem is getting there. If you had a car, you could even sleep in it, push to shove." I agreed that might work. "You'd come back smelling like trolls, but you wouldn't notice, 'cuz you'd both smell the same."

"Okay, I gotta draw the line on the smelly part." I clicked my fingernails.

"So we got food and sleeping. What's next?" she asked.

"Lots of things." I counted fingers. "My parents. School." I hesitated on the third, but I asked, "The guy that found her, he's a pretty good guy? At what he does, I mean. The information, we're sure she's there?"

"You don't want to go on a wild goose chase." She took a breath. "I don't know, Sam. I think it's good. John and I were still together when he got the dope on Jean, so he had no ax to grind."

"Okay, thanks." I couldn't look her in the eye so I scratched at something on the bar.

"There's something else." It wasn't a question. She knew. I shifted my weight, then turned back and forth on the bar stool. I looked toward the juke box.

She put her hand on my knee to stop my fidgeting. "Sam, what is it?"

A long sigh. "I don't even know how to say this." She took her hand off my leg and waited. "We... Diane and me, we were dating for over a month. And you know how, with you and me, I didn't even know you for like five days and it didn't matter, because well, I guess we just hit it off—"

"You haven't had sex yet," she said.

I tented my fingertips across my forehead then dragged them down over my face. "Yeah, that's it. No sex."

"But you've done some of the…"

"Opening acts, yeah."

"And they went pretty good?"

"Sure, yes. Just never been, you know, the headliners."

"No pun there." She laughed a little. I did too.

"Listen, you're making too much of it. She's already made the decision. She's asked you to go on a road trip—alone, right?" I said yes. "Then it's just a matter of when. And I'll bet you a hundred dollars it's Memphis… If you ever get there."

I took a breath. "I'm going to miss you so much."

"Me too." She slipped off her stool. "I better be going."

"Let me walk you out."

For whatever reason, I can recall every step between the barstools and the car—holding the door for her, walking down the porch steps, approaching the Corolla. She turned and said, "Goodbye, Sam."

We gave each other a kiss on the cheek and another hug. She got in the car and drove away. She was the first, and up to that time, the only girl to take me to her bed. When it happened back in June, I didn't have to tell her, she knew. But I never heard a careless word from her, not a single put-down or tease. Highest marks, Erin, then and now. I was lucky, very lucky.

---

Diane called about an hour after Erin left. I knew she'd be eager to talk about her sister and what our next step should be. "Eager" didn't even begin to describe her state of mind. She'd already mapped out the morning for us and a plan to get to Memphis. The first thing she was going to do was talk to her mother and father.

"They've got some money," she said. "They can pony up some cash for us. I mean, it's their daughter. Carter is up with his coffee. And I can hear Ethyl clomping around upstairs." When I asked about getting there, Diane was vague, skipping from borrowing a car to taking the bus, she even mentioned hitchhiking. I put a hard stop on the last idea. She gave me the "get out and live" argument, but only for a second, then let it drop. I thought the bus idea was a groaner. The idea of being cooped up like that for almost a day sounded terrible.

"Never mind that," she said. "We're meeting someone for lunch who might help us." When I asked who, she became evasive. "Keep an open mind. You've never met her. I have, and she liked Jean, so don't be surprised or upset." I said I wouldn't be, if she'd just give me the name.

"Deborah Manticore."

"What! Willard Sr.'s wife. Are you crazy?"

"Sam, she's still Jean's mother-in-law, so she's got skin in the game. Now, you promised to give it a chance."

I hadn't promised anything but I saw no point in arguing further. "Fine. This oughta be good. Where?"

"Porterfield's Resort and Outfitters. I'll pick you up."

Diane arrived at Noquebay Resort around 11:30 a.m., later than expected. I went out to meet her. She got out of the car. We said a tentative hello then hugged like we meant it. I asked, "What took you so long? I couldn't stand the waiting."

She closed her eyes, exhaled through her teeth, and said she got into an argument with her mother about going to Memphis to find Bethany Jean, which is what she was now calling her sister. Her mother didn't believe Erin's story at all. In fact, once the body in Red Wolf Lake was identified as someone other than her daughter, Ethyl had concluded that Jean wasn't anywhere but dead and that she'd never be found, in Memphis or anywhere else. Wanting desperately for closure on the fate of her daughter, Ethyl had put all her eggs in one basket, and when the body in the lake didn't pan out, she'd lost all hope. Therefore, she wouldn't help Diane with expenses on what she thought was a waste of time and money.

"What about Carter?" I asked. "Did you ask him?"

"By the time my mother and I were talking about this, he was gone. But it doesn't matter. If I was dying of thirst, I wouldn't ask him for a sip of water."

We got into her car and headed for our lunch date. Diane's

expectations about going to a big city like Memphis and tracking down a single person who had lived a vaporous, vagabond existence were optimistic in the least, and in some ways, off the wall. This was no less true than when she told me the reason we were meeting Deborah Manticore for lunch. If she was going to help us, we were going to need an awful lot of it. I couldn't figure why she'd be interested in the first place. I could have asked Diane these questions, but they would have spurred another argument, and we had just gotten back together. Another spat was the last thing we needed.

When seen from the air, the West End of Red Wolf Lake looks like a profile of Charlie Brown's Snoopy dog facing down and left. Snoopy's neck is the Narrows. Here, Noquebay Resort sits on top of the dog collar. Walnut Creek, the lake's only outlet and the town by the same name, reside by his south-pointing snout. Opposite this, where his ears would be, Crabalocker Creek brings spring runoff from as far away as Crabalocker Mountain twenty-five miles to the north. Between lake and mountain are acres of forested wildlands, the town of Ellis Junction (which lies right on the creek ten miles north of the lake), and several sections of the Manticore Farms land empire thru which the stream flows.

The Porterfields didn't run a resort, they operated a complex that included a supper club, outfitter for kayaks and canoes, and resort lodge all under one roof. The building was huge, constructed of rough-hewn logs, and set squarely at the joining of the lake and Crabalocker Creek. The outfitters faced the creek. The lodge faced the lake and had a great view of the West End. The supper club had to be toward the back because that's where the kitchen was, along with all the offices.

Diane parked the Chrysler on the gravel lot outside the restaurant door. She pointed at a Lexus. "That's Deborah's model, but it's the wrong color."

We went inside Porterfield's Country Inn. There was a woman sitting alone at a table near the window. "Is that her?" I asked.

"No," Diane said. "Deborah is a brunette." She looked about, worried. "We're a few minutes late. I hope she didn't bolt on us."

A woman, who I later learned was the owner of the place, approached, tapped Diane on the shoulder, and asked us to follow her. Naturally, Diane recognized her, so I thought nothing of it until we were taken to a private office far in the back, where a small lunch table had been set up for three. The woman showed us into the room and we sat down. Seconds later, another person came down the hall.

"That's Deborah Manticore," Diane whispered. She was younger than her husband by fifteen years or more. That would put her in her late fifties, but she wore it well: erect posture, skin clear except for a few lines and blemishes. But her eyes couldn't complete the effect, they looked tired and care-worn. We stood as she entered the room. The woman closed the door. Diane introduced us. I shook her hand and we sat down. I sat opposite Deborah.

The simple lunch was already on the table—sandwich, small salad, water. Neither Diane nor I touched anything though, wondering why we were called to a public place then whisked to a back room.

Deborah started on her salad as if nothing were amiss. She noticed our quiet hands immediately. "Hope you haven't lost your appetites."

I looked at Diane, then said, "No ma'am." I took a drink of water and buttered a roll, just to be polite.

Diane selected one of the prepackaged dressings and put it on her salad. "Thanks for talking to us. I guess it must be kinda bad over at your place right now."

"You guess correctly." She used her napkin. "Everyone thinks they know your business when it's in the paper every week. In a way, they do. But they don't know all of it. I'm sure both of you have heard about Mitchell and Willard so I won't bore you. But that's not the worst of it." She took a sip of water.

I had a bite of bread in my mouth by then. "So, what's the worst?"

Deborah cut her sandwich in half but didn't take a bite. "Diane, you called this morning about your sister. What's that all about?"

Diane put her hands on her lap and recounted the story Erin

had told about the discovery of Bethany Brooks in Memphis by facial recognition and how it was thought to be a match for Jean.

"Ah huh," Deborah said. "And how does a girl from Chicago get her hands on this kind of information?"

Definitely a question for me to field, but she'd caught me again with a hunk of bread in my mouth. Deborah saw my problem and gave me a couple beats. I took a sip of water, then told her about Erin's government connection and that she and I were friends. Given her husband's history of working with organized crime, I thought it was an explanation Deborah could relate to, since the mob and government had some similarities.

"From what I can see," Deborah said. "At the very least, you have to go down there and take a look around. It's been a long time, six years. If she's alive, maybe she's there. Maybe not. But if you're looking for the answer from me, you're going to be disappointed." She picked up half of her sandwich. "Because I don't know where she is."

Diane looked at me. I blinked. Had Diane requested the meeting or Deborah? At that point, I wasn't sure. I'd just met the woman and coming to the meeting was Diane's idea in the first place, so she was going to have to make the next move. I was only there for moral support.

Diane straightened the knife and fork next to her plate, then looked up. "I've already decided, or I mean, I agree with you, Mrs. Manticore. But we, neither Sam or I, have the money or the car to get there, to Memphis, I mean. I know you and Jean always got along pretty well, so I was wondering... I was hoping, you could help us out."

Deborah finished her salad as she listened and considered Diane's request. Very deliberately, she took a drink of water and dabbed her lips with a napkin.

"Sam, I never answered your question. The worst thing is, I don't know where... I think I've lost Scotty. After the TV story, they arrested everyone in the house except me, Steve and Scotty. Oh, and the dog, I got to keep him. He left a couple days later, Scotty I mean, not the dog. I haven't heard from him since."

"You don't think he's looking for Jean?" I said. "Technically, they're still married."

Deborah blinked away a tear. "I don't know what's in his head or where he went, but if Memphis is a possibility, I want someone down there on my side."

Diane sat forward, eyes alight. "That's us, Deborah. Just give us a hand."

Deborah shook her head. "Impossible. For god's sake, I can't even have lunch with you without all this cloak and dagger crap. Why do you think we're in this office? It's for your protection as well as mine. Don't say a word about this meeting to anyone. Terri Porterfield," she waved her hand toward the hallway. "is my bff. We can trust her. But here's what I can do." She wrote down a name and address on a napkin and handed it to Diane. "Talk to her. She'll know what to do."

"Where is this address?" I asked.

"Ellis Junction Water, Track, and Trail. It's right in town on the creek."

# CHAPTER EIGHT

# Ellis Junction Water, Track, and Trail

As the name implied, there had been a time when the train stopped in Ellis Junction, but no more. The town did remain a confluence in its own right, however. Though the tracks had been moved to a new bed a quarter mile south of town, the old rail line had been converted into a popular bike trail, part of which included a quaint, old railroad bridge that crossed Crabalocker Creek. State Highway 64 still skirted the town limit on the north side and the creek was the border to the west. The town hadn't known a growth phase since WWII, but if any new homes were built, they went up north and west of the highway.

The drive was about twenty minutes from Noquebay Resort. Diane had been to Ellis Junction any number of times but not recently; me only once. She drove directly to Water, Track, and Trail, situated right where you'd expect, next to the bike trail on the banks of Crabalocker Creek. Old growth poplars and maples surrounded the building, which looked like a converted school house right down to the concrete steps and elevated front door, high ceilings, and peaked roof. There were a few picnic tables in front, parking on the side, and a gravel lot with a bike rack that went unused. Three bikes rested separately by the front door, over which a sign hung on rusty iron that marked the place with its name. On the bottom it said, *Betty Toscana, Proprietor.*

Diane stopped me. "Look at the name, Sam. Toscana is Deborah Manticore's maiden name. Got to be relation." We walked inside.

The front third of the building was retail space. If Betty Toscana was using the back part as living quarters, I couldn't tell. Customers got an eyeful of country-kitchen deco right down to the checkerboard cloth covers on the jars of jam and pickled vegetables that lined the pie chests and wooden kitchen pantries. On the other hand, the tables and chairs were more of the soda-fountain white, wrought iron variety. A girl I recognized from school named Kelly Thompson was behind the counter, tending the cash register. The three bikers were off to the right, standing near the window, drinking something from a bottle. I approached the checkout empty handed.

"Hey, Sam, what are you and Diane doing out here?" Kelly asked. "Did you bike?"

"No, we drove." I turned to Diane. "Have you met Kelly Thompson? She's a junior this year." They both said hi and I went on. "We're here to see the owner, Mrs. Toscano. Is she around?" Kelly said she was out back and she'd go get her.

A minute later they both came through the door. Betty looked a little disheveled and in need of a nap, as opposed to her store, which was well kept and bright. She eyed me up immediately, then Diane, seeming to make a calculation and finding the answer she wanted.

"I'm Betty Toscano. Sam and Diane, I presume. Did I get a call about you two today?" Betty asked.

"Ah, probably." Diane hesitated. "From—"

"That's all I need." Betty waved us over to a table opposite the bikers. "We can talk here. Want a drink? Pull something out of the cooler there. It's on me."

We both begged off.

"All right." She raised her hand. "Kelly, bring me a lemonade."

She was older than Deborah, and though there may have been a little family resemblance, it wasn't obvious. The pale slacks and shirt outfit didn't do her any favors, but I had the sense she didn't care.

Betty said, "Okay, fill me in. Deborah couldn't talk for very long."

I asked her how much she knew about Jean's history, her

marriage to Willard Scott Manticore Jr., or Scotty as his mother called him, and her disappearance.

Betty sat forward. "I lost my son, Trent, about twenty-five years ago. Since then, Deborah has always been there for me and vice versa. She's my niece but we're really more like sisters. So yeah, we talk, and I know about Scotty and his marriage."

It took us a few minutes more to fill her in on the story about the buckle, the body in the lake, and ending with the Memphis information.

"Do you know why Jean left town back then?" asked Betty.

"Oh, yeah. Like we said." I nodded at Diane. "We think she found the pump and was going to turn them in. The Manticores, I mean."

Betty took a drink of lemonade. "Look, I've known Willard Manticore all my life, knew his father too. He was so crooked, when he died, they had to screw him in the ground to bury 'im. There is nothing I'd put past that bunch. You hear me? Nothing. Anything for a buck, be it legal or otherwise, it don't matter. I know Scotty too. To my way of thinking, he's the only one over there has a shot at getting out of that ranch without wearing orange." She tapped the table with her cup. "That's why I never bought the body in the lake story. I think there's a different kind a stink here, I just wish I knew what it was."

She scratched her shoulder. "Money for the trip is no problem. Just don't ask where it came from and remember, if anyone asks, cash is not traceable." She raised her hand again. "Kelly, the envelope."

It was manila and there was a definite bulge. She slid it across the table. "You found it in a ditch."

Diane was wide-eyed, stunned. I picked up the envelope and said, "Thanks. Thanks a lot."

The decision to go to Memphis, it seemed, had been made for me. But was I ready? I stood, along with Mrs. Toscano, my stomach in my chest, fully believing the meeting was over.

"We're not done yet." Betty held up a couple fingers. "Two, transportation. Come with me."

We exited through a side door and went to a double garage on the back of the property, obviously newer than the school house. She opened one of the bay doors to reveal a car covered by a black, fabric cover.

"This car used to belong to Trent." Hands on her hips, Betty stood in a very clean, well-kept garage. "I've kept it up for all these years. Oil changes, tune ups, ran it every year for a month then put it back here. It's time for it to get out and really stretch its legs." She nodded at me. "Go ahead, pull the cover."

# CHAPTER NINE

# Driving a Stick

The windfall from the visit with Betty Toscano had convinced Diane that a trip to Memphis was meant to be. I was in another place all together, in a trap, or on an island in the middle of the sea, the water rising, and no boat to row. After we left Water, Track, and Trail we'd stopped at a county park to talk about our options, and for the second time in less than a week, we both raised our voices, and I don't mean to Heaven.

She had no idea where my life was at. She was a legal adult, I was not. She'd graduated high school; in eleven days, I would begin my senior year. I had responsibilities to my family; so far as I could tell, except for Jean, she felt none toward hers. And though I could hear her voice in my head saying, *Are you bragging or complaining?* the fact was, each of those was an anchor tethered to my ass, while hers walked wild and free as you please.

I'd have given my left arm for fifteen minutes on the phone with Max. He'd have been the perfect pop-off valve, the objective eye-in-the-sky I needed to sort this out. Betty had handed us enough cash to make it to Memphis and back. The car, though not as sound as the dollar, looked to be in pretty good shape. The red, 1986 Volkswagen Golf three-door had an 85 horsepower engine and a five-speed manual transmission. The body had minimal rust and the interior only a few dings. Betty had indeed taken good care of her son's car.

I drove the Golf home Friday night so my folks didn't see it until Saturday morning, the busiest half-day of the week at the resort. We put off talking about it until after lunch. I was in no way worried about speaking with either of them. They might actually give me the excuse I needed *not* to go on the trip at all. Because I had another reason the trip scared me, one I hadn't mentioned to Diane and wouldn't bring up with my parents. The relationship between Diane and I was on shaky footing at best. After the contentious discussion about Memphis, we'd parted without a kiss, for god's sake. If we weren't careful, a 700-mile road trip could very easily be the swan song for her and me together, forever. If it came down to rescuing Jean or keeping Diane, the choice was obvious. The real question was whether I could do both.

Our family had the usual lunch, and I corralled Mom and Dad right after. Dad was set on checking the work done by the electrical contractor on the mobile home park, so I almost had to lasso him to keep him at the table. Mom and Allison put away the leftovers from lunch while Dad and I sat at the table.

I said, "I want to tell you what Erin had to say when she was here."

Mom paused a second. "Okay, Allison, that's enough. You can go."

Allison stopped suddenly. "But I want to hear, too." Mom repeated her order. "Ahh, I never get to stay for the good stuff." Allison marched out the back door.

Mom sat down across from me. "Go ahead."

My heel tapped the floor. "She told me… she thinks she knows where Jean Warren is."

"Yeah, we know," Dad said. "Memphis."

"What!"

Mom said, "She told us when she was checking in, but wanted us to keep it secret until she told you. We've been wondering when you were going to let us in on it."

I exhaled. "It's been a ton to think about, I'll tell you that. For Diane too."

"Have you tried calling her?" Dad asked. "Jean."

I shook my head. "No phone we know of. She's off the grid. We think she's still in hiding, so she probably doesn't know what's been going on with the Manticores and the pump."

Mom said, "That's one possibility."

I blinked. "What else could it be?"

"Don't know," Dad said. "There are a lot of reasons you might not find a phone number on her, or why she wouldn't have a phone."

"How did they find her?" Mom asked.

"Erin didn't tell you?" I asked. They both shook their heads and I thought, *Of course she didn't tell them that.* "Facial recognition. Her ex-boyfriend knew a guy who knew a guy. That kind of thing."

I put my hands on the edge of the seat and straightened my arms. "Diane wants to go down there and find her and bring her back home."

Mom and Dad looked at each other.

"And that's where the red car comes in," I said. "It's a loaner from ah, from an aunt."

"Fanny?" Mom asked.

"No," I said. "A different one."

"Can she afford the trip?" Dad asked. "Memphis is hundreds of dollars away. We're talking gas, food, lodging, whatever else comes up."

"No, Diane couldn't go without help. We, I mean she, got money from the same aunt."

Mom added, "And she, Diane, not the aunt, wants you to go along."

I'd never blushed so hard in my life, and I didn't know why. Diane and I had never slept together, but the implication was all it took. I couldn't find any words at that point so I nodded.

"What do you think?" Dad asked. "Is this a good idea?"

*Dirty trick*, I thought. I cleared my throat. "I know what you're thinking. I'm not eighteen. I got school. You could make a list." I paused. "But yeah, I think I should go with her." And in that moment, in my head, the sentence finished itself. *I should go with her because she needs me.* I opened my hand and counted the reasons. "We have money. She has her phone. I'll call every day. Every hour, if you want. Joe and Kevin can cover for me around the resort." I turned my hand into a fist and tapped it on the table.

"And mostly because, she doesn't have anyone else. Her brother won't do it. She'll never ask her father in a million years. She's got girlfriends but they won't go, not for this."

They grilled me on some more of the details. How long would I be gone? Did I have Jean's address? I said I didn't know the length of the trip, and the address was suspect. Dad said, "Then you'll need some luck."

I blinked twice. "You mean… it's okay?"

"We didn't say it's okay," Mom said. "But yes, you can go. You and Diane have showed us who you are this summer. We wouldn't be running Noquebay Resort right now without your ingenuity and persistence. You're only months short of your eighteenth birthday, so—"

"Don't prove us wrong." Dad got up and went out the back door. In that moment I wasn't convinced that he and Mom were one hundred percent in agreement on this one.

A couple minutes later, I was in the Golf on my way to pick up Diane. She couldn't drive a stick. She was fine with me as the only driver, but I wasn't. She had to learn how to use the manual or the deal was off. I picked her up. We found a lightly used town road and I put her behind the wheel. She stalled it a couple times, naturally, but kept it out of the ditch. There was nothing to hit out there and the lesson turned out to be quite a laugh. She played up the NASCAR driver angle for all it was worth, acting like she was winning the Daytona 500 at forty-three mph, downshifting and taking the curves like she was Junior Johnson. She learned fast, and well enough to drive rural highways. I'd be doing cities and Interstates, anywhere the traffic was heavy. She pulled over and stopped.

"When are we leaving?" I asked.

"I'm packed," she said. "In my head I'm already there. Tomorrow?"

I was lightheaded suddenly, and my ears were ringing. I didn't know what to say, so I looked straight ahead and didn't say anything.

She leaned forward, her eyes on me, as if to get my attention. "You want to go, right?"

I exhaled for the first time in a long minute. "You really think it's the right thing, this car, this trip, hundreds of miles…"

"Yeah." Her voice was soft but not a whisper. "I really do. And you're the guy I want to do it with."

I had to smile at that. "Then drive me home because I haven't packed a thing. We should leave early, no later than seven, I'd say, so we don't—"

She squeezed my arm, then put the back of her hand on my cheek, and I stopped talking. Her eyes were moist. "Whatever you think is fine with me."

"Yeah. Okay."

She smiled shyly. "Thank you, Sam."

I shrugged. "Haven't done anything yet."

"You taught me to drive the stick."

I put my finger under her chin and brought her mouth to my own. She rose to meet me. Her lips warmed on mine. It was the first kiss we'd shared since we'd been back together. It was worth the wait.

# Chapter Ten

# Road Trip

The next morning, I got up at 5:30 a.m. I'd gotten a little sleep the night before, more than I'd expected actually. Once the decision to go to Memphis had been made, I found it easier to relax. That didn't stop me from getting up earlier than necessary and repacking the small grip I'd put together the night before. I thought the most likely stay over was going to be two nights. Diane was more optimistic. We were going to walk up to this so-called address, there'd be a tearful reunion, and Bethany Jean (or whatever her name was) would pack her bag and jump in the Volkswagen, waving goodbye to Memphis forever. Diane thought we'd be on our way home Monday afternoon, with a possible overnight on the road depending on our departure time.

I walked into our kitchen just after six. I dropped my bag and went to the pantry to retrieve my usual breakfast of Wheaties, Frosted Flakes, and milk. Mom walked in from the bathroom, ready for the day well ahead of me. She took a seat at the table.

She said, "Are you all set? Got a water bottle, something to snack on?"

"Water, yeah." I poured both cereals into a bowl. "We're gonna stop in Walnut Creek for the munchies. Then I think we should turn some of the cash into credit cards."

"Good idea. Keep some cash, though."

"Oh yeah." I poured the milk. Mom seemed more at ease with the trip now than I did. Maybe because she'd taken a cross-country trip of her own with her girlfriends after high school. We'd marveled at the pictures of the California coast, San Diego, Monterey, and her friends crossing the American West. If I knew Mom, she was thinking if she could do it then, I could do it now.

Dad came in the back door and sat down. "I checked the Golf for you. Oil's good. Right rear tire pressure was low so I filled it. Keep an eye on that one. Washer and wipers work."

"Thanks, Dad."

"In good shape for the shape it's in." He knew me well enough to know I wouldn't have checked any of those things until they became a problem somewhere in the middle of an Illinois cornfield and not a service station for twenty miles.

I finished my breakfast, put the bowl and spoon in the sink, and picked up my bag. "Diane's expecting me early."

"Good luck, son," Dad said.

"We love you, honey," Mom said. "Remember, call every day."

"I will." I embraced both of them, and left.

When I walked in the back door of Diane's home she was sitting alone at the kitchen table, a cup of coffee in hand, a small suitcase at her feet. She looked up when I walked in. I said, "Hey, babe, ready to roll?"

She bit her lower lip and shrugged. "I'm packed but..." She turned the mug in her hands. "I've been doing a lot of thinking, Sam. Up all night, actually."

I sat down at the table. With a closer look I could see the tired eyes, her usually dark complexion had lost some of its color. "You're worried."

Her leg bounced, half a smile came my way. "You think?"

"Well, what is it? You still want to go to Memphis, right?"

"Oh shit, Sam. I do and I don't. You're right. Everything you said about finding her in a big city like that. What the fuck do I know about Memphis? Not a damn thing. Even if we do find her, what then? She's not going to be the same person. I'm not the same person. She might not even recognize me. How could I be so stupid?"

I put my hand on her arm. "Wait. Wait, babe. Is this the Diane Alyssa Warren that I know? The one that found the paint that colored the corn that put the old man in jail? Yeah, I know that I was saying all that stuff. But that was yesterday, and you can't listen to my bullshit. I was just thinking out loud. Listen to half of what I say, at the most."

Her fingertips tapped on the coffee cup. There was never any rhythm to it. More like Morse code or the rapping of a tree branch on a window pane during a summer storm. "Yeah, but which half?"

"Good point. Ethyl and Carter still asleep?"

As if to answer the question, Carter came down the steps draped in a threadbare bathrobe that must have been saved from before his incarceration. It'd been a week since I'd seen him, and it didn't look as if he was taking to life outside of prison very well. Instead of gaining weight on home cooking, he looked a few pounds thinner. Diane had also told me he'd lost his taste for alcohol and that he'd cut way back on the cigarettes, now only lighting up when he was alone, maybe three or four times a day. Nothing like the two-packs-a-day he used to smoke. He got to the bottom step before saying both our names in greeting; we answered back with a good morning.

"Suppose you two are fixin' to leave."

Diane said we were talking about it. Carter shuffled over to the coffee maker and poured himself a cup. He drank it black. He sat down, wrapped his bony fingers around the mug, and said, "Your mother is in no way approving of this trip of yours."

One side of Diane's face twitched. "Yeah, Carter, I'm aware. That's because she's not a positive person. Born that way."

"Diane," Carter said sternly. "I told you. I don't want to hear that sour talk about your mother. Not in this house."

That bought the color back to her cheeks, but she seemed to push away her usual response and said, "We'll be leaving in a minute so she won't have to worry."

Carter exhaled and looked down. "That wasn't my intention. In fact, I'm more behind this trip than you think. Now's the time to do it."

Diane was dismissive. "Whatever."

Carter stood up and took his coffee upstairs, his gait defeated.

Diane apologized for her father.

I waved it off. "Actually, my folks said something like that. If we don't do it now, we never would. And we'd be wondering for a long time what would have happened if we *had* gone."

"Liz and Jim said that?"

I said yes.

"And they trust you with me? Alone."

"They didn't say that. But I have a condom in my wallet."

She slapped my arm. "I knew it! But is it the one Nic gave you, or a new one?" She lifted her cup for a sip and stopped. "Just one?"

I groaned. "You are going to drive me crazy."

"Well, something to keep you awake all the way to Memphis, anyway."

We got in the car. As always, I buckled in, she didn't. I kept the key in my hand. She looked at me and said to get going. I said, "Nope, I've put up with it long enough. I'm not going anywhere until you buckle your seatbelt." She groaned the same old song and dance about how uncomfortable they were, and she didn't believe in them. "Believe? What believe," I said. "It's not a religion and this ain't a church. Just put it on." She reached for the keys. I pulled them away. "We're not moving."

"For chrissakes, all right." She searched for the clip. "I gave up smoking for you and now this. What next?"

"Well, almost on the smoking," I started the car. She shot me a look. "Dee, I kissed you last night. You think I can't tell?"

"Damn it." She looked out her window. "Only when we were broke up. I quit again."

Diane was going to be my navigator, but within the first ten miles after leaving Walnut Creek it was obvious she was going to be offline for several hours. She inclined her seatback and closed her eyes. I turned down the radio and she fell asleep. I knew the roads well enough in Wisconsin to do the highway changes on my own, but once we crossed into Illinois I'd need the navigator on her phone. The engine was a sipper. We didn't have to stop for gas until we got to the state line. Diane was still asleep when I pulled into a station. After paying at the pump, I went inside and purchased a phone holder for the dash. Then I plucked the cell out of Diane's purse, set up the NAV screen and we were off.

It was the first time I'd ever seen her asleep. It's true what they say about a woman at rest, with their eyes closed and stress has flown. There's a different kind of beauty, observable only then. My appreciation came only in brief glances. We were in Illinois now. The roads were new and even though I'd plotted a course to avoid Chicago, I had to keep up with the map to know where I was. After over four hours of sleep, Diane woke up. She hadn't been kidding about her sleepless night before.

She squinted out the window. "Where are we?" I gave her an approximation and showed her the phone. I also said I needed a break. She agreed and wanted something to eat. We got off at the next exit.

It was a crossroads. There were multiple places to choose from. I selected a bagel and soup chain I'd been to before, because I knew Diane would like the coffee and salads. I had a sandwich and we spent more time there than we needed to. Since we were now in wide open farm country, I offered to let Diane drive. She said she would, but I could see her heart wasn't in it. There were too many eighteen-wheelers on the road, and so many others racing by even though I'd been doing seventy-five mph.

It was midday. I turned on the radio. There was a tape player in the dash, but neither of us owned a single cassette. The AM/FM bands were chuck full of Jesus rock and preaching, oldies and one hip-hop station. Talk radio was everywhere. Diane was more in to Country music than I was, and it seemed the least abrasive, so I left it on. About four songs in Diane started to sing along with a tune I later learned was "All Your Life" by The Band Perry. Diane matched the girl on the radio note for note. I was gob smacked both by how good she was and the fact I'd never heard it from her before. Not a single note. Even at highway speed, I took my hands off the wheel and clapped.

"That was amazing." I looked at her. "You can really sing."

She shimmied her shoulders a little. "Ah, that was nothing. I like the song is all."

"No, wait. Sing another one when it comes on, if you know it." She tried to beg off, but I persisted. "Have you done karaoke? You'd be killer. Hell, you could front a band. Think of it. Screw Memphis. I'll take the next exit. We'll go to Nashville."

"Now you're teasing."

"Ten percent, maybe."

She sat back in her seat and read her magazines. I did all the driving. In trade, she sang some more songs—one by Carrie Underwood and a couple more after that. At one point, I glanced over in the middle of a song and caught her singing with her eyes closed. I watched that performance as long as I could and still kept the car on the road. Just seeing that, I was good for another hundred miles.

Illinois went on forever, the highway bisecting miles and miles of cornfields. The asphalt intersected with or ran parallel to railroad tracks, their paths marked every twenty miles or so by a cluster of grain elevators tended by a church and two taverns, or any multiple of that ratio. We talked about our plans for the morning. The address we had for Bethany Jean, our chances of finding her there, and what to do if we didn't. We also fine-tuned the story we would use to convince her to come back to Wisconsin. We knew what she knew—that the Manticores had been illegally taking water from Red Wolf Lake. What she probably didn't know: they'd been brought to justice, so she could come home again.

Finally, we stopped in Sikestan, Missouri, where we picked up some supper and I-55. By that point, I was feeling the wear of the road. My legs were stiff and my shoulders ached. I didn't want to stop for a sit-down meal though, because I thought we'd lose too much of the remaining daylight. We hit a drive-in with good bathrooms, gassed up the Golf, and got back on the road. Our next destination was West Memphis, Arkansas.

The sun was setting as we turned east onto I-40, crossed the Mississippi River, and arrived in Memphis, Tennessee.

# Chapter Eleven

# A Long Night in Memphis

Neither one of us knew anything about the city we were driving into, its neighborhoods, the streets, or even what kind of food was served in the restaurants. We arrived as night was falling and decided that a hotel close to the highway was the safest for new-comers who didn't know any better. That was the easy decision.

I pulled into the parking lot and stopped the engine. "So, what's it going to be? One room or two?"

"Are your parents going to expect a bill for one room or two?"

"Bill? What bill?" I lowered my brow. "And what do they expect? Two rooms separated by three feet of concrete. But we're paying in cash. They're never going to see a bill, because we're going to forget to bring it home."

She huffed a little laugh. "I can see you've put some thought into this. I'm the only one can rent legally. I'll take care of it. You stay here."

She was the picture of cool efficiency. She exited the car and walked through the sliding glass lobby door. In less than ten minutes she was back in her seat, key card in hand. She had rented a standard room, second floor, around the back so we didn't have to walk through the lobby, eighty dollars a night. I drove to a side door and parked. We entered and carried our bags up. There were two queen beds with the usual set-up. Strung out from the road, I dropped my bag, collapsed on the first bed, and closed my eyes. She said she wanted the bathroom first. I extended my arm and pointed in that general direction.

She said, "I'll take that as a yes."

I fell asleep while she was in there. The sound of the running shower was like a sedative. I didn't hear her finish but I heard the door. She came out, in a night shirt and shorts, her long, dark hair wrapped in a towel. She shook me by the knee. "Your turn."

I sat up, grabbed what I needed from my grip and went into the bath. The mirrors were fogged, the counter populated by a dozen girl-things that shouldn't have taken me by surprise, but they did because I'd never seen such a display before. I heard the hair dryer in the other room. The shower was much better than it had any right to be, not in that place for what we were paying, or maybe I was just that needy. I'm sure I spent more time in there than I had to, skillfully avoiding the next of many traps on this trip: sleeping arrangements. Had I known then what I know now, I'd have had much less to worry about. What happens between the sheets and when was always up to the woman anyway.

After twenty minutes, I emerged in a t-shirt and boxer shorts. She had turned on the air conditioning and taken the bed next to the window. The line had been drawn. I slid into the bed near the bath. She was propped up on two pillows and had the remote in hand, clicking through channels but watching nothing. The only light was a lamp between our beds. I asked, "Do you want me to leave this on?"

"Are you gonna sleep already?"

"Yeah. I'm beat," I said.

"Me too, I guess. Turn it off."

I did and crawled under the sheets. My dreams of Memphis nights weren't going to come true. *Not tonight*, I thought. Diane watched TV for a few minutes longer then turned it off. The sound of the fan on the air conditioner was about to put me to sleep when Diane said:

"Do you think she'll be there?"

I had to wake myself up. "Wait. What?"

"Bethany Jean, whatever, anybody at all," she said. "When we go tomorrow."

"I don't know. That's why we're here. You have to see these

things in person." We were talking in a darkened room, the only light a crease down the center of the pulled curtains.

"But what if there's no one there?"

"I don't know. Ask neighbors if they know anything. Google her again."

"What if it's the right address and this Bethany chick is there, but it's not Jean?"

I sat up and looked toward her. "Dee, you got to stop doing this to yourself. If it's not her, okay, we move on. But no more 'what ifs' tonight. It's a dead end."

She was sitting up too, hadn't moved from her watching-TV position. "How can you be so calm about it? Don't forget where this address came from, Sam. We could be walking into a drug house. We don't even know what kind of neighborhood it is."

"No, we don't. We'll keep our eyes open. We see anything we don't like, just keep on goin.'"

"Come all this way, and don't even knock on the door?" she said with some finality.

I put my head back on the pillow. "Maybe." I'm a side sleeper, so I rolled away from Diane and drifted off. I was fully asleep when I felt the covers tug off and a hand push me to the center of the bed.

"Move over."

"What?" I asked.

"Just till I fall asleep."

"Fall asleep...?"

She pushed me again. "I need more room."

I didn't bother arguing. She spooned up against my back. I said, "Are you trying to kill me, here?"

"It's dumb, I know. Please."

It took a while to get my breathing under control. I took the hand she'd wrapped around my belly and held on. If nothing else, I congratulated myself for being in bed with *the* legs.

"She used to call me Dee Dee."

"Jean?" I felt her nod.

"That's one more 'Dee' than I use."

"I really didn't like the name, except when she said it."

"Maybe you'll hear it tomorrow," I said.

"You think?" she asked.

"Goodnight, Dee Dee."

"Goodnight."

---

I woke to the sound of Diane cursing the coffee maker. I hadn't felt or heard her get out of bed. Daylight was streaming in around the curtains and the bathroom light was on. She sucked on a finger, which she'd burned on the hotplate. She poured herself a cup and asked if I would like one. I shook my head and headed for the bathroom.

"Suit yourself," she said. "But you don't want to know me before my first cup of coffee. I'm pre-homicidal till I get caffeine."

From the bath, I said, "Then I'll lock the door. Go for breakfast after we dress? They have a free one here." She agreed.

A few minutes later we were on our way to the breakfast area. It was going to be a warm day. The choices were easy for me, shorts, t-shirt and tennis shoes. Not so easy for Diane. Her usual look wasn't going to play well in the parts of town we might visit. She dressed down with long-cut shorts and a baggy top in drab colors. She also went light on the makeup, especially around her eyes, which could be trouble any time of day in any city in America.

In the dining area there were ten tables at which to sit, only three of which were occupied. We picked one far away from the other early risers. I poured syrup on my waffles. "Did you finally fall asleep then?"

"Oh, yeah. Really good." She looked over the rim of her cup. "And you?"

"For crap, if you want to know. Something soft pushing on my back. Something hard poking my stomach. I couldn't get comfortable."

She grinned into her coffee cup.

I pointed my fork at her. "I'm serious. I can't put in another night like that. You're in my bed or not. It has to be one or the other."

She put down her cup. "Oh, I know. Neither can I. I mean, middle of the night, I woke up, you were on your back. I was next to you on my stomach. Somehow, I'd crossed one of my legs over yours. My hand on your chest." She slowly shook her head and took a spoonful of yogurt.

"Yeah. So?"

She opened her hands. "Do I have to say it? I was so wet, I damn near slid right out of bed."

I choked on a piece of waffle, then covered my mouth with a napkin and coughed. "Why didn't you wake me up?"

"I should have. If anything kept me awake it was your pecker, poking my elbow half the night." She straightened her left arm and showed it to me. "See any bruises?"

I laughed. "All apologies."

# CHAPTER TWELVE

# The Pump

Diane had preloaded the address for Bethany Brooks in her phone. She showed me the suggested route before I started the car. We were not headed for the older part of the city but about eight miles south toward the airport and, oddly enough, Graceland, which we had no desire to tour. The directions took us on major highways and weren't difficult to follow. Both of us were relieved not to be traveling into the inner city. The culture and the people who lived there were too foreign to us, and us to them. It reminded me of an old saying my father told me, if you can't see the bottom, don't jump in. In this case, I felt the water there was different on some molecular level, and I wasn't smart enough to figure it out.

In fifteen minutes we were nearing our destination. My stomach churned. Diane's eyes were on the road signs. We found our exit, took a left and immediately it was obvious that this was not a typical residential area. With an interstate and two major state highways intersecting within half a mile, the road noise was constant and annoying. Several commercial aircraft flew over at low altitude along an approach to Memphis International Airport. I didn't see any houses, not a one, and I wondered out loud if our address was going to come out a dud.

Diane said, "Don't say that. We're not there yet."

We went another quarter mile, took another left, and came face-to-face with our answer. The sign said Cedar Point, even though I couldn't see a single tree. We were at the entrance to a trailer park. I pulled in and followed the arrows directing me to the right. The asphalt was weather-worn, cracked, with an edge that had a jagged, moth-eaten look. There seemed to be no one about. The trailers were in various states of repair, there must have been about fifty of them, none new. Trash was everywhere. An all-white chest of drawers with chipped paint and all the drawers secured with duct tape sat in front of one of the trailers. Random pieces of shelving, toys, and small, rusting appliances were lying near or around others.

"What a dump," Diane said.

"Look at the rust on the trailers. That takes a long time. Some of these gotta be over twenty years old." I pointed ahead. "Look at that one. Windows boarded up. Are those scorch marks? Must have had a fire." Only about half the places had a vehicle parked nearby, and most of the cars appeared to be in the same state of repair as the trailers.

"Next one on the left. That's our stop." Open mouthed, she paused. "Holy hell."

"Diane."

"I know. I know, it's not the slums but... sheesh."

I parked and we walked to what we thought would be the front door. There was almost no lawn, just brownish patches and browner patches. No porch, just a couple of cinder blocks stacked under the door. The curtains were pulled behind louvre-type windows that were cranked open a bit. No sound was coming from inside. The trailer looked about average for what we had seen in the rest of Cedar Point.

"Do you think anyone's home?" I asked.

Diane hugged herself and looked around. "This place gives me the shivers."

"You want me to knock?"

She bit her lip. "Try the doorbell."

I pushed the button, but heard nothing inside. I pushed it again. "Doesn't work."

"Go ahead, knock."

The trailer was only about a foot off the ground so I didn't stand on the blocks. I rapped three times and waited. Silence. I rapped three more times but harder and called if anyone was home. Still more silence. I turned to Diane. She was standing close behind me, a fistful of my shirttail in her right hand. She frowned and said to keep trying. I went with a more methodical thump and harder, calling her name, Bethany, this time.

Suddenly, the door burst open. A drawn woman of about forty years, wearing a faded housecoat, abruptly filled the space, though not very well, as thin as she was. I felt Diane's grip pull me backwards. The woman wore no make-up, her hair was tussled as if she'd just gotten out of bed. The morning sun blinded her.

Her eyes were flat but focused. "Who sent you over here on a Monday? Even my cat knows I don't work today."

"Ah, so, we're... Hello, I'm—"

She put up her hand to shade her eyes. "What are you blathering about?"

I noticed she didn't have the accent we'd heard from the hotel people or anything like Fanny Van Zandt's southern drawl. Even though the light was harsh, this woman didn't look like any of the pictures of Jean that Diane had shown me. Jean would be thirty years old and this woman was well past that.

I cleared my throat. "What I mean is, we're looking for someone called Bethany Brooks. Does she live here?"

She shushed her cat inside with her foot. "That someone is me, but I told you, I'm not working, so get lost." She turned to close the door.

She caught me off balance, because I didn't know what she was talking about. I put up my hand to hold the door open. "We came all the way from Wisconsin. Could we ask you a few questions?"

Bethany was now in the shade of the doorjamb and saw me more clearly, and who was behind me. Her eyes narrowed on Diane. Bethany put a hand on the hair near her neck. "Wisconsin? Where?" Her lips moved twice before they uttered a sound. "Dee Dee, is that you? Dee Dee?"

"Jeanie?" Diane said. "Yes... yes it's me."

"Oh, for chrissakes." Bethany Jean dropped out of the door

to the ground and embraced her sister, who'd grown taller and heavier in the six years she'd been gone. What was there to do for the next few minutes but to stand back and let the sisters reattach the fiber optic connections they'd lost. Sparks flew, voltage arced, amperage surged, and circuits blew. It was getting hot standing in the sun. I suggested we go somewhere for coffee. Diane and I had agreed on this plan ahead of time since we didn't know what Bethany Jean's circumstances might be. Given the little bit that was viewable through the door, a coffee shop was far better than visiting inside Bethany Jean's trailer.

Bethany Jean looked at me. "Diane! Are you going to introduce me?"

Diane grabbed my upper arm and sidled close. "This is Sam Robel. Without this man, Jeanie, I wouldn't be here today, talking to you."

Bethany Jean put a hand on her hip. "I don't remember any family of that name around Walnut Creek." I told her about my family's recent arrival. She said she wanted to hear the whole story but she had to go inside, clean up, and change clothes first. Diane and I accepted her offer to wait inside. Bethany Jean apologized for the mess.

Diane and I sat on two of the four dinette chairs. Furniture in the living room was sparse, a TV with rabbit ears on a stand and a chair sitting on an area rug. A microwave was the only luxury in the kitchen. Dirty dishes peppered the counter space and filled the sink. One of the cabinet doors had lost a chunk of particle board, another was tilted on a broken hinge.

Suddenly, the front door opened and a broad-shouldered, thick-bodied black man came in the door, startling me half up and out of my chair.

He stepped into the living room. "Bethany!" Then he looked at me poised over my chair, 'halfway between a shit and a sweat' as my grandfather would have said. The man was about 6'2" tall, over two hundred thirty pounds, and wore a straw Fedora hat. His forearms were heavily tattooed and he wore a ring on his right hand that looked dangerous. "Bethany," he called again. Then he tossed his chin in my direction. "Either sit or stand. You're making me uncomfortable. And why are you two calling today? She doesn't work on Monday."

Bethany Jean's footsteps came down the hall. "Ben, what the hell you doing here already? It's not even ten." She opened her freezer, removed a plastic bag, and took out a thick stack of cash. She handed it to him.

Ben seemed unimpressed. He fanned the bills, counting as he went, then looked up at Bethany Jean. "This is light again. What's going on, B? You know what I'm saying. You don't produce, you come back to the Palace, that's the deal."

Bethany pointed at the cash. "It's better than last week. I told you before, it's gonna take a while. I got some new... people. Not as many, but they pay better."

"All right. I guess this arrangement will work, for now. But next week I'll be back, you can count on it." He tipped his hat to Diane. "Ma'am. You all have a good time." He walked out the door.

I looked at Diane, whose expression exactly mimicked how I felt. She said, "What the hell was that?"

"Sorry you had to see that. I didn't expect him until two." Bethany Jean's face was stern. "Everything has its price. Let's go."

She took twenty minutes for makeup, fixing the hair, and a change of clothes but it was worth it. She looked five years younger. I remember thinking to myself, *If she gets a little sun and puts on fifteen pounds, who knows?*

As we drove out of Cedar Point, I pointed at the burned-out trailer and asked if she knew what had happened.

"Oh yeah. They just took down the yellow tape yesterday," Bethany Jean said. "It was a crack house and they were cooking. You can't believe the smell. Then it blew up."

"You mean it exploded?" Diane asked.

The women were sitting together in the back seat. Bethany Jean pulled out a cigarette.

Diane said, "Sorry. This isn't our car, and the owner said no smoking."

"Really." Bethany Jean put the pack away. "Take a left here and go about half a mile. Then a right at the light."

In less than ten minutes, we were at the coffee shop.

The booth was comfortable enough. Diane and I were on one side of the table facing her sister. They both ordered coffee; I got a hot chocolate and two oversize scones we could share. In six years both of the women had gone through profound changes, Diane for the better. Bethany Jean, not so much. She wanted to focus the conversation on Diane. She obliged, and why not? There'd been a long time between, and a lot to catch up on. But eventually, Diane couldn't wait to ask the question that had bothered her for so long:

"Why did you leave? You haven't said. It was Junior Manticore, wasn't it. That whole family is crap to the core."

"Oh, honey, it was them, I guess, but not just that either." She rolled a napkin in her fist. "I wouldn't know where to start except, first of all, you can't blow my cover here. Does anyone else know?" She twisted the napkin. "About Memphis, I mean."

"No one important." I broke off a chunk of scone. "My parents know we're here, and so do Ethyl and Carter."

Bethany Jean straightened, her eyes narrowed. "Dad knows? How the hell did he find out. He's still in prison, isn't he?"

Diane's fingernails tapped the table. "They released him early, last week, on good behavior, *he* says." She looked away. "If you can believe that bullshit." She pushed the scone plate toward Bethany Jean, encouraging her to eat.

She turned up her nose at the food. "Good behavior. What the—"

Diane shrugged. "I can't figure it out either. He is not the same after ten years though, I'll give him that." Bethany Jean asked what she meant. "Drinking near beer now, none of the hard stuff for one thing. Cut way down on the smokes." Carter's oldest daughter was impressed, I could tell. Diane went on. "He can still be a jerk, that hasn't changed, but he seems more considerate of Ethyl, which he never was before."

There was a pause. Then I said, "And…"

Diane said, "Oh, yeah, well, right. He asked me to forgive him for, I don't know, all the bullshit in the past. You know, let's wipe the slate clean."

"Really," Bethany Jean said. "He has changed."

I asked, "What should we call you, Bethany or Jean or both?"

"No. Bethany Brooks. Don't use my other name. And what did you mean, 'no one important.'"

"The other person that knows where you are is the one who helped find you," I said. "She's from Chicago and doesn't actually know *who* you are, if you know what I mean."

Bethany looked at me. "Are you from Chicago?"

"No."

"Okay." Bethany waved her finger between Diane and I. "How did you two meet?"

Diane answered. "I sat next to him in history class." She whipped her thumb at me. "Supposed to be so fuckin' smart. I copied answers from him on a test and got a D, a big red one from Mr. Anderson!"

We all laughed, but I had to defend myself. "It was a D *plus!* She slapped the test paper on my desk." I smacked a napkin on the table. "Just like that. But I apologized."

"Oh, right," Diane said skeptically as she dunked a bit of scone.

"Yeah. I wrote 'Sorry, I'll get an A next time' and gave it back to you. Remember?"

"Oh, I remember and that's not what you wrote." Diane's voice was high and confident. "It said, 'Sorry, I'll do better next time,' which wasn't saying much; a C minus would have done it."

Bethany smiled but her hands worried the napkin again. Diane saw it too. She placed her hands on Bethany's. "You don't have to worry anymore. You can be Jean again. That's what we came to tell you. The Manticores are history. The old man is on house arrest waiting for trial. Mitchell is out on bail with a GPS locked on his ankle."

"Who busted them?" Bethany asked. "The DEA?"

Diane and I looked at each other, wondering what that was supposed to mean.

"No, no," Diane said. "You remember J.R. Cherhasky? Big

mansion over by Walnut Creek."

"Yeah," Bethany said hesitantly. "His wife was killed in a bear attack years ago."

"Guess who he married," I said. She shrugged. "Nadine Colum."

Bethany leaned forward and half-laughed the name, "Nay-Dine!" She sat back and popped a piece of scone in her mouth. At that point I noticed how bad her teeth were. She said, "That little whore. I can't be surprised. She never put out unless the price was right. I'll give her that."

"Trophy wife," Diane said. "Best gig she's gonna get."

"Hey, look at me." Bethany shrugged and shook her head. "I ain't gonna talk."

Diane said, "Anyway, here's the punchline, the whole lot of 'em were busted by the FBI."

"Stealing construction stuff, lumber, pipes, wire, by the truck-load," I said.

"But what about the farm?" Bethany asked.

"That was us," Diane said. "We busted his cows in the corn, egg-sucking ass. We found the pump."

Bethany blinked, her face was blank.

"You know," I said. "The one sucking water out of Red Wolf Lake. We figured you found out about it and that's why you had to leave town."

Bethany said, "What pump?"

# Chapter Thirteen
## Moving Day

It was the big reveal that fell flat on its face. The white-winged dove shot out of the sky. And for long moments Diane and I were stunned stupid in disbelief. We were sure that we had solved the mystery of Jean Warren Manticore's disappearance. Never did we consider we might be wrong. Indeed, for many minutes neither of us could accept it. We plied Bethany with more details about the pump, where it was set up, what it did, how we found it, hoping to shake loose a memory she'd somehow suppressed and left to rust in one of the backlots of her brain. It was a futile effort.

Bethany closed her eyes for a long second, then told us how much she appreciated everything we'd done, all the effort put forth on her behalf. Most of all she understood how hard it had been on Diane, alone with Ethyl for all those years, and Carter in jail. "But even if you'd somehow burned Crabalock—" She stopped herself, put fingers across her lips, then started again. "Even if you'd fixed everything, I'm still doing all right here. I mean, there's nothing for me in Walnut Creek anymore."

The answer to that was so obvious, I had to clench my teeth to hold it back. Diane had no such control, nor should she.

"Jeanie, come on. That trailer! I'm sorry, but it's, it's nowhere to live. And neither is that park. Druggies next door. And who the hell is Ben?"

Bethany had just refilled her coffee and was stirring in the cream. She tapped the teaspoon on the rim of the cup three times and set it down, then looked up at us under a furrowed brow that had become almost aggressive. "'Careful what you ask for.' Isn't that the old saying? Right now, let's say he's paying my rent and leave it at that."

Diane sat back. "Okay. I get it. We only showed up an hour ago. You don't owe us a thing. But we're family, and I'm not stupid, Jeannie."

I could feel Diane's temperature rising from a foot away. I put a hand under the table and discretely pressed the back of my hand against her hip.

"It's Bethany." She leaned forward and lowered her voice. "And I know you're not stupid. I raised you, remember? But be careful. Judge not, lest ye be judged."

*Scripture. Holy crap*, I thought. *Didn't see that coming.* And neither had Diane, who froze, her coffee cup halfway to her mouth.

Bethany went on. "I've come a long way. In just the last six weeks, I've got a counselor who's helping me get a job." She dropped her head. "Not great, at a grocery store, but better than what I'm doing now." She looked away. "They helped me get the trailer, move out of the city. You think this is bad, you should see that place." She paused. "They're helping me find furniture."

"Who's they?" I asked.

"The church I joined." Bethany broke off more of the scone. "Which brings me to a question. I don't have a car and I still have some stuff in town. Could you take me there and help me haul some of it back?"

Twenty minutes later, we were driving slowly past tenements and open lots with burned out homes. There was an occasional home with a porch and windows intact, but too few to loosen my grip on the steering wheel. It was my first experience in an inner city. I was hyper-vigilant. I scanned every home, every intersection until my eyes ached. My speed was slow but not too slow. Bethany was giving me directions which I dutifully repeated back to her. She knew every street like someone who'd lived in the area and not for just a little while. On the other hand, for the first time in my life, I felt I was in a place where I didn't belong. Finally, she told me to take the next right. Her old place would be the third house on the right.

I did as I was told. A car parked in front of me was never going to move again, even if the tires were replaced. The streets were littered with everything from empty Pringles cans to old tires. Outside of a mother pushing a stroller with a toddler in tow, the neighborhood appeared quiet, a huge relief. Bethany's former address was not quite an eyesore, but I cringed at first sight anyway. The porch tilted forward like an unfinished handicap ramp. The paint was faded and cracked, and the front window pane had two bullet holes in it. I asked how long she'd lived here.

"Three years in the Palace," Bethany said. "On and off."

"This is the Palace? Are we expected?" Diane asked. "This ain't a place I want to barge in, ya know, uninvited."

"It's cool," Bethany said. "You're with me."

Somehow, I wasn't reassured. We walked up the porch and into the foyer without knocking, but then Bethany called out, "Latoya, Bennie, you up?"

"Ben!" I hoarse-whispered. I looked at Diane, then at Bethany, and said, "Is this the same Ben?" She ignored me.

Bethany waited a second. "Toy, Ben, it's Bethany. I'm here for my stuff." She walked into the sparsely furnished living room. Empty beer cans were everywhere. A tattered rug on the floor was marked by several burn marks of various sizes and shapes. One, larger chair upholstered in red had a dusting of white powder on the arms. A few empty pizza delivery boxes were strewn on the floor. There were no pictures hanging anywhere but in at least one spot it looked like someone had put their fist through the wall.

There was some movement or noise in the back. Bethany stepped toward the kitchen which was at the back of the flat. A black woman, well-endowed both top and bottom, as tall as me and about my weight with corn rows and braids to the middle of her back came out of a side bedroom. Her silk nightshirt went to her waist, and the lace panties looked a size too small. "Toy, were you sleeping?" Bethany asked. "Sorry. I'm here for the rest of my stuff."

"Thought you was done wit dat." Toy walked toward the kitchen. "Ben be lookin' for you."

"Yeah, I know. Saw him this morning," Bethany said. "A couple more things. Bought friends to help."

She waved us off. "Just git it and go. And be quiet about it."

The room was so small I don't know how she fit more than a TV and a small mattress in there. Bethany said they used to use it as a sewing room. There were two boxes and a chair that had to go. Then she pointed at a pedestal table with a removable top. "I really want that. Sentimental reasons."

I said, "Can't have it all. Won't fit in the car."

"Can we come back for the table?" Bethany asked.

I could see Diane wanted to do it, and since the haul was going well at that point, I agreed. We took the first load out to the car and packed it up. Bethany Jean said we should bring the table to the front porch so we wouldn't have to bother Latoya or Ben again. I agreed. The less often I stepped in that living room the better. We went back to the tiny room. The girls took the table top and led the way out. I grabbed the pedestal, which was made of oak and as dense as a bowling ball. As we passed through the dining room, a gust of wind came in an open window on one side of the house and pushed open a partially-closed bedroom door on the other. A crescent of light followed the breeze into the otherwise darkened room. What I saw froze me where I stood. Lying on the floor, propped against the far wall, her head lolling to the side, was a half-naked, dark-skinned girl. Her only clothing was a pair of panties and a cut-off t-shirt hiked up around her shoulders. Her face was slack, like melted wax. I thought she was dead.

"What the hell?" I mumbled. Diane and Bethany must not have heard me because they didn't stop. I set down the pedestal and crept into the bedroom. It smelled like urine and sex and filth. The woman's arms were limp at her side, a tourniquet laying near an elbow next to a needle and syringe. I wanted to call for Diane and Bethany Jean but couldn't find my voice.

Did I see her take a breath? I thought so. I tapped her bare foot with the toe of my shoe but she didn't move. Finally, I said not in a loud voice but enough to be heard beyond the room, "Diane, get back here."

Another voice, from a girl on the bed, croaked, "What?"

I jumped against the door. I hadn't seen this second person because she was huddled in the shadows and tangled in bed covers. Her face was partially covered by hair that was reddish blond, long and kinky. All I could see on her was a bra, or some kind of swim top. Suddenly, her arm was gyrating in the air, her hand grabbing at something. Agitated by some dream or withdrawal, I didn't know, but she struggled again, her feet kicking at the sheet twisted around her legs as if she were riding a bike. From the waist down, she wore nothing.

"Sam, what the hell?" Diane stood in the doorway, Bethany Jean right behind.

"I thought—"

"You though what, Sam?" Bethany Jean asked.

The tone of her voice implied I was snooping around, which made me mad. "Hey, Bethany, I'm here because of you. That's all. I looked at *her*"—I pointed at the girl on the floor—"and thought she was dead."

Bethany pushed past Diane and took a quick look at the girl on the bed. "This is Anika. She never comes down easy. She'll be, not okay but... okay." Then she put her hand on the shoulder of the girl on the floor, gave her a shake, and called her name. "Carmel. Carmel, you there?"

The girl roused a bit, changed her position, but didn't wake up. "They're both hard cases, but Carmel..." Bethany Jean clenched her jaw.

"We can't just leave them here," I said. "Shouldn't we call someone? An ambulance or something?"

"Sam, you can't save them." Bethany Jean paused a second, sighed, and said, "Let's go."

Diane and Bethany Jean moved toward the door but my feet were stuck to the floor. I couldn't take my eyes off the pitiful, sad lost girl lying in front of me. Both of these people were in a family once, they were someone's daughters. Maybe they still were. I couldn't help but think that someone, somewhere was wondering where they were, if they were all right.

Diane paused in the doorway. "Come on, Sam. We can't stay."

And still I didn't move. She took two steps toward me, wrapped her hand around my arm and tugged me away from the scene. I took a single step. And then I couldn't get out of the house quickly enough.

We got in the car and headed back to the trailer. The drive back was uncomfortably quiet. I was still trying to absorb what I'd seen. We were back at the trailer before I'd regained control of my breathing. My hands were still shaking as we unloaded and helped Bethany Jean unpack. It was half past one by that point. She was ready for the return trip. I figured whatever was going to go down with Carmel and Anika had already happened. Bethany Jean said the heroin had probably worn off. If so, they'd have left and gone home. I had visions of driving into a scene with police cruisers and a couple ambulances parked around the house. If that was the case I wouldn't stop; the table would be history.

We climbed back in the car and headed north to the heart of Memphis.

By the time I'd parked the Golf, my heart was thumping in my neck, my palms sweating. In the afternoon, the neighborhood had changed in some palpable way but not in the way I had feared. More people were walking about. Three guys were talking together on the corner where we'd turned, our lily-white faces drawing their stares as we went by. It felt like even a look back on my part would provoke something, so I kept my nose straight ahead. I parked in the same place. Bethany and I went for the table top. Diane stayed and opened the tailgate. As we scaled the porch, I cast a wary eye toward the corner and the trio of men there, only three houses away. One of them was looking in our direction, the other two were having some kind of intense debate. "Sam, you got it?" Bethany was ready to lift.

"Yeah, sorry." I saw no sign of Anika or Carmel and, to be honest, didn't make any effort to look for them.

We took our first steps down when a black woman across the street yelled:

"Hey, what the hell. Dat ain't yours. Put it back."

My gut coiled like a prodded snake. This woman was drawing the attention of others in the neighborhood to our little operation; most likely the three men at the corner who appeared to be *waiting* for a reason to harass the naïve, white, country cracker who'd just driven by. I was sweating in all the wrong places by that time. My hands were so slippery with perspiration I might have dropped the tabletop.

Bethany said to keep going. Then answered the black woman, matching her in volume and attitude, "Yeah, it's mine. Ask Toy and Ben, they'll tell ya. I lived here for three years."

The woman was big-boned with short, tightly cropped hair and wore tight blue jeans and top. She marched across the street. "I will aks 'em, right after you put this back." She yelled. "Toy! Ben! Dey's takin' the table." She walked past us toward the porch, stopped, and grabbed the pedestal. "That table ain't no good without 'dis, now is it." She had me by forty pounds. In temperament she was my equal and then some, especially while holding a big piece of solid oak. If she had the three men backing her up, I was a goner. I looked down the street. The black men had just boarded a green bus with the name of a local produce farm on the side. They were on their way to work. I didn't have time to be embarrassed just then; that would have to come later.

Bethany said, "You're Makisha. You remember me." She pointed at herself. "Bethany Brooks. We talked only just last week."

"Yeah, *and* I remember you don' live here no more."

"Right. I'm moving out." Bethany looked at the house. "But I don't think Toy and Ben are home right now."

Makisha sat down, pedestal across her lap. "Den I'll wait."

I looked about the neighborhood. No one else had taken an interest in our tussle, but it was only a matter of time. I approached Makisha. "We'd like to wait too, but Diane and me, we're from out of town."

Makisha grinned. "No shit."

I sort of laughed too. "I know, right. Now if we take the top and you have the pedestal, neither of us got nuthin'."

"Maybe so," Makisha said. "But it ain't right, you takin' it like dat."

"All right. Let's say I give you twenty bucks for the pedestal and you give it to Toy and Ben when they get back." I pulled the bill from my pocket. "Now, you gotta say, it's an old table."

She looked down her nose at my offer. "No way I go to Toy and Ben with dat scrap. I need sixty."

I reached in my pocket and pulled out another twenty. "Last one I got. Make it forty. Deal?"

"Let me see dat."

As I walked toward her with the forty dollars, a red Mercedes Benz coupe pulled up behind the Volkswagen close enough to park us in. The driver's door opened and Ben stepped out of the car, still in his Fedora, this time with a toothpick in his mouth. He walked over to me, the bills still in my extended hand, then looked at Makisha and said, "You told me you was out of the business. If you're back in, we gotta talk, girl. You know that."

Makisha said, "Nah, nah, nah. Ben, yous gots a one-track mind. I caught Bethany and dees two tryin' to take dat table off you porch. I'm lookin' out for you is all. Got him to pay me forty bucks for the bottom part."

Ben surveyed the three of us—Bethany and Diane standing by the back of the Golf and the loaded tabletop. I was near the porch, a step away from Makisha. Ben took a look inside the Golf, and then said to Bethany, "You come all the way back here just for that table?"

"Yeah, I guess I did," Bethany said.

Ben nodded. "Hum. I see. Then I'd say it's worth more 'an forty dollars. Might even be worth more than a hundred." He took the toothpick out of his mouth. "But I'm a fair man. Eighty sounds about right."

Bethany bent at the waist. "Ben, you know I don't have eighty dollars. You just took everything I had this morning."

He pointed the toothpick at Bethany. "Like I always tell you, anytime you want to change back to the old way of doing business, just say the word, baby. I'm right here." He put the toothpick back in his mouth. "And just for the record, I didn't think you had the money, but I know your friend..." He opened his hand toward me as if to ask my name.

"Sam," I said.

"Sam." Ben nodded again. "I'll bet he's got it. Check in that pocket again, Sam."

———————

By the time we'd reassembled the table in Bethany's living room, it was late afternoon. We'd skipped lunch and I was feeling it. Diane, I had found, could skip a meal and not miss a step, so I couldn't rely on her to call time for food. Bethany was so thin, I didn't know if eating regularly was part of her life or not. There was next to nothing in her frig, just mustard, a sprouting onion, moldy cheese, and a couple beers. A Memphis barbeque diner was nearby, and we convinced Bethany to come with us for an actual meal. Besides, it was still too early to call it a day. I knew Diane wanted more time with Bethany, and what better way than over a meal. We also needed one more shot at turning Bethany back into Jean again, and bringing her home. The restaurant was in a strip mall on the highway and didn't look too fancy, but I was in no mood to be fussy. Again, we got a booth. This time Diane sat next to her sister. We ordered soft drinks.

The menu was wild. I could have ordered anything from a bologna sandwich ($5) to a "Whole Slab o Ribs" for two, including bread and two pounds of sides for $35. The waiter came. Diane had the pulled chicken, Bethany the catfish, and I got the half-slab of ribs dinner.

The conversation was lighter than the morning, but also subdued because Diane knew our time with Bethany might be coming to an end. Diane made another pitch for her to come back with us, if even for just a little while. Our food arrived, so Bethany didn't answer right away. She spread a napkin on her lap, put her silverware just so, and said:

"Dee Dee, right before I left, I did some stupid things. I was married to Scott, of course. I didn't know it when I married him, but I found out soon enough that he was the doormat of the family. The old man, Tapper, they both used him like a rented mule. It pissed me off and I told him so, told him to get a little spine. Even talked to his mother. She was on our side, but she coddled him too, and that wasn't good. But she never gave me any trouble. In fact, I think she liked me."

We had all dove into our meals, which were either surprisingly good or we were starving. Probably both. "That's pretty good barbeque." I dropped a rib bone and wiped my mouth. "He's still your husband, right? Technically, you're still married."

Bethany shrugged.

Diane asked, "What was so bad about that? The marriage, I mean."

Bethany finished her coleslaw. "I started talking smart. If Scott wasn't going to speak up, then I would. Got knocked around for my trouble."

It took me a little time to get used to Bethany calling her husband Scott. We always called him Junior, mostly because we knew he didn't like it. Looking back on it now, I think he was subconsciously distancing himself from his father, who he had never loved and actually despised in the end.

Diane said, "Junior—"

Bethany interjected, "Scott. His name is Scott."

Diane lowered her voice. "Okay, Scott, hit you for defending him?"

"Who said that?"

"Nadine Cherhasky, for one," I said. "She said you and her were tight before she got married to J.R. She was really upset when we found the belt and buckle in the lake. Everyone thought it was yours, from when you worked at the gift shop."

Bethany sat back. "Her again? Nadine's a drama queen, and she doesn't always know what she's talking about. At least when I knew her." Bethany picked up her knife. "Of course, I didn't back down. I was married to a Manticore. Thought I was bulletproof. The day came when I heard someone talking outside the window of the kitchen. By that time, I already knew the old man had connections to some kind of crime ring. I heard them say they'd killed this guy. I should have ducked away and never said a word. But I froze, right there at the window. I always knew the family was dirty, but to kill someone as a matter of family business? Then the dog walked in the kitchen and barked. The old man sent Tapper in to see what was going on. He found me. I probably looked guilty as sin. From the second I saw the look on his face, I was afraid for my life. I knew Scott couldn't protect me. Not long after that, I bolted."

Diane put down her sandwich. "Who'd they kill?"

Bethany stabbed at her catfish. "It was… It wasn't a name I knew, so I don't remember. It's so long ago, it doesn't matter now."

"It could matter," I said. "Just give me the name and I'll turn it over to the FBI. I won't give you away. Maybe they could track it down."

"Lower your voice," Bethany said. "I'm not sure of the name, and even if I was, I wouldn't give it to you. Too dangerous."

How were we going to change her mind? Nothing we said was gaining any traction. In desperation, I asked if she ever considered trying to get ahold of Scott.

"No. Why would I," she asked.

"You're his wife. He's the one person who's got the money to come down here and pluck you out of this situation." I took a sip of cola. "He's not working so he's got the time. Talk to him; go where ever you want. Anything to get you away from Ben."

Bethany pinched the bridge of her nose and closed her eyes. "Haven't you heard a single word I've said?" She opened her eyes and looked hard at me. "Both of you. Didn't I just say I left because I feared for my life? Does it sound like I married a man that I could hitch my wagon to? If I'd married a good man, a man I could've trusted, I'd have stayed with him in the first place."

As we finished the meal, I asked Bethany Jean about Carmel and Anika. "What would have happened if we'd have called 911, or taken them to the hospital ourselves? At least they would've gotten some help."

"They've been there, done that. Both of them," Bethany Jean said. "Last time Carmel went in, they didn't even keep her. Once she was able to walk and talk, they put her right back on the street. They know her on sight in every emergency room in the city. Anika? Not yet. But it's only a matter of time."

"You got out," I said. "Someone must have helped you."

"Yeah, that's right. But you have to want to do it." Bethany Jean wiped the sauce from her hands. "Let it go, Sam. Let it go."

The rest of the meal and the ride back to her trailer was quiet by comparison. There were so many things Diane and Bethany could have talked about but none of them seemed to matter in the wake of Bethany's stubborn declaration. We hadn't solved the problem of her self-imposed exile, which seemed to have more prongs than a virus particle, and that was disheartening.

It was well after six p.m. when we gathered in the slim patch of shade near the front door of Bethany's trailer. She knew we'd be leaving in the morning. We still had a lot of cash, and the money wasn't ours to give, but I took $500 out of the envelope and gave it to Bethany, telling her I was under orders to do so. We told her who gave us the car and where the money came from. Secretly I hoped the cash would allow her to give up prostitution.

I was standing behind Diane. She was about to give Bethany a farewell hug when I noticed the cellphone in Diane's back pocket. It struck me we hadn't called home that day, neither Diane nor me, and hadn't suggested it to Bethany.

"Oh, wait, before we forget." I pulled the phone out of Diane's back pocket and held it up. "Would you like to call home, Bethany? To talk to Ethyl and Carter? I'm sure they'd love to hear your voice."

"Oh my god, yes. How stupid," Diane said. "We gotta call home." She winked at me knowing, as I did, this might be the answer. Nothing else had worked. If Bethany talked to her folks, maybe she'd change her mind and come with us.

Diane took the phone from me. "Whadda ya say, sis? Can I call?"

Bethany looked at the cell suspiciously, inhaled through her teeth, and took a step back. "Oh, I don't know." She put her hands on her face. "I'm not ready... no."

Diane said, "Oh come on. Just to say hi. They'll be—"

"No!" Bethany shook her head, then repeated, "No," less

urgently and turned sideways to us.

I could see we were losing her. "Okay. Just a suggestion. My mistake. Another time, maybe."

Diane put the phone away and pulled her sister into her arms one more time. They kissed cheek to cheek. The tears and hugs came to an end. Bethany went into the trailer, and we drove away.

As we turned out of the trailer park, I said, "That was a tough one."

Diane shook her head and said, "Gawd, that woman."

"We gave it our best shot."

She asked, "Do you think so?" I nodded, then so did she. "I guess we did."

I knew if Bethany wouldn't come with us, the time after parting was going to be a bummer, so I'd planned something. The hotel had a pool. I hadn't brought a swimsuit and there was a department store on the way back where I thought I could buy one cheap. I pulled into the parking lot and told Diane my plan. Still too bummed about leaving her sister, Diane wasn't crazy about the idea. But I convinced her to come along and help me pick one out. She did and once we got in the clothing section, the women's department was calling with season ending closeouts that were not to be missed. She found a blue two-piece.

Three blocks from the hotel, we passed a liquor store.

"Pull in, pull in," she said.

I did, brought the car to a stop, looked at her and said, "You're not."

"I am."

"You're gonna use a fake, out-of-state driver's license to buy some beer?"

"Well, hard lemonade I thought, since you don't like beer."

"Just don't get arrested," I said, though I knew she'd pull it off. She looked older than her age and the I.D. was a pretty good knock off. Four minutes and some seconds later she was back in the front seat with a six-pack.

She clapped her hands. "Hot tub and cold lemonade. Watch out Memphis, here I come."

## Chapter Fourteen

# Taking My Bullets

No beverages of any kind were allowed in the pool area, so we each downed a can of hard lemonade, for rehydration purposes only, before we left the room. We took out the suits we'd just purchased and had another look at them. They weren't even worth the discounted prices we'd paid, but good enough for the one and done use we had in mind. We finished our drinks, put on the suits, shouldered a couple of towels, and headed downstairs. We had the pool room to ourselves. But then we saw the hot tub right next to the pool and any plans to actually swim went down the drain. The jets came on and put some life back in my tired muscles. But the moment she slid in to join me there was another energy, a voltage in the water, and amplified by the alcohol. The highs and lows of the day melted off our skin into the whirlpools of foam. Neither of us mentioned Bethany Jean, or Ben and Toya, and certainly not the scene in the bedroom. Although Diane briefly brought up the negotiation about the table and how she'd never seen anyone so quick to pay up, considering I had lost forty bucks just by standing speechless.

I said, "Hey! No broken bones. I think I got away cheap. Eighty bucks, I'd a paid twice that just to get the hell outta there."

She glanced sideways, suppressing a smile. "He had a pretty hot car, though. Red Mercedes coupe. Oh, baby."

"Oh, sure." I splashed a little water her way. "I suppose you wanted a ride. Next time we see him I'll ask... not."

"Would you? Thanks." She put her foot on my leg and gave

me a little shove. "I'm always up for a ride."

Two cycles with the jacuzzi and we were ready for another round of lemonades. We wrapped up in the towels and went upstairs.

After the hot tub, the air-conditioned air of our room felt good. I popped the tops on a couple more lemonades and handed one to Diane. We tapped cans and drank to shitty swimming suits and hot tubs in cheap hotels. I pulled the curtains on the window. "Drinking in public is illegal in Memphis," I said.

She stepped toward me, pulled me close, and took the can from my hand. "So is kissing." She went on her tiptoes, wrapped her arms around my neck, and put her lips on mine.

Her warmth went through me like a wave. Her arms, her mouth, her toes touching mine, I felt everything all at once. The moment had arrived. The door was open. I felt like a paratrooper diving into the great wide open without a chute. I tried to slow down by kissing her neck and running my hand around her waist, areas I thought less dangerous. I was so wrong. Her hands and mouth more urgent, I pulled back and said, "So what are you, the Memphis sex police or something?"

She smiled. "Undercover division." The towel, which had been wrapped under her arms, released and fell to the floor. She kissed me again.

The looseness I'd gained from a can of hard lemonade was gone. A sheen of sweat covered me in spite of the air conditioning. The towel I'd cinched around my waist followed hers to the carpet. Her hips pressed closer to mine. Even with my suit on, she didn't have to look. "Oh my, drawing the gun on me already? That's a felony."

"Guilty." I sighed. "Be careful. It's got a hair trigger."

She raked her fingertips down my chest. "Is that so. Easy fix." She freed my erection from my suit. "I'm taking away your bullets." But first, she grabbed her lemonade, and in one pull, polished off the can and threw the empty over her shoulder. Then she pushed me backwards, sat me on the edge of the bed, and knelt in front of me. Her hand clutched the base of my penis. She flicked her tongue. "Hmm. Memphis hot tub on a stick. I must be at the Tennessee State Fair."

I think I laughed. I probably did, but I don't really remember. Diane's humor always did it to me. What was certain was that for the next several minutes, I was breathless and speechless. My brain knew sounds but not words. When she'd done me and was done with me, I was barely able to continue upright. With a couple fingertips, she pushed me sideways onto the mattress, grabbed herself a fresh lemonade, and came to the bed. I made room for her. Still in her two-piece suit, she laid down beside me.

"How you doin', Sam bone?"

I took a long drink. "Someone stole my bullets and I didn't even see who it was."

"What? You weren't watching. You're so careless."

I rolled toward her. "I must've had my eyes closed." I gave her a quick kiss. "Or maybe I just don't remember." I interlocked my hands in hers and kissed her fingers.

"That's b.s. I know you were watching. You must have sexual amnesia. How lame. Never work before a judge."

"Yes, your honor." I kissed her neck twice. "Sexual amnesia." I kissed her shoulder.

"You better stop that."

"Why should I?"

She let go my hands and wrapped her arms around me. "Because it's already wet down there."

I slipped a leg under her and ran a hand up and down her belly. "Of course. From the hot tub."

She gasped as my hand slipped into her bikini bottom. "No, not... hot... tub wet. I'm wet like a storm front." I pushed a little farther. She moaned, took hold of my forearm and squeezed. "Don't slip off... the... spot."

Her grip tightened so that I could feel tendons and muscles flexing in my arm as my hand moved. Then, in one simple motion, she was astride me and I was sitting, her right arm behind my head, my left arm around her waist. As if clinging to a tree, she inched higher, her legs and arm working until, by no coincidence, her breast was just a kiss away. With my free hand I reached behind her neck and undid the tie that held her top and pulled it away. I nipped lightly at her breast.

"Oh, fuck." She pressed my face into her.

Again. "Oh, fuck."

I could hardly breathe. I squeezed her lower back. Her legs tightened around me. She clutched my head with both hands. "More, more, more… yesss."

Then, the air went out of the balloon. In parts and pieces, my body was released from her clutches.

Together, we laid our heads back on the pillow and she closed her eyes. I watched her, waiting for them to open. Many minutes passed before either of us wanted or was able to move. When finally, she opened her eyes, I said, "Hi."

She smiled, gave me a short kiss, and said, "Hi yourself."

"I'm going to the bathroom."

She sank into the pillow. "I'm going to sleep."

When I returned a few minutes later, Diane was sitting on the edge of the bed, dressed only in her bikini bottoms. Rifling through my wallet. I said, "I thought you were tired."

"No, I said I was going to sleep. And I did, for about three minutes. Now I'm awake. Is there anymore lemonade?"

"Good to have you back." I got the last can and popped it open for her, then pointed at my wallet. "What are you looking for?"

"Your condom."

I reached behind the back flap and slipped it out. "Secret compartment."

## CHAPTER FIFTEEN

# Empty Handed

I woke up early the next day. The two cans of hard lemonade had left me with a throbbing, early wake-up call right between the eyes. I took two ibuprofen and snuck out to the lobby for a can of cola. Diane was amazing. While I was sneaking around for a hangover cure, she slept like a princess on a cloud. How did she do it? She weighed sixty pounds less than me and had downed twice as much alcohol. I crawled back in bed and waited for the sugar, caffeine, and ibuprofen to kick in, and for Diane to wake.

We said goodbye to Memphis early Tuesday morning. The two days in Tennessee were about as bipolar as I could have imagined. On the downside, we'd found Bethany Jean Warren Manticore Brooks, but she was in poor circumstances, much worse than if she'd have been living in Wisconsin. In spite of that, we weren't able to bring her home. On the other hand, we might not have found her at all, and if we had arrived three months earlier it looked as if we'd have found her living in a crack house in inner-city Memphis, turning tricks to feed a drug habit. Now, she was trying to climb out of that blackhole, to find legitimate work through a connection with a local church, and she knew there was family in Wisconsin who still loved her.

As the car gobbled up the tedious, corn-lined miles of Illinois, much of our time was devoted to Bethany and how we missed on our biggest goal. We weren't clear on why it happened. Did Bethany want to stay in Memphis as she claimed, or was she afraid to come home? After talking to her for an entire day, neither of us could say for sure. Diane was suspicious about Bethany's mention of the DEA, which had slipped out while we were talking about the Manticores. I thought Bethany had just gotten her initials mixed up. Besides, if she'd been doing drugs, as we agreed she was, the DEA would have been on her mind a lot more than the FBI. And I thought she'd corrected herself, anyway.

"No, I did," Diane said. "I said FBI."

Bethany switched tracks later, and argued for her life in Memphis. She talked the good talk about new friends, a new job, and a church. But really, what was there to recommend about her situation there? Fear, we decided, was the deciding factor. But that led to an even tougher question. What was she afraid of?

At one point she'd almost said "Crabalocker," which in the Red Wolf area could refer to either the creek or the mountain. Crabalocker Mountain was located in a state forest about twenty-five miles north of Red Wolf Lake; what that could have to do with Bethany or the Manticores neither of us could imagine. Crabalocker Creek seemed a more likely suspect since, in part of its course, it ran through Manticore property and then emptied into northern Red Wolf Lake in an area called the West End.

I said, "Okay, here's a question for you: biggest surprise from last night?"

The wicked grin and the flashing eyes this question provoked are beyond my ability to describe. "Oh, come on. I mean besides the sex," I added quickly.

She laughed. "Well okay, what do you mean? About Jean and her trailer or what?"

"The whole thing. I'll tell you what mine was. Bethany Jean still has feelings for Scott, Junior, or whatever his name is."

"Really? Why do you say that? She sounded pretty down on him to me."

I took a drink from my water bottle. "Because of what I just said. She corrected us on his name. She wanted us to call him Scott, not because she liked it, but because *he* didn't like being called Junior. And *he* wasn't even around."

She opened a bag of trail mix. "Yeah, you're right. She was

really strange too, when we talked about the spouse abuse. She never denied it, but she dissed Nadine pretty hard when we told her she put the finger on Scott. You think Jean and Scott are texting or emailing?"

"No idea."

Diane was tiring of the topic, so I asked if she was hungry, something banal like that. Unfortunately, we drove past a sign directing drivers to an Illinois State Penitentiary, which reminded her of Carter. Suddenly, my growling stomach was on the back burner. Diane's mind was on something else. I could always tell in the way she became quiet, and at the same time, motionless.

"What are you thinking about, Dee?"

She stepped out of the trance. "You wouldn't understand."

"Try me."

"We haven't talked about this since the night we broke up, and I don't want to talk about it now, really. But I... I don't know how to put it."

I waited, but the start wasn't encouraging.

"The reason I... I want the job in Green Bay is because I'm ashamed."

All at once, I was choking up. "Of what?"

"My father. Yeah, Carter. Mom's no walk in the park but I've seen worse. It's..."

I looked away from the road, toward her. "Yeah..."

"I thought bringing Jean home would make a difference." She pulled a tissue from her pocket and dabbed her eyes. "Now, that's not going to happen. And I'm mad at her because she's too stubborn to even talk to them on the phone, much less come back to Walnut Creek. I can't do it, Sam. I can't walk around being angry at everyone in my family. What's the point?"

I didn't know what to say. Lame words of consolation would have fallen flat, and I've never been a poet, I wasn't going to smooth over that kind of rocky emotional terrain with what I had in my vocabulary. So, I sat there and waited and told her she was right, anger was not her jam. It didn't suit her. And that she'd figure it out.

When I thought she was ready to hear it, I told her the up-side to the trip: she and I were back together. For me, that could counterbalance just about anything you could put on the other side of the scale, short of nuclear winter. Though she was only a year older than me, I'd always had the idea she was more woman than girl, and that if I ever got too close to her, she'd ruin me for any of the other girls at Red Wolf High School. I wasn't right about much, but I was right about that.

We'd made love again that morning before breakfast. I'd asked her about using another condom, because she told me she was on birth control. Because of the unexpected pregnancy and the miscarriage, she didn't have confidence in the pill.

"Were you on birth control before you got pregnant?"

"No." She paused. "Do you think I can trust it?"

"Are you taking the pills every day?"

"Yes."

I Googled the question on her phone. "Says here 99.7% effective if you take them as directed. So yeah, I think you're good."

---

When we arrived back in Walnut Creek, I dropped Diane at home and then headed to Noquebay Resort. I talked to Mom and Dad for an hour and told them everything we found in Memphis and why we came home without Bethany. Business at the resort had slowed, only about half the cabins were rented, partly because schools were getting back in session down south, and partly due to the misinformation spread about Noquebay Resort by the Manticores before they were arrested. The slowing family business wasn't good news, but I was too worn out to worry about it just then. I went to bed early and was dead asleep in minutes, which was a good thing because...

---

... the next day my four-day vacation abruptly ended. Right after breakfast, pitchfork in hand, I was unceremoniously dispatched to the shoreline where a southern breeze had deposited a slithering mass of seaweed and kelp. In the past, Joe and Kevin would have been there with me, but they were at football practice, a fall ritual I was missing for the first time in three years. Looking back now, I've never regretted the decision. Football was a game I have always enjoyed watching, but not from the inside of a helmet. I could think of no better way to scramble my brain than to catch a knee upside the head while trying to bring down a two hundred twenty-pound fullback.

I was more worried about Diane and how her day was going. What kind of reception had she received and how did the story about Bethany Jean sit with her parents? I was supposed to pick her up later that afternoon so I guess I'd find out soon enough. I was trying to figure if the burden on Diane was lessened after our trip to Memphis or not. As we got closer to home, I think the inevitability of her family's presence in Walnut Creek without her sister started to weigh on her. I sensed that she thought, as far as the saga of her sister was concerned, we were nearing the end of the road. I threw in my two cents, of course. We still had some loose ends to track down; Bethany had given us clues, whether she wanted to or not, and we shouldn't throw them away. I wasn't sure Diane was convinced. These things were more than enough to occupy my mind, not to mention the night of the lemonades, the memory of which sent my heart spiraling to the clouds anytime I thought of it.

By late afternoon, the weather turned breezy and a little cooler. I drove the Golf over to the Warren house to pick up Diane. She about ran out the back door as I pulled to a stop. Before I turned off the engine, she was in the front seat, buckled in, and ready to go. She leaned over, put her hand behind my head, and gave me the best, longest, hello kiss ever. Then she said:

"Get me the hell out of here."

Both Carter and Ethyl were rather indignant about the fact that Jean (both refused to call her Bethany) hadn't come home with us, but for different reasons. Ethyl took umbrage at a perceived slight in Jean's attitude; took it, in fact, as a slap in the face. If Jean thought living like a tramp in Memphis was better than being in Walnut Creek with her family, well, then to hell with her.

Carter wasn't quite so resentful, but was still offended. He thought his daughter was afraid of something, and immediately asked if Jean knew he was home. Because how could she think that he, Carter Warren, would let anything hurt his "little girl?" He'd "walk through the fires of hell" before allowing anything like that.

Diane said all she could do was sit, listen to the two of them, and keep her feet out of the horseshit.

Diane had dinner with my family. It was my night to help Dad in the tavern, so after the meal she and I went out and opened the front door. There were no customers immediately which was good, because the floor needed a vacuuming. While I got out the Hoover, Diane cleaned the back-bar area. A.J. McTibble was the first one in. He took his usual spot at the bend in the bar. He always started out a little cranky because being first meant he had to buy his own beer, and maybe even his second if he couldn't mooch one off another customer. Dad came in when he heard the bell over the door, and joined Diane behind the bar.

A.J.'s luck was good. In the next couple minutes, Wes and Fanny Van Zandt came in and took their usual spots at the open end. Though several stools away from A.J., they never failed to buy him one.

I still had the vacuum in hand when Nic Vedder came in the door with his typical burst of energy. We all called out his name, even A.J. I wrapped up the Hoover and went behind the bar.

"Hello all, good vibes," Nic said. "Long weekend on tap and the very two people I was looking for—right here." He walked over to Diane, who was standing on the open end next to her uncle, and put his arm around her. "Diane, you and Sam, skiing, tomorrow. Whadda ya say?"

I turned to Dad and raised my eyebrows. He said, "Sure, after the work is done."

Nic whispered something in Diane's ear. If I'm any kind of lip reader, it was "I got beer."

Diane said, "I'm down." She took the seat next to Fanny.

"Well, all right." Nic slapped the bar. "Come down whenever you can."

Wes said, "Can't you stay for a quick one?"

"You buyin'?"

"Of course he is," Fanny said.

Nic stood behind Fanny and Diane. "Then I'll have a cola."

It was a pretty good crowd for a Wednesday night, very good considering the time of year. I heard the porch door open, saw who was coming in, and said under my breath, "Holy crap, here we go."

Fanny was the only one who heard me. She looked over, then answered, "You mean holy shit."

The bar door opened. Standing next to the bowling machine was a man in a wrinkled denim shirt, belted Dickies work pants, and a pair of boots. Carter Warren shut the door behind him and took a seat between A.J. and Diane. Dad said, "Hello Carter, what can I get you?"

Diane spun on her barstool. "Looking for someone?"

Fanny put a hand on Diane's forearm and whispered, "Easy now."

Carter looked at Diane and said he was looking for her, and that Ethyl said he might look at Noquebay first.

"Okay, you found me. What do you want?"

"Talk for a bit. Have a drink with you."

Diane looked at him side-eyed. "Thought you gave it up."

"I did. I'll have a root beer." Carter played with a bar napkin, his eyes focused there. "A lot of years in there we didn't talk at all. Oh, I know, that's on me." His fingers tapped nervously on the bar. "But, well, you left tonight before I could say thank you."

Diane froze for a moment. "Thank you for what?"

"For going down there, finding your sister. I know your mother feels the same." He took the root beer in hand.

"Yeah, then let her tell me."

I grabbed a bag of pork rinds and tossed them next to Diane's diet cola and said, "Here you go."

It broke her concentration. She looked at the bag, then at me and grimaced. "I didn't ask for those. They're gross. You know I hate them." She knew very well that I knew very well, she hated them. Diane had already turned up the heat and seared her father on both sides in an earlier confrontation, no point in repeating that now, especially in a public place.

"Oh, yeah. My mistake." I picked up the bag and raised my eyebrows.

She took a breath, then pushed hair behind her ear. She turned toward her father for the first time and said, "You're welcome." Then in a low, even voice, "I can't change how I feel."

Carter said, "Everything you've said, I've thought about a thousand times and more. Wasted time. Wasted lives. Another man dead." Finally, he was able to look at his daughter. "I can't ask that man to forgive me unless I see him in the hereafter. That'll come soon enough." His eyes went back to the napkin.

Diane hadn't taken her eyes off of him. I could imagine the narrowed eyes scrutinizing her father, the skeptical set of her mouth. She'd be looking for that crease of insincerity, a flinch to show the whole speech was nothing but a put-on. Unless she was sure his repentance was real, she wouldn't risk being hurt again. A prolonged silence ensued between the two of them. Carter took a sip of root beer and asked:

"What do you think? Does your old man deserve a second chance?"

"Maybe." She looked forward. "We'll see."

I stepped closer to her, leaned forward and reminded her that she'd told me Carter once worked as a ranch hand for the Manticores. Perhaps he would know something about Crabalocker Creek, how it connected back to Bethany Jean, and why she was afraid to come home. Diane said she was at the end of her rope with the whole thing. "Burned out." She doubted Carter would know anything of importance after being away for so long anyway. I still thought it was worth a try.

She nodded sideways. "He's all yours."

I shivered my shoulders, stepped in front of Carter, and told him what we knew and didn't know about Jean and Crabalocker Creek.

He clasped his hands together and slowly massaged his palms. "There's a lot I could tell you, but how much is still true, I don't know. I worked there a long time ago. But I was like their private FedEx and UPS. Traveled down to Chicago and back with deliveries. What was in the packages? How the hell would I know?

Didn't want to know. But I have eyes in my head, and I damn well figured there was something going on over there. But I never really knew until four years ago."

"What?" I asked. "Four years ago, you were in prison."

# CHAPTER SIXTEEN

# Jailhouse Confession

I started work early that Friday morning, cutting grass mostly, so that I had all my chores completed well before lunch. I called Diane, told her we were on for skiing with Nic, found Mom and begged off lunch. I told Mom to avoid any objection from Dad, who had an Italian's predisposition for family gatherings in the presence of food. The Vedder boat would be fully outfitted with everything we needed from lifejackets to towlines, wakeboards to skis. It had been so long since I'd spent a day on the water, since Max and his boat went away actually, that I could hardly wait for it to begin. I jogged over to Nic's place and went directly to the pier.

I knew Diane was there ahead of me; her car was parked in back. I found her, beer in hand, lying on the boat's sundeck, working on her tan, which was like saying Meryl Streep needed to study acting. I put my foot on the gunwale of the boat and said, "Dee, the sun called. Your minutes are up. He's cutting you off." Nic's wave boat was a beautiful white, red, and black hulled inboard with a ski tower. I jumped in, bent forward, and gave her a kiss.

She smiled. "You better hope not. I gotta have my sun."

"You're as brown as cinnamon, for chrissakes." I shook my head. "Where's Nic?"

She said he was still up in the cabin.

I went up to see if he needed a hand. He pointed to a huge freezer chest stocked with beer and water, cheese and meat and who knew what else. Carrying it was a two-man job. No sooner had we got it in the boat, Nic popped open a beer. Diane got a fresh one. I got one too, not because I liked the stuff but to keep the vibe alive.

Nic backed the boat out of the boatlift and drove us to a deep part of the lake on the north side of the West End between Crabalocker Creek and Dark Horse Inlet. Deep water made for higher waves for surfing and wakeboarding, shallow water just the opposite. Diane and I had been on a wakeboard only once before. Nic was well beyond us, in fact, wake *surfing* was his jam now. He would go first. I got in the captain's chair. Diane sat on the transom. Nic set the rope to twelve feet, got in the water with his surfboard, and paddled behind the boat. I put down the surf gate. The engine rumbled to life. Nic was up and out of the water in seconds, surfing the wake. He tossed the rope to Diane, who gathered it in, and then grabbed another beer before sitting next to me. One leg jackknifed beneath the other, she had a hat on her head and wore an oversize pair of sunglasses with lenses larger than her bikini top.

The sun warmed my skin. Was it the blue sky and a warm breeze that made summer, or the tan legs and flat midriff of the girl in the next seat? I cranked the music on the audio. Nic was an AC/DC fan. "It's a Long Way to the Top (If You Want to Rock n Roll")) played. The bagpipes were killer; perfect for surfing.

"Oh! Hang on." She called to Nic. She held up a fresh beer in my direction. "You need another one?"

I shook my head. "I'm driving, and I'm a cheap drunk. But you oughta slow down. We haven't had lunch yet."

"I know. Chill a little, will you? And don't worry, I'm not my sister, doing drugs, for god sake. All the stress I've got. This stuff is like water." As if to prove her point, she took a long draw on the beer.

She asked if I was going to try surfing. I thought I might. "Nic makes it look easy. One more beer and I won't even need the rope."

Nic looked tireless, but at one point he got down on his knees and motioned with his hands. "What's that mean?" Diane asked.

I looked in the rearview mirror. Nic had crushed the empty can and tossed it into the boat. "Oh, for chrissakes. He wants you to throw him a beer."

More than any wave grinding, carving, or 360 degree turns he'd done, a beer toss was something Diane could appreciate. She laughed all the way to the cooler. Beer in hand, she sat on the back end of the boat and tossed the can… right into the middle of the motor wash. "Oh shit. I missed." Nic almost fell off the board trying to make the catch.

"Try again," I yelled.

"You do it," she said. But of course, I was driving. She grabbed another beer, but this time she slid off the transom and stood on the swim deck, a rigid, two-foot wooden platform attached to the back of the boat and set above the waterline. Nic stood too, and bought the board forward. Now the toss was only a few feet rather than twelve. Nic caught the can. From the swim deck, Diane did a little cheer.

"Get back in the boat before you fall in," I said.

She stumbled a little coming back to the ski-dog seat. "Mission accomplished." She pumped her fist in the air.

Nic was done soon after that. We took a break, opened the cooler and broke out the cheese and sausage. There was a box of crackers in the storage bay. We had a floating feast.

Nic asked what we were going to do now that the Memphis trip was behind us. Diane mentioned how frustrated she was, knowing where Bethany Jean was and having her father home unexpectedly. She wasn't sure if she was any better off now than she was two weeks ago.

"I can see why you think so," Nic said. "In the long run it'll be different. Wait and see." Then he looked at me. "What the hell were you and Carter talking about last night. Kinda on the downlow."

I hadn't told Diane any of this yet, and I was going to wait until we were alone, but Nic was a close friend and trustworthy, so I decided to tell them both what Carter had heard in the penitentiary. "He told me about a guy he met about four years ago. He didn't remember his name. Thought he was from Milwaukee or somewhere down there, doing time for breaking and entering, armed robbery, or drugs. He wasn't sure about any of that. Anyway, this guy gets to talking and, it was one of those jailhouse confessions. This guy he was talking to, he said he heard about this operation 'up North.' The guy got the name wrong, too. Thought it was Mannitol, or Minotaur, something like that, but he meant Manticore because he mentioned Red Wolf Lake and all that. He said this family was growing it like a cash crop right in the middle of the woods, then hauling it south, or wherever." I ate a cheese and sausage.

"You mean 'it' as in marijuana?" asked Nic. I nodded.

Diane was open-mouthed. "Maybe that's what she heard. Bethany Jean heard something to do with a drug deal that went bad. They'd kill her for that." She cut herself some sausage. "Maybe that's what this Crabalocker crap is all about."

"Heavy shit." Nic took a drink of beer. "You done any surveillance? I got a great set of binoculars and a tripod at home. Camera, high power lens. Would be perfect."

"No. Nothing like that," I said. "Where would we do it from? Manticores own all the land in that area to hell and back, at least where we want to see."

"Where is that?" Nic asked. "High ground is the key."

"Where the Crabalocker runs through Manticore Farms. Don't ask why. It's just that Jean seemed to clam up when the name was mentioned." Diane dug in the cracker box. "There's wooded public land north of Manticore's ranch. We might be able to see something from there."

"Let's go tonight." Nic slapped his hands together and looked at me. "You ready to try a little surfing?"

"No, I'm not. But I want to wake board like you surf, to get the feel of it."

The water was bracing after sitting in the sun. Bindings on my feet, rope in hand, I yelled for them to go, and I was "surfing" on a wakeboard, and completely fine about it. After about five minutes, I was ready for a beer toss. I gave Diane the International Signal for "Toss Me a Drink," which she immediately understood. This time she was going to make a show of it. I was off the left side of the boat. She stepped onto the swim deck again, but instead of just tossing me the can, she started dancing to the music blaring from the boat speakers. To her credit, in only her bikini she could really bust a move, but I yelled, "just the can, Dee." In defiance, she put her feet together, put her arms out like wings, and took a bow. Just then the hull hit a wake from another boat. She lost her balance and fell in the lake.

"Down!" I yelled. I dropped the rope, sank into the water, and slipped my feet out of the bindings. The boat's wake washed over me. "Diane, Diane." I swam to where I thought she should be. She was a good swimmer. I'd been in the lake with her a few times before so I knew, but this was deep water, sixty feet or more, she'd been drinking, and she was not wearing a life jacket. Nic was already circling back. After doing five or six strokes I hadn't seen nor heard anything from her. My next thought was that I was going to have to dive after her, and I couldn't do that in a life jacket. I undid the zipper, pulled my arms free, and shed the jacket. Then I dove in the direction where she'd gone in.

Visibility was terrible. The churn from the prop on Nic's boat and the huge wake it produced had clouded the water for at least ten feet in all directions. I had swum to about six-feet deep, and if Diane was nearby, I couldn't see her. Panic rose in my chest. I lost my breath. I could hear Nic coming closer with the boat. He couldn't see where I was. I had to surface.

My head popped out of the water. I sucked in a deep breath. Nic was a few feet away, his elbow resting on the gunwale, the boat idling.

"Where's Diane?" I asked.

He didn't look at all concerned, which sort of pissed me off. He pointed over my head, behind me. I turned. She was floating about twenty feet away, paddling easily, hanging on to my life jacket.

"We were waiting for you," Nic said.

I swam over to her. "You okay baby?"

"Of course." Diane said. "Where were you? And why did you take this off?"

"Because, I didn't know where you were. I thought… Never mind."

Nic idled the boat alongside. "Things happen quick between you two, don't they? Listen, if you want to be together, just tell me to get lost. No need to scare the shit out of me."

We called it a day after that. Nic pulled the boat into the lift. We drained the cooler and stored the equipment. There was still time left in the afternoon. The Vedders had a hammock strung in a shady spot between two trees. Diane and I thought to take a ten-minute break there. She'd put on a cover-up. I'd put on a t-shirt and shoes. My arm around her, we laid side-by-side, her head on my chest. The dappled sunlight played above us. Sea gulls sang over the water. I could still smell the lake on our skin.

She scratched absently at the fabric of my shirt. "He asked me for a second chance again. This morning, at breakfast."

I knew she was talking about Carter. "What did you say?"

"Do you want another coffee?"

I lifted my head a little. "You know I don't drink... Oh, that's what you said to him. You were at the table." She nodded. "Well, it wasn't a 'no.'"

"No. It wasn't no."

"So, you're thinking about it."

"I guess. Maybe."

I shifted my shoulders. "But you'll let him know, at some point." I paused. "Even a 'no' is better than no answer at all." She glanced up at me. "My nickels worth," I said. "I'd do it."

"Easy for you to say."

"Suppose so, but what's to lose? Play your cards close to the vest like they say, and still be in the game. Don't go all in. You already know he could screw the pooch again. So, a small bet, to make him show his hand. He can't raise the stakes, he doesn't have the chips. Fold now and you never know what he's holding."

"Your so-called value bet?" Her hand moved down to my belly, her eyes followed. "This isn't Texas Hold-em."

"No, but life's a gamble. Heard that somewhere too."

"So it is, Sam bone. So it is."

A lake breeze tossed our hair and freshened the air. Far away an outboard motor started, then gradually the sound faded away. My left hand found her right hand on my belly. We slept for an hour.

# Chapter Seventeen

# Striking Out

A spam call set off Diane's cell and woke us up. We got out of the hammock, stretched and walked up to Nic's cabin. There, on the porch, just inside the front door, Nic had set up a huge pair of binoculars on a tripod. Both Diane and I took a look through the lenses and were impressed. Nic came out and asked what time we wanted to head out to the stake-out. No one knew much about the lay of the land or how accessible it was, so Nic led us into the kitchen and opened his laptop.

"Google Earth," he said. It was a great idea, but once he zoomed in on the acreage we wanted to see, not quite the bonanza I was hoping for. I'd thought out loud the satellite pictures might have picked up a marijuana farm somewhere along the creek, but no such luck. Different shades of green abounded everywhere. We found a couple of old logging trails that came off a town road that went in the right direction. They stopped well short of Craba-locker Creek, but we could go in on bikes and hike the rest of the way if we needed a better view.

As Nic panned along the creek, something else caught my eye. The Manticores had put up some kind of wall along the west edge of the field where it abutted the creek. Now, stone walls were common in that area. Rock picking was a springtime ritual for all the farmers in northern Wisconsin, and usually the rocks were deposited along the fence line. But on the Manticore property, solid fence lines were few except for this extended, formidable location.

Nic asked Diane to check the time for sunset on her phone.

"Seven forty-five," she said.

"Then we should leave before six." Nic pointed at each of us. "I got a bike. You two?"

"I got a couple a old bangers we can use," I said. "We'll use the old Ford to get to the trailhead."

---

We were all in blue jeans and long-sleeve shirts. Diane between us on the bench seat, bikes loaded in the back, I drove the garbage truck out of Noquebay Resort at six p.m. Never before nor since have I seen a woman more at home or carefree with men. You could say it was because she knew both of us and there was a mutual affection and respect, and that was true. But it went beyond that. She complained on occasion that, though she liked having all the guy friends, she wished she had more girlfriends. I told her, half joking at the time, that her personality only had an obvious effect on males, but not on members of her own sex, unless they were lesbian. I got a shot in the ribs for that. Then she thought about it for longer than I expected and said 'Really' with too much curiosity. I didn't bring it up again. Now, in my mid-twenties I realize I was closer to the truth than I knew.

The logging trail we were looking for started on Wildberry Road. I took the long way around because I didn't want to drive past Manticore Farms and run the risk of being spotted. The loud muffler on the old Ford made us an easy mark. Coming from the north, I took a right onto the logging trail but was able to go only half a mile before the woods became too overgrown. I parked nose-out just in case we needed a quick escape. Nic backpacked the binoculars, me the tripod, and Diane the flashlight. The trail bed was in pretty good shape, probably because it was used as a snowmobile trail during the winter. We got on the bikes and rode single file for about three or four miles when a fork in the trail appeared. We knew to take the left fork bearing southwest. Another mile or so and we were at its end. We stashed the bikes and walked south toward the Manticore property. We'd be coming upon pastureland, some of the most distant from the farm itself, often used for grazing cattle, which made the solid fence even more peculiar. Rock picking was usually only necessary on crop land. Now we were going to see with our own eyes if it really was a long wall of rocks.

We were on public land that hadn't been logged for decades. The trees had fully recovered, as had the understory, making the comparatively short walk to the forest's edge the toughest part of the trip. There were obstacles everywhere: twist an ankle in a hole, get poked in the eye by a broken twig, or tripped by a vine. We found the pasture all right, and the wall of stone, which was high enough to make observation beyond from where we were difficult. There was higher ground to the west, closer to the creek, but if anyone was working the wall or the pasture, we'd be easier to spot. We found a clump of buckthorn to hide behind on the higher ground and moved there. It was quarter after seven p.m.

Nic set up the tripod and the binoculars and took the first five-minute shift. For almost a half hour, we saw nothing but some eagles flying overhead. The beef cattle were not close by. We stayed as quiet as the woods. Dusk was beginning, and we were starting to think we'd come to witness nothing but a sunset. Then Diane noticed some small, downward-shining lights coming on at intervals along the stone wall. I trained the binoculars on distant fence posts. Similar down-facing lights were showing on them as well, likely hooked up to a light sensor. In the distance, the sound of a truck, a rather large one, was coming our way from the general direction of the farm. It reminded me of the type of truck I'd seen hauling corn or soybeans after harvest, only shorter. Using running lights only, it moved slowly.

Diane took the binoculars and trained them on the stone wall. "It's moving. A section of the wall or fence or whatever."

Nic took a look. "She's right. There's a section, must be, I don't know twelve or fifteen feet wide, it's swinging in toward the trees like it's on a hinge. Fake rocks for sure, right there anyway."

The truck approached the opening. Diane got out her phone. "I'm going to video this." Though the gate was all of a quarter mile away from us and more, I thought she'd get something usable, even as the sunset crept along.

"Make sure your phone light is covered," I said. "Or they'll spot us."

"Got it."

The truck took a farmer's left turn through the opening in the stone wall and disappeared into the woods. Nic wondered out loud how they were going to cross the Crabalocker. A second truck appeared on the far side of the field, following the same path next to the fence line. Diane's cell battery had been giving her trouble lately, and was running down again. She asked Nic to video the next one. Nic pulled out his phone. The second truck approached the gate. Nic turned on his phone. The light shone like a beacon. The watchmen at the gate saw it and looked straight in our direction.

"Nic! Stop. Stop," I said. "The light."

"Oh shit. Busted." He shoved the cell in his pocket. "Let's get the hell out of here."

We packed like there were bears invading our campsite and we were covered in honey. Getting slapped and scratched and poked and bumped by very unfriendly underbrush, we hot-heeled it back to our bikes and hit the pedals; our wheels scorching the trail like lava. The fork in the trail came and went. We swallowed the ground streaming before our wheels in breathless gulps until the body of the baby-blue pickup took shape before us. There were no words spoken. We all knew the drill. Nic was first with his bike in the box. I had mine at chest height when I heard the engine; we all did, coming down the logging trail. A red pickup, lights on, including a row of four spots on roll bar over the cab. I dropped my bike in the box then helped Diane with hers. By then, the pickup had stopped three feet away, nose to nose with ours. The driver turned off the engine. Nic stood by the open passenger's door. Diane and I walked to the other side of the cab and waited for the driver to make the next move. By that point, we'd all recognized him.

"Tapper," I said to Nic and Diane.

Nic nodded. Diane inched closer to me.

Mitchell "Tapper" Manticore got out of the truck, baseball bat in hand. "Sam Robel and Diane. Why doesn't that surprise me?" He pointed the bat. "Didn't expect you, Nic. Are we a threesome again, Diane?" He laughed, a fishy gleam in his eye.

"Too bad that shackle on your ankle doesn't have a microphone, hey Tap?" Nic said. "If you're looking for the softball game, I think there's one in Walnut Creek tonight."

Tapper slapped the bat in the palm of his hand. "Very good. Funny. You're a funny guy." He walked between the trucks. "You ever watch Louis CK? He's good. Too edgy for some, but I love him." He paced back and forth between the trucks, slapping, slapping, slapping the bat. "I was just watching him tonight when I get this call." He stopped. "I hate after-hours calls." The pacing resumed. "A very disturbing one, from one of my employees who tells me someone," he pointed the bat at Nic, me, then Diane. "was recording their operation." He spread his arms in an attempt at fake conciliation. "Now understand, as a legitimate businessman, I have to protect my interests or our competition, well, they'll run me into the ground."

"We're not your competition," I said.

"No, I don't suppose you are. That's why I'm asking myself, why, why am I here? Why are you here?"

"Just out for a nice ride in the woods," I said. "This is public land. No law against—"

"Shut the fuck up."

There was no talking our way out of this. He was sniffing around like a wasp on a soda can, and he'd already had a taste.

"Get to the point, Tapper," Nic said. "We haven't got all night."

Tapper took a step back and pointed the bat at Nic. "The point. The point! Here's your point." He swung at the truck and smashed the right headlight. Diane flinched.

I said the wrong thing. "Hey! Knock it off."

"What? Knock it off? Be happy to," Tapper said. He banged the front of the truck. Another swing like a tomahawk and he creased the crown of the hood. "Don't even think of taking that phone out of your pocket." One more blow to the grill. He dusted off the barrel, then pointed his chin at me and said:

"Next time, it'll be your head. Now, let me see that phone."

I'll always credit Nic for his quick thinking. Before Diane even moved her hand toward her pocket, Nic had pulled his phone and thrown it at Tapper's feet. He picked up the phone, set it on the hood of the Ford, and with one single-handed thump reduced the cell to a shattered mess. He brushed the electronic remains into the grassy turf of the woods and crushed them further with his heel. "You might be needing a new phone, Nic. Send me the bill."

Tapper got back in the truck, backed up, and drove away.

As the taillights faded, we walked up to the front of the Ford F-100 and checked the damage. The right headlight and directional were dangling like a zombie's eye. There were two large dents in the grill, one much worse than the other. The crease in the hood was just off center to the right and probably wouldn't lead to any trouble with running the truck; neither would the grill damage. The problem rested with the lights, and replacing those would probably mean finding a new grill assembly on that side, if not the fender as well.

"Okay, fine," I said. "But shit! How am I gonna explain this to Dad?"

"You hit a deer, man," Nic said. "Big motherfucker, a buck. Killed him dead, right on Wasko Road. A farmer came along and took the deer for his freezer. Didn't know his name. Agreed?"

High fives all around.

"Sorry about your phone," I said.

"Replaceable. Don't forget the most important thing," Nic said.

"What's that?" Diane asked.

"Tapper's reaction tells you all you need to know." Nic poked his chin toward Crabalocker Creek. "Something's going on over there."

# CHAPTER EIGHTEEN

## The Iron Arm

Seven days to Labor Day Weekend and Noquebay Resort was drifting slowly toward fall. Even though summer didn't officially end for over three weeks and the weather was still warm, one could feel the inevitable creep of sundown getting closer to the dinner hour, the snap of cool in the morning air. If I had any ideas about spending Saturday with Diane, those plans were summarily dashed at breakfast. Two new mobile homes were coming, one in two days, another in six days, and Dad wanted "all hands on deck" to prepare the spots in the mobile home park for their arrival. A load of river stone had been hauled in and dumped on each of the lots. Shovel, rake, and elbow grease were needed to finish the job. That could only be done after the cabins were turned over for the new group of arrivals and the garbage collected. The cover story about hitting the buck with the pickup had worked. Running into a whitetail deer was a constant worry when driving country roads, especially at dusk, which is when this "accident" was supposed to have happened.

By late afternoon, most but not all of the work had been done. I called Diane and told her that even after a dip in the pool, I was beat. We decided to get together Sunday night. Besides, it was my night to help Dad in the tavern.

Mom and Grandma made lasagna for supper, which always had a way of recharging me. I think the garlic bread had something to do with it too. I opened the tavern at six p.m. and in a half hour Fanny had the jukebox playing country songs, Wes had bought

A.J. McTibble his second beer, and Nic Vedder was sipping a root beer next to Wes. Just before seven, the couples from #1 and #2 came in and took the spots between A.J. and Nic. They were four people vacationing together, set in a world of their own, who clearly had an inexhaustible range of topics and common experiences to talk about, and required nothing from me but to keep the beer cold. The perfect customers. After a couple rounds, the men went to the pool table; the women stayed at the bar to chat. I dropped in on Nic.

He said, "So what now, Sam? With Crabalocker, I mean."

I cleaned a couple glasses. "I don't know. I was thinking, if they have a drug operation back there, best thing would be to get a picture of whatever they got, and get out."

"You know the sheriff around here. You'll need something solid, or don't bother." Nic gazed out the window. "Right now, you really have nothing to go on. She said, he said. Pictures of a truck. The Manticores will argue their land goes beyond the fence because it does. They own both sides of the creek through there."

I bent over and lowered my voice. "But they can't own the creek, right? That's public land, or access, or whatever."

Nic held up a finger. "Navigable streams. Can you float a boat in Crabalocker there?"

"Hell, if I know." I looked at the women and their beers. They were still half full. "Let's say it is. How do we get there without them knowing?"

Nic moved closer. "Same way as yesterday, except you'd have to take the other trail at the fork. Takes you farther north, but at least they won't hear you." I wondered why they would hear us. "Because you'll go in on an ATV. Leave it someplace hidden, go get the pics then get the hell out." Nic glanced at Wes and Fanny, who were in their own conversation. "ATVs are a lot faster, because you might need it."

"If the creek is so dry, why not come down from Ellis Junction? Then we don't have to fight the woods. From what we saw on Google Earth, that logging trail doesn't go all the way to the creek."

"You could do that, but you'd be sorry. That creek bed is a disaster waiting to happen. The less time spent there, the better. I know, I kayaked it about ten years ago in the spring, when it's supposed to be at its best. Never again, my friend. Now, in August, with the drought we've been having, I wouldn't even consider it."

"Okay, fine," I said. "But I don't have an ATV."

"I'll take care of that." Nic tapped Wes on the shoulder. "Hey guys, you know that ATV you use for ice fishing? Sam wants to take Diane for a ride tomorrow. Can he borrow it?"

Fanny smiled. "Of course, he can. Right, Wes?"

"Sure, we even got helmets," Wes said. "Diane can wear Fanny's. Mine oughta fit you, Sam."

Nic caught me off stride. "Wait. What?" I lowered my brow. "Not Dee and me. You and me. That's what I thought."

"Nah," Nic said. "This is your bag of tricks. Plus, I'm running up against that trip with my dad." I didn't know what he was talking about. "Oh, I didn't tell you? We're leaving Monday night on safari. Flying from Green Bay to South Africa. Kinda of a welcome home from the Army trip."

"But you were gone for a month," I said.

"Yeah. I can't wait."

"When do you need the ATV?" Wes asked.

"It wouldn't be tomorrow, Monday, maybe." I had to talk to Diane about it before making it a date.

Wes said, "It'll be ready to go."

---

Diane called Sunday afternoon and said she couldn't get the car until after supper. She arrived wearing her swimming suit under shorts and a shirt, ready for a swim in the pool. The day had been warm and humid. Their house had no air conditioning and she felt sticky all over. I put on my suit. There was another couple in the pool at the time, but they left soon after we jumped in. The water was warm and the breeze, too stiff for comfort for most of the day, had started to calm down as the sun set. We sat on the edge of the pool, our feet dangling in the water, towels over our shoulders.

Diane ran her fingers through her tangled mass of brunette hair, trying to loosen it up. I ran my left hand up the back of her neck and shimmied my fingers. "Here, let me help."

She said, "Ooh, I like that. A little higher." She pushed her head back into my palm. "You know, I talked to Carter today."

"That so."

She hummed a yes. "Kept it low key. No over the top everything's-all-right after all these years crap." My fingers slowed. She went on. "More like, okay, the debt is forgiven but don't expect me to forget. That's not who I am. Forgetting is something you have to earn." She shook her head against my fingers as if to tell me to pick up the pace.

"Wow, that's pretty good." I moved my lips near her ear, kissed the side of her face and said, "You're something else."

---

When we got to her place, the sun was down, the last shades of dusk were feathering the western sky. An evening breeze prodded the screens of the back porch and swept away the heat of the day. The almost-antique couch seemed noisier than usual, and so, more fragile.

We were kissing, nothing more, when Carter came down the steps onto the back porch dressed in a denim shirt and jeans, a working man's look I'd not seen on him before.

"Where are you going?" Diane asked.

"Got a job. Ain't much. Part time. I'm on call, second shift mostly."

"A job." Diane's eyebrow jumped. "Seriously. What kind of job? Where's it at?"

"Driving truck." He exited the porch.

"Hey, wait," Diane said. "You can't take the car. I have to drive Sam home."

"Got a guy pickin' me up." Carter's voice faded as he walked around the corner of the house.

"Huh, imagine that," Diane said.

From a room away, the flickering images of the TV reflected in the picture window right above us until ten p.m., when Ethyl tracked slowly up to the second floor. In the meantime, I had told Diane about the plan Nic and I had cooked up regarding the Manticore property near Crabalocker Creek. She was excited again about getting something done, especially after the disappointment following Memphis. As long as there was a reasonable plan, and she believed in the cause, that woman was on board.

My biggest worry was escape. We needed more than one way out, like a kayak or a canoe. That way we could shoot the rapids going south if they somehow boxed us in on the north side. But to drag either a canoe or a kayak through the woods wasn't practical, it was too much work. "Unless we had one of those inflatable kayaks," I said.

Diane was quiet a moment, then asked me if they used inflatables for duck hunting in the marshes on Red Wolf Lake. I told her that's exactly what they're used for. She said, "I think my brother has one of those stashed in the old hay mow."

We went out the door and walked to the very place I'd tried to take her for a tryst only a few weeks earlier. We were going there now for all-together different reasons, but the bad vibe remained, at least for me.

Access to the second-floor mow was up an earthen ramp that led to two, large doors on the far end of the barn. There were also two chutes, one on each end of the barn, through which bales of hay were dropped to the main floor. Each chute had a wood-slat ladder and a recessed light in a cage just above. Ben Warren used the mow for storage now, renting out the space over the winter to boat and pontoon owners. He had his snowmobiles up there as well, along with a small but impressive collection of antique farm machinery.

We stood at the base of the ladder. Diane turned on the switch for the light then climbed; I followed. We were at the end farthest from the house but closest to the double doors. The air was musty and warm but, because sunlight never entered, not as hot as I thought it would be. We looked about for a folded, portable kayak, but didn't see it right off. Ben's collection of tractors was truly old, but not in showroom condition. An old rake and plow that must have been pulled by horses caught my eye. The contraption had a catcher's mitt seat attached to a long, arching arm of iron, two, huge iron wheels, and a couple of control levers at hand-height when seated.

As I circled the old plow I found in the shadows a neatly folded kayak in a rectangular case, a hand pump and collapsible paddles attached. I called Diane over.

"Oh, checking out the old plow, are we?" she asked.

"Yes, I was, until I found this." I dragged the case into the angular light. She confirmed the find with a high five. "Do we call your brother and ask if we can use it?" As long as we were only using it for a day, two at the most, and would return it none the worse for wear, she didn't see the point of bothering him with the details. At that time in my life, I was only vaguely familiar with hunters and the connection they had with their gear, but I was aware enough to know if I were Ben, I wouldn't appreciate what we were about to do with his property without prior knowledge. But I wasn't about to get in the middle of anything between Diane and her brother. I was up to my ass in the Warren family drama as it was. I didn't need to drown in it.

I didn't pick up the case right away. The three-bottom plow fascinated me. I couldn't picture the life of a farmer back in the day. I kicked the wheel of the plow, got up in the seat, and grabbed the levers. "This is pretty cool. But can you imagine sitting here all day long, behind a horse, just to plow a single field?"

"No, I can't."

I tested the flex in the seat. "Neither can I." There was still plenty of spring left in the iron arm. "But I can imagine something else." I half-winked.

She stepped inside the wheel, put her hand on my belt buckle, and proceeded to push; bouncing me in the seat, the iron arm squawking like a rooster on each downward thrust. Her hand moved down. I was ready for her so fast, it was embarrassing.

She said, "Whoa, horsy," and continued with the rhythmic cadence.

I looked down at her shorts and slapped her on the rump. "Take those off and get up here."

Her shoes, panties, and shorts were soon in a tangled pile. I pushed my cut-offs to below my knees. She straddled me face to face, and for the first time in decades, the plow came to life. She kissed me then, wrapped her gorgeous, long legs around my waist and, with a tilt and roll of her hips, breathtaking in its effect and marvelous in its simplicity, the pace was set. My hand was in her hair again, which still smelled of the chlorine from the pool. We tested the temper of that arm of iron. Louder and louder it complained, but there were only the mice to bear witness to what became one of the most erotic moments of my life.

# CHAPTER NINETEEN

# Crabalocker Creek

Except for a little extra tavern clean up from the weekend, Monday morning was generally a slow day for work around Noquebay Resort. I was able to get all the day's work done in the morning, which left time for the ATV ride Diane and I had planned for the afternoon. A mobile home was due for delivery that day, but there was little I could contribute to parking one of those behemoths, so that had no influence on my schedule. I asked Nic to come over early in the afternoon so he could help me with Wes' ATV, show me the controls, and give me a few pointers on driving. I'd driven a snowmobile before, and the concepts were similar, but not the same. The weather was good. It had rained overnight but was clear by breakfast time. I didn't want my parents to suspect there was anything unusual about our afternoon plans, so I made the morning as typical as possible, right down to separating linen in the laundromat and arriving on time for lunch.

I met Nic next to the Van Zandt's small machine shed by #5 at one p.m. Wes and Fanny had gone back to Green Bay, but had left the shed unlocked and the gas tank full on the ATV. I had bought along the kayak case, paddles, and handpump, which we strapped to the rear platform. The Warren's rusting Chrysler stopped on the gravel road in front of the cabin. Carter was behind the wheel. He coughed, spit a putrid wad of yellow-brown phlegm out the window, and then tipped a couple of fingers in our direction by way of greeting. We waved back.

Diane got out of the passenger side and said, "Thanks, Carter."

He lit up a cigarette and puffed the smoke out the window. "Hope you guys know what you're doin.'"

"We'll be fine," Diane said.

"All right." Carter made a U-turn and drove away.

I stepped to her and gave her a kiss. "Hey, Nic was just going to show me how to drive this thing."

She gave Nic a kiss on the cheek. "Thanks for setting this up. Sam told me you're going on a trip to Africa. So awesome."

"Leaving in about an hour. Going to be epic." He nodded. "Got your phone for pics?"

She pulled it out of her slacks. We'd agreed on long pants and long sleeves in drab colors to reduce exposure to mosquitos and protect against brush and branch scrapes. Water shoes to navigate the stream, mosquito repellant singles, a granola bar, bottle of water, and I bought my pepper spray on general principles.

Nic showed us the controls on the ATV. My biggest worry was the transmission, but it turned out this one had an automatic, so nothing could have been easier. I got on, started it up, and took a couple of slow laps around the resort, along the mobile home park road, then back to #5 again. Diane wanted to learn to drive as well. She'd never driven a snowmobile, so getting used to the controls and the feel of the throttle and brake took a little time. She was too aggressive with both of them at first. In fifteen minutes, she was doing much better, certainly good enough to take over if something happened and I couldn't drive for whatever reason. We were itching to get started, get on the road, and be done with the whole thing, so she called an end to the lesson. We packed it up, waved goodbye to Nic, and headed down the road.

In the town of Red Wolf Lake and most of those surrounding, ATVs were legal on township roads, and trails were available in many other areas. Even with those choices however, I was not able to get to the logging trail via the same route that I took with the pickup. This time I'd have to take the back way, which would mean driving past Manticore Farms and Square M Construction. Following the FBI raid on both addresses, the people there knew both Diane and me on sight, but with the helmets on I thought detection would be difficult. We cruised down Loomis Road, right past the enemy, got to Wildberry, and took a right. Another few miles and we were at the head of the logger's trail.

Even on the paved roads, I was far short of a speed demon. I didn't have the experience nor the inclination for it. And I had Diane behind me, her arms squeezing my chest, her thighs tight on the outside of mine: distraction enough minus the speed. I rolled onto the right rut of the trail, which somehow felt rougher now than it had when we rode it on the bicycles. It took only about ten minutes to reach the fork in the trail.

I got off the ATV to stretch my legs and get a drink of water. Diane stayed onboard and drank as well. I took one more swig and asked if she was ready. She nodded and we were off into uncharted terrain, on the much-longer right fork, heading northwest. The farther we went, the rougher it became to the point I wasn't sure where the trail ended and second-growth forest began. The transition was gradual. There were times I thought the trail was done, only to have it reappear then vanish a few seconds later. Finally, I knew I'd better start checking for landmarks because the trail was gone. I stopped and said so to Diane, who reminded me she had GPS on her phone. "When they work they're fantastic," I said, my cynicism none the worse for the fresh air and sunshine. She gave me a rap on the arm. With that I thought to stop. The going was slow and the machine noisy. We were probably within walking distance of Crabalocker Creek. And who knew how far the sound of a revving engine would travel through the otherwise quiet woods. I parked the ATV.

Diane got out her cell and indeed the GPS worked beautifully. It looked like we were only half a mile from the stream, but about four miles north of where the stone gate was, and therefore, our destination.

"I hope the stream will float our kayak," she said. "That's a hell of a hike on a soggy riverbed if we end up draggin' that thing."

I grabbed the keys to the ATV and the kayak case. Diane took the pump and the paddles. We set off. My first miscalculation became apparent within a quarter mile: the water shoes were doing a damn poor job of protecting our feet as we walked the woods. They didn't safeguard our feet from rocks, sticks, branches, or anything else that poked us below the ankle. True, we hadn't encountered the creek yet, but if we spent any time in the kayak at all, the usefulness of the shoes was that much diminished. And the fit was too loose. I slipped and slid all over the place, and because I wore no socks, the perspiration only made it worse. Diane suffered in silence. I bitched all the way to the water, where we ran into some good news.

The overnight rain had improved the current in Crabalocker Creek well beyond what we expected. Brush and undergrowth were heavier along the stream. We looked for an area to break through to the riverbed without ripping our clothes to shreds. We found a spot that looked promising. I busted through a dense hedge of greenery composed of large, heart-shaped leaves the size of dinner plates. The leaves sprouted from long, hollow stalks that looked like greenish bamboo. This was the heaviest bed of Japanese knotweed I'd ever seen. We'd had some of it growing on the shoreline at Noquebay, and staying ahead of the fast-growing weed was hard as hell.

I got through the hedge only to step ankle deep into some tenacious, stinking mud. My feet sank so fast and the ooze covered so quickly, I had a difficult time extracting my foot without losing my shoe. I tossed the kayak case backwards and warned Diane away. Then I plopped doggedly toward the water until I hit the firmer stream bed. The mud was unbelievably sticky and it took several minutes of rubbing in the middle of a brisk current to clean it off.

Back on dry land again, we inflated the kayak. I stuck three, sturdy broken tree limbs in the mud to mark the spot we entered the stream, and left the pump hidden behind them. We rolled up the cuffs of our pants, got out a couple of insect repellant singles, and rubbed our exposed skin. Avoiding the mud, we launched the empty kayak and hung onto its tether. The water wasn't deep enough just yet to float the both of us, so we had to walk downstream until the we hit a deeper, more centralized channel. We soon passed a couple of feeder streams with robust flow. With their contribution to Crabalocker we were able to get in the kayak and paddle with only minor scrapes and bumps, most of which occurred in our first mile onboard. Though the current was less than brisk, after that we were free and clear, and making better time than we would have on foot. The collapsible paddles weren't sturdy, appropriate for pushing water only. I had to be careful not to push off logs or rocks lest it break. A sandbar stopped us at one point. We used the opportunity to check our time and position. We were only about a mile north of where we thought the trucks came through the rock fence. It was four p.m., more than two hours since we left the resort. Where had the time gone? If we didn't get moving, it would be well into the evening by the time we got back to the ATV. And I didn't want to find my way back upstream at dusk, which comes so much earlier in the middle of the woods than it does on the shore of Red Wolf Lake. Furthermore, when the sun goes down, nothing looks familiar, especially in strange terrain. Searching for three sticks stuck in the mud, or a four-wheeler hid in the bush of the county forest might be near impossible.

I looked closer at Diane's cell phone and swore.

"What?" she asked. "Are we that far off?"

"No. Your battery. It's below half."

She looked. "That damn thing. It's for shit. I need a new one."

"It's all right. All we need are a few pics and go home."

The sand bar extended for almost two-hundred yards. Finally, we were afloat again. We slithered along silently, following the creek which was becoming more and more tortuous in its course. We were not out to surprise anyone. The bigger worry was that we would out-stealth ourselves—sneak in too close and inadvertently startle the bad guys and ourselves at the same time. We'd have to get off Crabalocker Creek soon. Even with the meandering curves of the stream, we were too easy to spot in the kayak.

I'd considered hiding in broad daylight, cruising right down the middle of the stream, acting like a couple of naïve tourists out for a little fresh air when... OMG, we lost our way! Given the state of the creek from Ellis Junction, the only logical launch point to the north, no one would believe that story, even from city slickers.

When we judged our position a half mile north of the mysterious trail, we stopped for water and a granola bar. Diane put her phone in a secure pocket, a small flashlight in another. I had pepper spray and a cigarette lighter in my cargo pants. The kayak fit nicely behind a copse of brush and a fallen poplar on the east side of the stream. The camo pattern made it hard to spot, so I planted three more limbs in the muddy bank. There was a game trail that ran almost parallel to the creek on the west side. Staying low and quiet, we followed the trail south. For the first ten minutes, there was nothing to see or hear. Squirrels ran through the woods ahead of us. Birds called occasionally and then swooped across the trail before or behind us. The smell of the stream and its recent revitalization by rain and the sound of the water was easier to follow than the sight of the creek itself.

Suddenly, I had the sense we were being watched, that they were the hunters and we the hunted. I had to stop, take a knee, and look in all directions.

Diane stopped too. "What?" she whispered. "Did you see something?"

"No. I don't know. Just checking. Don't like surprises."

She grabbed my arm. "That sister of mine. Do you believe the crap we go through for her? She better show some appreciation."

I tapped her knee. "Let's go. If anyone asks, we're nature photographers."

She rolled her eyes. "With a cell phone."

We must have gone another ten minutes when Diane tapped me on the shoulder and stopped. She whispered, "Look there, through those poplars." I did, but didn't see what she meant. "The green, it's a different shade, and it's all the same."

She was right. Where the undergrowth should have been, something else was growing. The game trail wanted to take us toward the creek; we had to go the other way, so we left the beaten path. The closer we got, the more obvious the odd, green color became until... there was no question. We stood still in a heavily wooded area bordering a huge, irregularly shaped clearing. From where we stood, I couldn't judge its size. It could have been from twenty to forty acres all told. The area had a little roll to it, but was otherwise flat. There were trees interspersed, poplars and a few stray maples sprinkled throughout what appeared to be a very healthy, well-tended, near-mature crop of marijuana.

"Wow," Diane said under her breath.

"Yeah. See those lines on the ground?" I pointed. "Irrigation. Manticores, those bastards never stop." I tapped her pocket. "Camera."

Slowly, she withdrew her phone and took a quick series of six shots. "I'm gonna do a quick video too. The DEA is going to love these."

"Hey, that's what Bethany said." Diane looked at me as if I were crazy. "No, I mean when we said the Manticores had been arrested. She said something about the DEA. We didn't know what the hell she was talking about."

"Now we do." Diane lowered the phone. "Now we do."

"I don't see anyone. Do you?" I stretched my neck toward the back of the plantation.

She grabbed my arm. "We got our shots. Let's go."

"There's a trailer or something back there. It sorta looks like the one from Cedar Point. No one's around. We'll stay out of sight." I waved her on.

We stayed well over one hundred feet away from the edge of the clearing and kept our heads down. About a quarter of the crop had been harvested. As we circled around the back, two small trailers parked well apart and painted a sickly pea green came into view. We moved to a spot where we could get a good shot of each trailer. Both still had their hitches and wheels in place. The closer one looked like it might be used as an office of some kind, but the other one was strange. The windows were blacked out. Blue metal cans and cardboard boxes were strewn about and, whereas the closer trailer had weeds growing high all around, the ground around the far trailer looked like the backside of a chemical plant. A breath stopped in my chest. The vent on the roof was spewing steam or smoke. Suddenly, the door opened and two men walked out, both wearing gas masks.

The first one was about six feet tall. In t-shirt and jeans, he looked wiry-strong. Even in the mask he looked familiar.

The second man was shorter by a couple inches, heavier by forty pounds, much darker of skin, and wore coveralls with a long-sleeve shirt.

The door shut. We ducked behind a large tree. They both pulled off their masks. I didn't know the stout one. The other was Steve Manticore.

Diane gasped.

The men turned in our direction.

My stomach dropped.

# Chapter Twenty

## On the Run

An expression of shock froze Steve's face, then came recognition, followed by a rictus of anger. Diane and I made a lame effort at ducking behind a tree. We were busted, we knew it. We should have bolted right away.

Steve's voice, "What the fuck. Get Staples over here. Now!" Then footfalls.

I grabbed Diane's hand. "Run. Come on."

Four strides later I rammed a toe into a log. A flash of pain shot through my foot and into my shin. The damn water shoes again, they gave me no protection at all. I limped along for a bit, the pain in my left big toe throbbing with every step, until a gun shot over our heads straightened out my stride for good.

"Jesus Christ," Diane said. "He's shooting at us."

I looked back. The forest here was good cover. They hadn't gained any ground. "Keep going."

We barreled through brush, broke limbs, and stepped on rotting logs on a general path back to the kayak, but more generally toward the creek. Looking back now, I really can't say why we ran in that direction. Little or no thought went into the decision, that's for sure. It wasn't a great option, but there was no easy escape. Had we headed straight west, away from the creek, there was nothing but cedar swamp for over ten miles. The prospects straight north were about the same. Had we gone south, toward Red Wolf Lake, the distance was shorter and the terrain friendlier, but much of the land was owned by the Manticores. We knew they had aggressively posted the land and could get some of their own people there very quickly.

So we headed back to where we'd come from, east by northeast, more by reflex than anything else, obviously giving the plantation wide berth and arcing gradually back to the stream.

I put my hand up to deflect a branch. "How you doin,' Dee?"

"How do you think?" she gasped. "I'm scratched in a thousand places and I can hardly breath."

I was gasping too. "Glad you gave up smoking."

"Should've given up you,"—a breath—"and kept the smokes. They're not as dangerous."

I coughed a laugh. "Sorry, babe, this is it. This is the—"

Automatic rifle fire ripped the bark off a tree right in front of us. We froze. Within seconds, deer flies circled our heads. On our right flank, fifty feet away, a tall, skinny, poorly shaven man in work slacks and a dirty, torn t-shirt under a stained vest with pockets full of rifle shells walked toward us. Diane was in front of me. I pulled the small pepper spray from my left pocket and palmed it.

"Hands on your head." He looked like security, or what I thought security for an illegal drug operation would look like. We complied. Steve finally caught up, wheezing like a fireplace bellows and coughing. His face was flushed. A 9 mm handgun was in his right hand. He bent over, hands on his knees, and said, "Fuckin' breathin.'"

"Near drowning will do that," I said. What better time to re-mind him that, only a month earlier, he'd have died in Red Wolf Lake had I not fished his sorry ass out of the water.

He straightened. His bloodshot eyes bore in on me, the pupils widely dilated. I'd spoken too soon. Somehow, this Steve had either forgotten about last month or didn't care. He swung his right hand and hit me in the face with the but end of the gun. I staggered sideways, put my left hand to the ground, but somehow managed to hang on to the pepper spray.

"Now we're even." Steve sniffled, then twisted his head and neck about. "I could have shot you."

The guard grunted something derogatory. It looked like he was parroting one of the characters from *Breaking Bad* but was never going to get his actors card.

Steve scratched his temple with the barrel of the gun. "Maybe I still will. Because, you dumb fucks, you've seen too much. What the hell you doin' round here anyhow? It's nothing to do with either of you, for chrissakes." He looked at the other man. "Go back to work, Marty. I'll take care of these two pixies."

Marty said, "Sure, boss." He shouldered his weapon and headed back toward the stream.

When Marty was out of earshot, Steve went on. "You morons. Don't you see my position here? I'm not an undertaker, but you guys are pushing me to it." Steve couldn't stand still. He shifted his weight, shaking out his shoulders and arms one second to the next.

"The scam is over, dude." I moved my head to avoid a fly. "People know we're here. We don't come home, they'll come looking."

"Keep your hand on your head, dipshit." He aimed the gun at me, his arm quivering. It looked as if his bones were moving too fast for his muscles, his muscles too fast for his skin. I thought he might blow apart at any second. "Come looking? I don't think so. Not your style, Robel. The paint job, the break-in, you did that on your own. Don't tell me your old man gave his blessing on either of those lucky shots."

He was right, of course.

"Besides," he said, waving the gun now, "what have I got to lose? I can't let you go, man. I'd be screwed. You made my decision for me." He was looking at me.

"And you." He glanced at Diane. "Guess you bet on the wrong horse, sweetheart."

"Screw you, Steve," she said. "This drug operation is what drove my sister away, isn't it?"

His lips pulled into a nasty, sneering line. "So, you can add, even if it's only two plus two."

She gave him the finger.

He laughed, waved the gun at her hand. "Back on your head."

I dodged another horsefly.

"What the fuck is wrong with you?"

I swatted at another near my ear.

"Hands!"

"I'm allergic!" I moved my head like a soccer player. "One of them bites me, I go into shock. I don't have my epi-pen with me." Diane side-eyed me, wondering.

"Good, let 'em bite you," Steve said. "Less work for me."

I'd never heard of an allergy to fly bites, and I was sure Steve hadn't either. But if he confused it with a bee sting allergy for even a couple seconds the diversion was worth it. At that point I had four or five flies buzzing my head. I waved my right hand about like a crazy person.

Steve stepped closer. "Knock it off or I'll shoot you where you stand."

I raised my left hand and pepper sprayed his eyes. Steve cried out immediately and collapsed to a knee, his left hand rubbing his eyes, right hand with the gun at his temple. I stepped forward and kicked him in the face. The gun flew out of his hand. Diane picked it up. Steve cried out, alerting Marty, who called another name. They came in pursuit. I saw more security coming on from the creek.

I tapped Diane on the shoulder. We ran inland.

The guards must have attended to Steve, because there was no one running after us. In the distance, we heard a more ominous sound, the rev of an engine that sounded just like the one on our four-wheeler. In a different terrain, it would have been a huge worry, but I wondered if they could gain serious ground passing through the kind of heavy woods we were in. Once the cedar swamp came into play, it would all depend on how much water we encountered, how many downed trees and marshes. The sun was out, but as the afternoon walked into night the shadows were stretching their legs; and using the sun as a compass point was becoming more and more difficult. But really, that became less and less a concern. We worried more about our pursuers and where they were headed. We tried to keep the sound of the ATVs right behind us. If they got off to one of our flanks, we changed direction accordingly.

I continued to pay the price for the water shoes, and though she said not a word about it, I knew Diane was feeling the pain as well. We hadn't hydrated or eaten enough; our energy was starting to wane. I was aching everywhere, so I stopped, grabbed a low-hanging limb with both hands, and tried to catch my breath. Only a couple steps behind, Diane leaned against the trunk of the same tree.

"Next time," I said, "when I say I want to take a couple more pictures, hit me in the head with a two-by-four."

She looked down, left and right. "How 'bout I use that log over there right now and avoid the rush."

I could only nod. "You're not gonna be happy with that one. Looks rotten." I waved at her pocket. "Check your phone. Call for help."

She held up the handgun. "Take this." The cell came out and she tapped the screen. She swore. "No signal." She dialed 911 anyway.

I tucked the handgun under my belt, midback. "Anything?"

She shook her head. She hit redial, listened, and swore again. "What happened to the ATVs? I don't hear them."

"Tracking us on foot maybe?" I lifted my head. "I don't know. Gonna be tough in this light if they are. Question is, do we try and get out of here tonight or hunker down?"

She stood away from the tree. "Keep going. It's not like we can camp out here. No food. No water."

I sat down and took my shoes off. "Are your feet hurting as bad as mine. Gawd, these water shoes, what a dumb idea. The guy thought a this oughta be shot."

"Careful what you wish for." She inspected her feet too.

"Oh shit, yeah." My feet were red in all the wrong places and swollen, too, especially the balls of my feet where blisters had formed. There was an angry looking bruise under the nail of my left, big toe. I poked around the heel on my right foot. "Man, my feet are trash."

"Yeah, mine hurt too. Nothing we can do now," she said.

I put my shoes back on.

They'd been driving us away from the creek, or so it seemed; with no landmarks or sun to guide us it was hard to tell which way we were going. The GPS on Diane's phone was out because we had no signal. We took a course a little the right of our last bearing, which should have been north by northeast and a little toward the creek. But really, in the middle of a dense forest, how much could we really tell? The territory was all new. Had it been seen by human eyes at all in the last fifty years? For all I knew the answer was no. That evening, the sound of the ATVs did not return.

We walked deeper into whatever wilderness we were in and came upon a meadow-like area about half the size of a football field. The trees were sparse here, the ground level and covered with long grass. In the middle was a pond surrounded by pussy willows and numerous patches of Japanese knotweed. Crossing the meadow would be easy, but would expose us as well. I wanted to get a glimpse of the western sky to reorient myself. I decided it was worth the risk. The west wasn't where I thought it would be. I was off by an entire quadrant, ninety degrees. Looking south, the sky was darkening too fast, not a friendly sight at all. A stormfront was approaching. I was about to mention this to Diane when she held up her hand for quiet and froze.

"What is it?" I whispered.

"Shh." She nodded straight ahead.

In the dusk, a large, black shadow emerged from the tree line, a four-legged behemoth, its ponderous head swaying back and forth as if on a scent.

"Holy shit," I whispered. I put the pepper spray in my left hand again, and pulled the hand gun from under my belt. Whether he could see us or not, he must have had our scent as he was follow-ing the path we'd walked to enter the meadow. The bear closed distance slowly but steadily. Still facing the black bear, we started backing away. "This way," I said. "Against the wind."

"No, he'll smell us," Diane said.

I showed her the pepper spray. "Yeah, but if I have to use this."

I'd heard making noise could scare off a bear, but we didn't want to go over the top and give away our position to the other carnivores in the area, even if they'd parked their ATVs for the night. I chanted, "No bear, no bear," every three or four seconds. It had no effect. He kept closing the gap from fifty feet to forty, to thirty-five feet.

"No bear." We backed into a fallen log and stumbled.

The bear angled left. "No bear."

We backed to the right. I didn't want to shoot the bear for several reasons. First of all, the sound of the shot would give away our position. Second, I doubted a 9 mm slug would stop a determined black bear. In fact, it might just piss him off. I'd heard plenty of bear stories just like it. I could miss the shot entirely. Who knew what would come of that?

We backed to the right again. For the first time he followed us, as if he were trying to cut off our escape route. We backed straight away. Thirty feet.

He lunged left. My voice now shaking. "No bear."

Twenty feet away. "No bear." He lunged straight at us. I sprayed at his head as long and intense as I could. The bear howled. Diane was about to break and run. I grabbed her arm. "No, walk."

The bear turned sideways, stopped, and looked in our direction as if he was considering whether to charge us again. I raised the handgun, aimed at his massive, bobbing head, but couldn't steady my aim. My hand, my wrist, my entire arm was quivering like a clothesline in a windstorm. Would another cloud of pepper spray do the trick? I sent another blast in his direction; whether it found its mark or not I couldn't tell. A second or two later he shook his head as if to clear it, and walked away. I sighed with relief and dropped the gun to my side, my arm numb with exhaustion at holding the gun on the bear for only a minute or two.

In the distance we heard, "What was that?"

An answer, also distant, "A bear, I think."

"Crap," I said. "They're still out there, and the bear just marked us."

The first clap of thunder ran across the sky. For the next half hour, lightning lit our way. The rains were coming. The storm front had robbed us of any remaining daylight. If the rain came hard, we'd need to find shelter, but the voices sounded too close to overnight where we were, especially near an open area like the meadow. We headed northeast again, away from the plantation, angling toward the creek so far as I could tell. On the other hand, we might not hit anything for more than ten miles and finally run into Ellis Junction or Highway 64. If we survived long enough to get there.

For a few more minutes we made steady progress through fairly dense forest, dodging heavy underbrush when it showed itself, but having more and more trouble seeing where it was. Diane had a small flashlight but I was afraid to use it. One turn in the wrong direction and the beam could show us to our pursuers. We could hear the rain coming in the distant trees, raindrops battering the leaves to our south and approaching fast. Our search for shelter was becoming desperate. I'd been looking for a stand of pines but had seen precious few. Diane noticed a ridge off to our left running roughly in the direction we were walking. Come morning, putting an elevation like that between us and Steve would be an advantage. As we hit the crest, the rain came down in wind-blown sheets. By the time we descended and got to the other side of the ridge we were wet through to the skin. We had to stop and get out of the weather. I jogged over to a trio of pines I'd spotted, but the prospects there were poor. Diane had found something at the base of the ridge. She called my name and waved me over to a spot where the ground had been scraped away. There was a slab of sod overhanging what appeared to be an opening, a rather large oval hole, that was dug out of the hill. I lifted the sod which was heavy with wet.

"What is it?" Diane asked, rain dripping across her face.

I opened my hand and asked for the flashlight. I gave her the pepper spray and told her to hold it at the ready in case it was needed. With no small amount of trepidation, I lifted the sod again and flashed the light inside, fully expecting to see an animal in there—a fox, a coyote, or even a bear—alive or dead. It was empty. And clearly large enough for both of us to fit inside.

# CHAPTER TWENTY-ONE

# The Bear's Den

From what I could see, we'd stumbled upon a bear's den, possibly used the winter before because there still lingered the unmistakable, rank smell of bear which, once you've had a whiff, you never forget. The second I saw the size of the dugout and that it was empty, I knew this was it, we'd found our shelter. I was ecstatic at the prospect of getting out of the rain, so when I saw the anguish on Diane's face, I was taken aback.

"Really?" she said. "You want me to crawl in there?"

I couldn't believe she was asking. Rain was pouring off both of us. We had to raise our voices to be heard over the roar of a thunderstorm in the woods. I was getting cold; I'm sure she was too. "Well, hell yeah. Why not?"

"Why not! What if it caves in and we're buried alive?"

"Dee, it's been there for a long time and it hasn't caved in yet," I said. "Okay, I'll go in first, then if it collapses, you can still crawl out."

She kicked the flap of sod. "What about this? It's in the way."

I said, "We need it to keep the rain out. We can get out anytime."

She looked down. "I'm claustrophobic, and this looks like a fuckin' grave."

"It's a bear's den from last winter. Maybe the bear we just saw." I knew that was a mistake, the second I said it.

"Oh, great!" She hugged herself. "What if he comes back?"

I shrugged. "So, pick your poison, buried alive or eaten by a bear? But hurry up. Freezing to death is the last thing I wanna do."

She huffed her shoulders. "You go first, and give me the pepper spray."

The soil appeared to be clay and sand but more importantly, dry and relatively warm. The dimensions were adequate for us to lay on our sides, like spoons in a drawer, and that was about it. The height was about two feet more or less. The biggest challenge was our wet clothing, which made it hard to feel the warmth of the earth, but there was nothing to be done about that. Teeth chattering, bodies shivering, we clung to each together, facing the opening. She had the spray. I had the flashlight and, if push came to panic, the hand gun in my belt.

We talked for a while, an attempt, I think, to calm ourselves down. It also kept my teeth from chattering. I said my family would already be wondering where the hell we were. I learned later, they'd already called Fanny and Wes Van Zandt and Ethyl and Carter Warren. The one person who could've brought them right to us, Nic Vedder was somewhere over the Atlantic Ocean, flying to South Africa and would be for another fourteen hours.

Lying in that dank, musty den, the shivering was starting to abate. Diane didn't know what to think about her family. She doubted her folks would have noticed her absence at all. She admitted that was partly her fault. Her schedule had always been erratic, so much so that it had become the norm and a few hours here or there, even a missed night, would not be out of the ordinary. I thought the discussion would end there, but she shifted her head, which was propped on her folded arm, and said:

"But then again, what was there for me at home?"

I asked, "Was it better when Carter was home, you know, when you were little? Or don't you remember?"

"It wasn't that he was *bad* when he was home. He just wasn't around, not that I remember. He was out drinking most of time, when he wasn't working. And obviously, he got a bad case of beer brains one too many times, killed a guy, and got what he deserved."

"So, are you pissed at him for being a drunk or for being gone?"

"Shit, I don't know. Both, I suppose."

"Sounds like you really haven't let him off the hook."

She was quiet for a minute. "Don't know if I have it in me, Sam."

"It's there, just a little lost and looking for a way out, like we're doing right now."

"Do you think there's a chance?"

"Of you forgiving Carter or us outsmarting these drug dealers?"

"Both."

"Hell, yes."

She said, "I don't even like elevators. That's how much I love this cave."

I gave her a squeeze and said we had to talk about our plan for the next day. We knew Steve Manticore wouldn't give this up; he couldn't afford to let us get away. Diane knew him better than I did, and for a longer time. That's why she wondered about our chances. My answer was optimistic because I didn't see the point of painting a black picture. After all, we were lying in a dirt hole, wearing wet clothes, our bellies empty, and we had gun-toting drug desperados on our tails: it didn't get much darker than that. Adding a black border to that picture would only make it bigger, not clearer. And, we couldn't plan a thing until we knew what Steve and his band of thieves had cooked up overnight. On that thought we closed our eyes and tried to get some rest.

I shifted my hips and nuzzled my face against the back of her head. "Did you notice anything different about Steve today? I mean, outside of the fact that he seemed hell bent on shooting us."

"Yeah. What the hell was that. I couldn't believe he hit you with the gun, for chrissakes. And that was only the start."

"Right? And the way he was acting. He's always hyper, but today, I don't know. The hyper was on speed."

"And what about his eyes?" she asked.

"Yes, yes! Bloodshot. And his pupils were huge; like looking at the wrong end of a shot gun. Marijuana don't do that."

"Cocaine, you think?"

"Could be," I said. "But you know that other trailer, the one with the blacked-out windows. It reminds me of the one we saw down in Memphis by Bethany Jean. It was a meth house. I'll bet Steve's cooking over there, and he's using his own stuff."

"Oh my god." She shifted her legs and took hold my hand. "Meth heads, they get totally out of control. Holy hell."

I was just about to nod off when Diane said, "Sam?"

"Yeah, babe."

"How do we know there aren't any creepy crawlers in here?"

"Didn't see any," I said sleepily.

"Yeah, but what if…"

I walked my fingers up her arm. She slapped aggressively at my hand. "Asshole."

"Sorry. My bad."

Then we listened for the sounds of the woods, the ones that only come out in the forest dark, the kind so thick you have to part it with your hands to find your way.

Though unbothered by animals—arachnoid, mammal, reptile, or otherwise—we slept poorly that night and woke early, still wet and shivering, hungry and thirsty. We'd become used to the nasty bear odor, which I would've thought impossible. After taking a look from under the hanging sod, Diane crawled out of the den. I followed. The rain had stopped during the night, but everything around us was still soaked. The forest, like us, was waiting for the sun's rays and an August breeze to dry it out. Both of us were stiff as old leather. We tried to do some stretching, but it's hard to do when your muscles are damp and cold. We were feeling better though. The treetops were glowing in sunshine. Our bodies were loosening up, and getting out of a hole in the ground will always improve your point of view. Diane and I had just sat down on a log to plan our next move when we heard it: in the distance, first, the engine of a large truck sounding as if it were coming across Crabalocker Creek. Then the barking of dogs, tracking dogs, I was sure, soon followed by the ATVs again. Though the dogs would probably be tended by handlers on foot, our chances of staying ahead of them had dropped lower than swamp water.

We looked at each other. I said, "Shit."

"That about sums it up. What now?" she asked.

"How do we fool tracking dogs?" I asked. "I don't know."

Diane raked her fingers through her hair, but not to comb or tame it; we were both beyond that. She was thinking. "I had a boyfriend, few years ago. His dad had dogs."

"Yeah, so…"

"I don't know if he was trying to impress me or what, he was kinda the type. He told me it wasn't that hard to fool them." She sat forward, scratching her scalp as if to make the blood flow. "What did he show me?"

"Come on, Dee. What?"

"Shut up. I'm thinking."

I waited. The barking hadn't stopped. The ATVs were no longer idling. "Scratch a little harder."

"No. Yeah. He told me… you walk in a circle. Start small, then bigger and bigger. They get confused, or frustrated, or whatever. Then they give up."

I put her dirty, smudged face in my hands and kissed her on the lips. "You're a genius. We'll lead them away from here. Make our circle, then double back. But we can't hide in the den. They'll sniff us out."

It was my turn to scratch. My scalp did itch. I needed a shower… bad. But I had to come up with something. Then I remembered the pond. "All right. Let's go. The circle first."

The sun was now high enough in the sky to guide us. We trotted north about a quarter mile and found a small clearing that was relatively flat. Starting from the middle of an imaginary circle, we walked in gradually larger concentric rings.

"One of your former boyfriends, huh," I said as I stomped along. "Anyone I know?"

"I don't think so. He graduated last year. Before you came here."

That was believable. Diane usually dated older guys. She claimed it was because they always had a car and money to spend. This was another one of those times when I could never tell if she was bluffing or telling it straight. "Just as well you don't tell me," I said. "Your boy list is out of control anyway."

"Is not!" She kept walking. I followed. The dogs kept barking, getting closer.

"Diane, come on. I can't swing a dead cat in Walnut Creek

without hitting one of your former boyfriends."

"Oh! My! God! You are so full of crap. And saying this shit while we have killers on our ass. Are you nuts?"

"Sorry, Dee. I'm as scared as you are. Joking around is my way of dumping my stress."

"Okay. As long as I know where your head is at. This circle is big enough."

"Yeah, we gotta get back to the pond before the dogs get to us."

We followed the same path back to the ridge, and then again to the meadow and the pond.

"Are you sure you're up for this?" I asked her.

"Do I have a choice?"

"No."

"How do you know the stems of those knotweeds are hollow?"

"I cut 'em every week. They're like huge straws," I said. "All we have to do is find a couple of dry ones so we can break them off."

We stepped through the border of pussy willows and knotweed at waters edge, careful not to leave any clues we'd walked through to the pond. I didn't know how deep the water was, only that it would be deeper after last night's rain. I thought we'd need at least two to three feet to hide effectively.

Amongst the hundreds of plants, you'd think finding a couple, mature, browning stems would be easy. It wasn't. I found one fairly quickly, snapped it off into a ten-inch section and handed it to Diane. "Practice breathing through it. You only have to do it for a few minutes."

I scrambled about, more and more desperate for another brown stem. The dogs got closer. I tried a green plant with predictable results—the stem would bend but not break off. I threw it away. I saw a brownish shoot a few steps away in the shallows. I stepped in, pulled the plant, stripped the leaves, and broke off the base. A foot higher, I tried again, but it didn't crack off. The dogs were very close. I told Diane to get in the pond and lie back. I bent the stubborn joint back and forth, then put it in my mouth and bit down on the weakest point. The stem frayed once, twice, then the third time gave way. The piece was only six inches long, but it would do. I looked for Diane's stem but didn't see it. Then I slipped into the pond, put the stem in my mouth, and sank onto my back.

I had only the vaguest idea where Diane was. The depth of the water was good, but still my biggest worry was not breathing but floating unintentionally. If my foot or face broke the surface, the dogs or one of the posse might see me and we'd be done. Of course, I could see nothing and heard very little. A few foot falls, a bark here and there, and then silence for a long time. The wall of pussy willows was working for us. They'd grown to about six feet tall and formed a good sight barrier.

I'd heard nothing at all for several minutes. I was getting cold in the water and anxious about Diane. I counted to one hundred twenty and still hadn't heard anything. I raised my head. We were alone. Still half immersed in the pond, I located Diane's stem, crept over to her and tapped on her shoulder. She came up slowly, eyes blinking then wide, wondering, I'm sure, who had found her out. "What? Are they gone?"

"I think so. I hear them on the other side of the ridge. Let's get out of here."

Gradually we climbed from the pond. Heads low, our clothes clinging to us like second-skin, we stepped lightly away. On a quick look back, I couldn't see any of our pursuers but the dogs and ATVs were making enough noise to easily tell us where they were. We started on a trot straight east, or what we generally approximated to be toward Crabalocker Creek and the kayak. As we slid through the woods, we had to make a choice. We wanted to get to the kayak as soon as possible, but if we went too fast and made excessive commotion, we could tip off the posse or possibly someone still at the plantation. It was hard to imagine us being louder than an ATV, but a cracking limb at the wrong time could resonate a long way in the woods.

The distance to the creek stretched out longer than I expected. Either that, or exhaustion, and the lack of water and food was finally catching up with us. We'd already done at least a mile and there was still no sign of water. We stopped to catch our breath and take a listen.

"How you doin'?" I asked.

She gulped a few breaths of air before replying. "How's it look like I'm doin'?"

She was a mess, of course. Filthy, really. I'm sure I looked no better. We both smelled like bear and pond scum, though neither of us could tell anymore. Her usually gorgeous brunette locks were a matted mass of sand and sweat. The only thing that kept her face from being completely tinted pond green were the stripes of perspiration beading down from her brow and long eyelashes.

I used my thumb to wipe away one of those sweaty beads from her cheek and kissed her. An unusually dry one as our lips were parched and our mouths like cotton. "You look fabulous."

She laughed. "I worry about you, Sam. I really do."

The deer flies and horse flies made a return appearance. Our long sleeve shirts had been cut to shreds. As a result, we'd suffered dozens of small nicks and pokes on our arms and torso. Our pants and legs had faired only marginally better.

I checked the sun again for direction. "Ready?"

"As I'll ever be," she said. "How much farther. I'm dry as a bone."

"Dee, I wish I knew." I held up my hand. "Hear that?"

"Hear what?"

The dogs were ominously quiet, but the ATVs were in full throat and seemed to be coming our way, or heading toward the creek, I couldn't tell. "They're trying to cut us off." I took her hand. "Come on."

# CHAPTER TWENTY-TWO

# Up in Smoke

The reprieve from the barking was brief. Within ten minutes the dogs were back; their baying howls echoed through the woods directly behind us. It sounded as if they were coming straight along our path. As we jogged toward the creek, we talked about diverting the dogs one more time. Since the path north would have been on foot, their presence eliminated that escape route once and for all. If we didn't find the kayak immediately, our scent would be all over the bank of the creek, and if we were delayed in finding it, the chase would be over all together. There was no time for another diversion. We had to find the kayak, and quickly, it was as simple as that.

As it turned out, we'd taken our break near the halfway point. We still had about a mile of trail busting in front of us. We were ahead of the ATVs, but they were probably sending armed guards toward the creek on foot, or so we assumed. The underbrush became heavy and tangled; it slowed us down and sapped our strength. We stopped for a breath. That's when we heard it: the sound of rushing water. Even though we couldn't yet see the creek, our ears told us which way to go.

We stepped through a dense stand of cedar and poplar, most of it young and small and densely packed, and suddenly, there it was—Crabalocker Creek, deeper, wider, moving faster than we'd ever seen it before.

"Yes!" I exclaimed.

Both of us went to our knees and drank in the cool water,

probably more than we should. There were no muddy banks to worry about this time, Crabalocker had overrun them. We washed our faces. I stuck my feet in, shoes and all, just to feel the cooling effect on my over-heated blisters.

Diane had found a good place to sit, it was dry yet accessible to the creek. "Which way to the kayak?"

I sat down next to her. "Don't know. The river looks the same everywhere. Except that tree overhanging the creek over there. It look familiar to you?" She said no. "Me neither. It could have fallen in the thunderstorm last night, but I don't think so." I pointed my chin north. "I think the kayak is upstream."

I asked Diane to check her phone again. She hadn't had a signal for almost twenty-four hours. She looked at the screen. Her battery was dead, no surprise she said after its immersion in the pond.

The current in Crabalocker was transformed by the rain. In fact, because our kayak was stashed on the opposite side, we'd have to be careful about where to cross. This wasn't the case a day earlier, when we could ford the creek at will, even in the deepest sections. Now, we'd have to look for a wider, shallow area or risk being swept away by the current. The course of the stream was tortuous and didn't allow for a long line-of-sight in either direction. We couldn't see what was happening, whether it be north where the posse would likely be, or south where the bridge that connected the plantation to the Manticore property should be located.

We found a good spot to cross the river about one hundred yards north. A similar distance more and we discovered the kayak and paddles. The three, large tree limbs I had stuck in the riverbank as markers were long gone. We climbed in the kayak, found the middle of the current, and headed south toward Red Wolf Lake. I would like to say we felt a sense of liberation as Crabalocker sped us along at a much brisker pace than before, but such was not the case. We knew the posse was in communication with whatever manpower was still stationed back at the plantation, and that they'd be on the alert. They may not have known about the kayak, but they would have guessed at an escape downstream after they had sealed off the north. Watching the creek would only make sense.

I estimated the distance to the bridge at less than a mile, no more than four or five minutes at the rate the current was taking us. We heard what sounded like an ATV again, but this time it was coming from near the plantation. By the sound of it, the vehicle was going to a spot in front of us, likely the bridge or somewhere nearby. We had no choice but to beach the kayak before the creek straightened enough for them to spot us. We pulled into an eddy on the same side as the plantation on a stretch where the brush was overhanging the creek.

Diane wondered why we were pulling up. "We can't just hide. The dogs will find us."

We pulled the kayak under the overhang. "You're only going to be here for ten minutes, maybe fifteen, tops."

"Me! What about you?"

"We need a distraction. A big one. I'm going to sneak over to the plantation and blow something up. You'll know it when you see it. That should pull all the guards off the bridge. They'll think it's both of us. That's when you get back on the creek and paddle like hell. I'll meet you on the other side of the bridge. Okay?"

"Jesus Christ on a bicycle, Sam."

"I know. It's the only thing I can think of. What do you think? Can you do it?"

"Hell, yes, I'll do it. Just make sure you're there. I'm not paddling to Red Wolf alone."

"I'll be there." The exchange sounded more upbeat than we had a right to be, but optimism didn't cost anything, and we had little else to spend. We knew we were surrounded by a group of brutal drug dealers bent on saving their business and staying out of prison.

I gave her a kiss on the forehead and said, "Wish me luck." I checked for the handgun tucked in my waistband and was on my way.

I found the same game trail on which we'd approached the plantation a day earlier. The kayak turned out to be a little over a quarter mile from the bridge. I stayed low, going from tree to bush to tree, already knowing the general lay of the compound I was approaching. Vehicles would most likely be found parked near the creek side of the plantation or in the back, near the two trailers. From the edge of the woods, I couldn't see anyone walking about.

I slipped from the cover of the forest, across the cleared area that encircled the plantation, to the nicely ordered rows of marijuana. Keeping my head below the top level of the plants, I worked my way to the back of the compound until I got to the edge of the field. To my left was the strange looking trailer with the blacked-out windows that I assumed was a meth lab. To my right was another trailer about one hundred feet from the first one. It looked more like a typical, middle-of-the-woods go-away-and-leave-me-alone place for a single male to live out a solitary existence, but was more likely an office for the operation. Right in front of me was a crop truck similar to the one we'd seen driving in at dusk a few nights earlier, and near the office trailer, a couple SUVs that probably had brought in the dogs. A large skid-steer that was used to carry containers of harvested marijuana sat near the truck. I was hoping to find gerry cans of gasoline to dump under a car and light, but there were none I could see. I could shoot a bullet into a gas tank but then how to light it? I wasn't going with to stand with a cigarette lighter next to a gasoline spill and touch it to flame. Would a spark from a slug be enough? And what about the sound of the gun? Well, I was trying to draw attention, anyway.

I worked my way toward the meth lab. There were half-a-dozen blue, metal cans sitting near the single access door, and a similar number of propane tanks, their top valves a peculiar blue color. I knew the tanks were tough, probably thick enough to deflect a 9mm slug and produce a spark. I jogged to the skid steer, where I found a small tool box next to the driver's seat. I wanted a claw hammer; what I got for my trouble was a screwdriver; it would have to be good enough. I jogged back to the meth lab; it wasn't far but it seemed like a four-hundred-yard run. Smoke wafted aggressively from two vent pipes on the roof. Ventilation fans loud enough to hear from fifty feet roared from inside. As I approached the trailer, the chemical smell became intense and made my sinuses burn. I stepped around a garbage can full of empty, lithium battery casings and a cardboard box full of cold-tablet foils. I tipped three of the empty propane tanks into the shape of a teepee right behind the trailer door. The blue, metal cans contained acetone. I took three of them, punctured each twice with the screwdriver, and let the clear pungent liquid run out on the ground.

Suddenly, the door of the trailer flew open. I drew the handgun and held it on the man standing in the doorway. He wasn't supposed to hear me. I was going to call him out of the trailer right before I blew it up. But maybe this was better. I said, "Pull off the mask." He did. I waved at his gun. "Drop it. Pull it slowly and drop it behind you, in the trailer. Slow-ly. Make a sound and I'll shoot you."

He was sweating, from drugs, fright, or heat I didn't know. When he complied, I said, "Cell phone. Two fingers, out of your pocket, then throw it over here, at my feet." He took it slowly from his pocket as I told him. Then, with a flick of his wrist, he threw it somewhere in the back of the trailer toward the kitchen. He grinned in a way that held no humor, showing a mouthful of wasted teeth.

"You son of a bitch." I had the feeling he had a stake in the operation. He'd calculated he wasn't yet worth a bullet, and he was right. I had to give him that. "Pick up that empty propane tank and walk toward the truck until I tell you to stop. Say a word and you're dead. Either that or I leave you in the trailer. What's it gonna be?"

I think he knew what was going to happen because he moved briskly enough. When we were a safe distance from the trailer, I told him to stop and crouch down. I got ready to shoot and had the sudden thought, *This gun was under water. What if it doesn't fire?* I pulled the trigger. The gun recoiled. The first attempt, a shot at the teepee of tanks, was too low. The second hit, but had no effect. The third drew a spark and blew the trailer off its frame. A fireball sent a plum of black smoke skyward.

I waved the gun at the cook. "Put that propane under the gas tank on the truck." This time he hesitated. "Now! Or the next bullet is in your shoulder."

"All right, all right. Don't shoot me." He jogged to the spot and placed the tank as instructed. He quickly backed away.

"Stop," I said. "Now, give me one reason why I shouldn't put a slug in your leg, right now."

He put out his hands. This was not the same man that came out of the trailer with Steve the day before. This guy was tall and rangy with a stooped posture, his hair long and disheveled. He wore long sleeves and blue jeans, but the clothing looked as wore out as his expression. "I got nuthin'. No gun, no phone. I can't hurt you. You go. Do whatever. All I can do is sit down right here."

He could do a lot more than that, but I didn't have it in me to maim an unarmed man who wasn't threatening me, and I had no time for anything else. "Go stand behind that SUV."

A shot into the truck's gas tank produced a stream of gasoline that spewed onto the ground. I had no idea how many rounds were left in the gun. It didn't matter as long as I had at least one more. If it was there or not, my time was running out. I had to head for the creek and wait for Diane. She'd be at our rendezvous point in minutes, and that was about a quarter mile away through the woods. I took aim at the propane tank and pulled the trigger. The gun fired. Flames engulfed the cab. I hit the ground. The gas tank exploded.

For moments—two seconds, ten seconds, twenty? I really don't know—I laid prone on the ground. My head throbbing, ears ringing, my chest empty. Finally, I pressed my palms into the dirt, pushed my body off the ground, and tried to run.

# CHAPTER TWENTY-THREE

# The Cook

The explosion had knocked me out for crucial seconds. My ears rang. My head felt full and I couldn't run in a straight line. It looked like the cook was in worse shape than I was, still sprawled on the ground, trying to gain his feet, then falling back down. I made it to the edge of the woods but for the first fifty feet after that, I was bouncing from tree to tree like an alcoholic lumberjack who'd just rolled out of the saloon. Multiple ATVs, which had started up near the bridge after the first explosion, were roaring down the trail. They had less than half a mile to cover before arriving at the burning truck. The flames near the trailer were already receding but the column of black smoke they produced was impressive. The truck burned black as well, with an even larger flame.

Over the next few minutes, my head gradually cleared. My hearing was still bad, but my balance had returned and the disorientation was passing. I don't recall how long it took to get to the creek, but it was longer than we had planned. My hands grasped for branches, pushed away vines, and then, all at once, Crabalocker was there. I tripped on a tree root and tumbled into the water. The splash alerted Diane to my location. She'd been waiting for me about one hundred feet up stream. She came quickly and before I knew it, she was yanking on my sleeve. The cold water of Crabalocker braced me. I shook my head and heard her call my name. An ATV started from around the plantation. It seemed improbable that one of the guards from the bridge would already be there. I'd seen the trail from the bridge; it was not paved, was quite rough in fact, with pot holes and roots crossing, and full of turns.

Diane came alongside me in the shallow water of the riverbank, pulled the kayak on shore, and stood up. "Sam, what happened?"

I crawled on shore too. "What?"

"I said, what happened?"

"I don't know. The explosion, I guess."

She took a quick inventory of my chest, belly, head, arms and legs. "Still got all your parts. Can you move?"

"Got to. They're coming." We climbed in the kayak, grabbed the paddles, and shoved off. The turbulence of the water, the speed of the current, and the fullness in my ears made my head swim. I had to put the paddle crossways on the kayak in front of me to regain my balance.

"Sam!" Diane said. "What's the matter?"

I raised my right hand. My head was in a spin, but it was slowing down. I closed my eyes and it got worse. I opened them and looked down at the paddle, which I knew wasn't moving. A few seconds later, the spinning went away. Slowly, I raised the paddle again. By this time, the kayak was half in, half out of the current, almost stuck in an eddy. I put the paddle in the water and started stroking. "Okay. Better. I had a dizzy spell."

Seconds later, we were in a race for our lives. I pointed my paddle at the ATV, which was heading on a parallel course with the creek. There must have been a trail, because he couldn't have been making those speeds through virgin woods. We put every-thing we had into every stroke. The current was strong but the creek continued its habit of turns and oxbows which slowed us down. We'd gone about half a mile when we spotted the ATV again, now on a diagonal headed for a spot on the creek ahead of us. We redoubled our efforts with the paddles, but with the short-handled versions we had, getting any torque in the stroke was hard to do. I still couldn't figure out who was chasing us. We came around another sharp, right-handed turn when we spotted a trailhead on the shore. As we passed it, I looked down the path and saw the ATV and its rider only yards away.

"The goddamn cook," I snarled. "Should have shot him when I had the chance."

The cook skidded the four-wheeler to a stop at the water's edge. He jumped off. We paddled hard through a left-hand turn. We had to get down stream and around another righthand turn to gain cover before he could get off a shot. We turned. The nose of the kayak and Diane were around the bend when he opened fire. The first shot hit the kayak. The second hit my paddle and knocked me into the churning water. The creek wasn't deep and, like a fool, I stood too quickly. The third shot hit me under my left arm. It spun me around and down. I heard Diane scream my name. Stunned and in pain, this time I stayed below the surface of the water and scrambled toward shore. Diane had taken cover out of sight of the gunman. She got hold of the sagging kayak and pulled it onshore.

I dragged myself from the creek, up the bank, and sat down.

Diane crab-walked to my side and said, "Did he hit you? Where? Let me see."

"I don't know. I guess so. It stings like a bitch." I lifted my left arm and immediately my rib cage was on fire, radiating around to my back. I cried out and dropped my arm. My eyes watered.

She took my elbow and raised it slowly. "Come on, I've got to see how deep it is." She lifted my shirt and took a look. "Oh shit, Sam. It's bleeding like stink."

"Did it go in the lung? As long as it didn't go in the lung."

"How the fuck should I know?"

"I'm still breathing. Must be okay." With a grunt, I got to my feet. "We gotta go."

I thought we were about two hundred feet away from the cook. I grabbed her by the hand. We ducked into an area of heavy bush, sat low, and waited for a sound, movement, inspiration, anything to tell us what to do next. What the cook knew, and what he didn't know, was not clear to us. He might have assumed we were still floating downstream. If so, he might speed by us on the ATV. That would give us time to regroup and plan our next move. After only a minute or two, we'd heard no engine revving, so that idea died. Maybe he was waiting for reinforcements. Not knowing was killing us. Diane was as antsy as I was, I could tell by the expression on her face. I said, "We should go."

She was on her feet before me. "Which way?" She motioned toward Red Wolf Lake. I nodded.

The bush was so dense we couldn't see where we were going. We could hear the creek, and that was about it. Walking on a game trail would make us more visible to the cook and whoever else might join him. On the other hand, thrashing through limbs and leaves would make more noise, so in the end it was pick your poison. We walked quickly along, off the beaten path. Breaking trail was a bitch with my left hand and arm; any movement of the shoulder produced sharp pains in my chest. Diane stopped me and took another look under my shirt.

"Holy hell."

"Is it still bleeding?" I asked.

"Yeah, some." I asked her how bad. She dropped the shirt. "I don't know. But you're moving your hand and arm. That's good."

"Won't mean a damn thing if we don't get out of here." I ducked through the last wall of greenery into the open; Diane right behind. The chambering of rounds in firearms stopped us cold. I looked to my right. Steve Manticore was there, his hips hitched like a cowboy, gun in hand. The cook stood on one side of him, his sidearm aimed at Diane. A security man on the other side had an AR-15 pointed directly at my chest.

"It's been a long run," Steve said between heavy breaths. "A marathon. Time for a rest. A long rest for both of you."

"Shoot them here, boss?" the guard asked.

"No, then we'll have to drag their sorry asses back. We've got heavy equipment back at the farm for digging. March 'em back and make it quick, before someone comes about all the smoke." Steve sniffed then wiped his nose on his arm. "Frisk 'em. He's got my 9mm."

Steve, the cook, and the guard rode ATVs. Diane and I were driven like cattle up to the camp, a distance of about a half mile, and taken to the area where the meth lab used to be. There was a crew there, hosing down the embers and cleaning up the mess. The vehicle fire had been put out as well. The explosions were not done for diversion only; obviously, I was trying to alert the local authorities—the fire department, police, DNR, anyone—to come out and take a look, and to save our asses. It hadn't worked. There was no sign of the dogs or the handlers. They must have been sent home once our capture was secured.

They got off the ATVs and walked us toward the trailer blast site. Steve led the way, in front and to my left. Diane was on my left too. The cook was right behind me with a hand gun. The guard was behind Diane, the AR-15 strapped over his shoulder.

With all the manpower focused on cleanup, I didn't see anyone in the marijuana field tending the crop, much less harvesting. The skid steer was idle and I didn't see any crop in the storage bins, so when, in late afternoon the crop transport truck arrived, I was surprised.

Our time was growing short and our options few. I had to make some kind of play to get out of this mess. "Hey, Manticore. You can't kill us, and you know it." I winced and grabbed my chest. "You think we'd come out here without telling our families where we're going? They're already putting together a search party. Count on it. And the Manticore Ranch will be the first place on the list."

Steve stopped, turned in my direction, his shoulders tensed, his stare wild. The last time I saw that look, he hit me on the face with the butt of his gun. My cheek throbbed evermore with the thought of it. If you'd have asked me six months before that day, would Steve Manticore hit a defenseless man, I'd have said no. This new, damaged, impaired version would do it in the blink of a raven's eye.

Steve stepped in front of me and shoved his finger in my face, his jaw clenched so tight it pulled on the muscles in his neck. The pupils of his eyes bore through to the back of my head. "Who the fuck told you to open your mouth? Keep your mouth shut or I'll end you right where you stand." His eyes traveled down to my bloodied shirt. He threw a punch into my left chest. I folded in agony. "That's what I think of your search party."

I put my hands on Diane's shoulder as if to hold my balance. A few seconds later I whispered to her, "I'm all right."

"Hey, boss," said the guard from behind Diane. "You knocked him into next week."

Steve sniffed twice. "Get moving. We got to get this over with. We'll bury them under the old trailer site. Any police dog sticks his nose in that shit, it'll come out with his brains on fire."

I could hear the cook snickering behind me. He nudged me in the ribs with the gun, to get me moving. Though it hurt very little, I responded much the same as I did from the punch. I let go of Diane's shoulder, staggered into the lanky cook, and caught him completely by surprise. I grabbed his gun hand, pointed it at the guard, and fired; hitting him flush on the right shoulder. The guard cried out, dropped his weapon, and went down, writhing in pain. The cook was taller than me by four inches but no heavier, and in poor physical condition. Spending all that time bent over a meth stove will do that, I suppose. I put a foot behind his leg and bent him backwards until he plopped to the ground. Diane kicked the AR-15 away from the guard then jumped in, pinning the cooks left hand to the ground. I wrestled the gun away from him. Suddenly, there was cold steel behind my ear.

"Drop it," said Steve.

I lifted my hands off the cook and dropped the gun. He immediately retrieved the firearm and stood next to me.

"Sorry, boss," the cook said.

"Shut up!" Steve said, then motioned to his right. "Diane, get up, move over there." Then he looked at the cook. "Think you can watch her without losing the gun?" Steve pulled hard on my hair. "You first, Robel."

"Sam!" Diane cried.

"Shut up!" Steve said. "Another word out of you and it'll be ladies first."

I licked sweat off my lips. "You owe me, Manticore. You owe both of us."

Steve laughed derisively. "For what? Blowing up my trailer?

Blowing up my family? For being a constant pain in the ass?" He pushed my head forward, his hand still ahold of my hair, the gun behind my ear again. "Which one? Come on, tell me so we can get this all straightened out."

"Cut the bullshit, Steve," Diane said. "You'd a been pulled out of Red Wolf with grappling hooks if Sam hadn't pulled you out first."

The guard groaned, his shoulder bleeding profusely. "Thirsty. Water."

Steve didn't even look at him. "Yeah, in a minute." Then to us. "See, Diane, I must a had one a those things where you die and then you come back. They say you lose your memory when that happens, 'cuz… I don't know what you're talking about."

There was a siren in the distance. I closed my eyes and begged for it to be coming our way. And then cursed to myself. *Why had it taken so long?* "Hear that, Steve? Better think twice. Gonna have company soon."

Steve addressed the cook. "As soon as we're done here, gas up the ATVs. If we're busted, we'll take the northwest trail out of here. We'll find out soon enough. But you won't be here to see it, Robel. If I ever have to do time, and you're out walking in the free world, that would make any sentence seem like life without parole."

Diane said, "Steve, are you crazy? That's exactly what you're going to get if you murder us, you dumb ass."

"Shut up, bitch. No worries for you. You'll be right behind your boyfriend."

"What the hell is going on back here?" The voice was stern, commanding and drew Steve's attention immediately; I could tell because the pressure of the barrel against my skull lessened and wavered a bit.

"Tapper!" Steve used the nickname for his oldest half-brother, Mitchell. Was he the driver of the truck I'd heard minutes earlier? "Your bail monitor. You can't be out here."

"It's either be here and clean up the goddamn mess you've made of this operation, or sit back at the house and wait for the feds to do it for us." I recognized the voice from an encounter I had with Tapper and his baseball bat on the trail a couple days earlier. He was almost as obnoxious and arrogant to me then as he was to Steve. "Looks like you've got a classic cluster fuck going here, bro. Nice work. And what the hell are these two doing here? Isn't that the Robel kid that blew up our irrigation system?"

The muzzle of the gun was again hard behind my ear. "Yeah. And you know Diane, Jean's sister."

Mitchell said, "Do they have something to do with—"

"Yeah," Steve said. "Sam blew them both."

"Then they've seen the operation. What the hell are you waiting for?" Mitchell asked. "Get it over with. Goddamn it, give me a gun and I'll do it."

Mitchell walked to the cook and took the gun from him.

"No! Tap," Steve said. "This is my operation. I'll take care of it."

Mitchell lowered the gun but didn't give it up.

I looked at Diane one last time, to say goodbye in some way. As it turned out, she was trying to catch my eye, and when she did, her expression changed. As usual, she was unreadable, and now always would be to the very end. I remember thinking, *just look at me one more time with those gorgeous, dark eyes*. But there was a light pulsing there, not entirely on Steve, nor me. It made me a little sad.

Steve said, "Say your prayers, sucker."

The muzzle hard on my skull, I heard the hammer click…

# CHAPTER TWENTY-FOUR

# The Last Stand

Silently, I said goodbye to my family, and apologized for getting myself into the stupid mess I'd so foolishly made for myself and Diane. Then I wondered if I'd hear the sound of the shell firing before entering the great void. But I didn't hear an explosion or even a click. I heard a raggedy, familiar voice:

"Make another move, Manticore, and your brains will on the ground right next to his." A short pause. "Put it down, Steve. There's been enough shootin' today. You too, Tapper."

The pressure behind my ear lightened a bit but didn't go away.

"Dad!" Diane exclaimed.

"Stay there, honey. I'll get this figured out." Another pause. "Drop your piece, Mitchell, right now."

But nothing happened. I could see Mitchell to my right, the gun still at his side. The pressure behind my ear was still there. Mitchell said:

"It's two on one. Do the math, Carter. You're standing, but you're already dead."

"You're closer to the truth than you even know, Mitchell, but I ain't dyin' today and neither is my daughter. Now, I'm giving you one more chance—" Two seconds later, a shot rang out. Mitchell dropped the gun and grabbed his chest. A blood-red petal bloomed on his shirt. He collapsed.

"Tap! Jesus Christ, Carter, you shot him, you shot my brother."

Carter picked up Mitchell's Smith & Wesson and tossed it over near the skid steer. Then he waved his gun at Steve and the cook.

"Now step aside, both of you." The cook took a few steps back.

Steve said, "I ain't movin.' And if you make a move, I shoot Robel. This is none of your business, Carter. Go back to the truck, and drive it back to the farm. That's all you're paid to do."

"I didn't sign up for this. Explosions. Crystal Meth. All I was supposed to do is haul weed. Now you're going to kill my daughter and Sam here, and you think I'm going to stand back and watch it happen?"

"You're going to turn around and get the fuck out of here because I told you to." Steve's hand was shaking, I could feel it through the muzzle of the gun. "You're in violation of your parole right now. They'll throw you in the slammer until your bones are nuthin' but dust. Your P.O. is only a phone call away."

There was movement to my left, and finally I could see the cook and Carter. He was dressed in Manticore Farms work clothes. He didn't seem to be bothered by the threats regarding his parole. The sirens were closer, louder.

Another shot, from my left this time. Carter sang out in pain. The guard had recovered enough to pull a Glock from his waistband and fire at Carter. The shot hit him in the mid-thigh. He dropped his gun and collapsed. In that second, I rounded on Steve, knocked the gun away from my head, and gut punched him. He fired and missed. A kick to my chest produced a blinding pain and forced me to the ground. I was on my back. Steve was on his knees next to me. I grabbed for his gun with both hands. He swung wildly with his free hand and grazed my face. We grappled for control of his firearm. My advantage over him was my weight, but he was above me so I was in no position to use it.

As soon as the guard shot Carter, Diane kicked him in his bloodied shoulder, then kicked the gun out of his hand. He uttered a guttural moan and passed out again.

The cook and Carter saw the free gun at the same time. It had skittered closer to Carter, but he was wounded and the cook was fast. They made a play for the gun at the same time. Carter managed to get a hand on it, but the cook's quicker response made the difference and he snatched it away.

Steve's brawn was all I'd remembered it to be, and more. I'd heard stories of superhuman strength in meth users, and wondered if that's what was fueling him now. My only hope was the wheezing deep in his chest. Maybe the trauma of the near-drowning and his heavy cigarette and marijuana use would catch up to him in time to save my life. I was still on my back. He moved his left forearm to the base of my neck, inching ever closer to my windpipe. My right hand was wrestling for the gun. My left arm was not strong enough to stop his forearm so I went after his ribs. Over and over, I pounded his chest, trying to take away his breathing before he ended mine.

He bore down with the gun. Flexed his wrist. The angle of the barrel inching steadily downward toward my head. From nowhere, a shot ricocheted in the grass right next to my ear. Steve and I stopped. I looked up. The cook stood over us, gun in hand, the muzzle aimed at my head.

Steve stood up and laughed demonically. "Good work, my man. Shoot 'em and let's get the hell out of here."

The cook grinned at me like a possum, raised the gun, and…

Suddenly, there were two reports. I thought it was the guard again. But this time, one shot was aimed at Steve, the other at the cook. Both found their mark. The gun flew out of the cook's hand. Steve's hand was more than empty, because where there was once a gun, there was now a bullet hole. I sat up and turned. Diane, in a shooter's stance, had the Glock in both hands, still trained on Steve. She nodded toward me. "Come and get this thing. I hate it."

I got up and went to her. "Okay, babe. Got it. Holy shit, you saved my life." I pointed at Steve, who was bent over in pain, his left hand holding his right at the wrist, blood streaming off the middle fingers to the ground. "Get your cell out and drop it to the ground." He did so. "Now step away. Move over there, by the guard." I motioned at the cook. "You too."

I said, "Dee, can you get that phone and call 911?"

"No need," grunted Carter, still lying on the ground. "I already did."

# Chapter Twenty-Five

# An Ordinary Life

The sirens had become extremely loud and incredibly close, then suddenly silent. And yet there was no rescue coming down the access road, no cavalry coming to save the day. Clearly, there was a problem and we needed someone to check the trail and the gate at the stone wall. I retrieved the AR-15 and had the cook, the guard, and Steve sit back-to-back-to-back on the ground. The guard was still semi-conscious so I had him propped against the other two, facing away from me. There were three other farm workers on site that I ordered into a similar formation near the first group. In spite of her training with a hand gun, Diane was not comfortable guarding the six men.

I asked her, "Can you take an ATV down the trail and see what's going on out there? I'm worried the cops or whoever's out there might be stuck at the stone wall."

One of the ATVs was a small, four-wheeler that looked more like a golf cart. She climbed in that one and drove away.

She was gone for ten minutes. During that time, I had to put up with Manticore's seething, whining threats and then, at the end, a pathetic attempt at making a deal. By then, I could barely bring myself to look at him. So far as I knew, he was still hopped up on some kind of meth and marijuana cocktail with an alcohol chaser, and I wasn't about to poke that bear unless I had to. If he went on another rant, made a play at an escape, or tried to rush me, the only option I really had was to shoot him, and I wasn't anxious to fire on anything or anyone.

Waiting for Diane's return was as hard as anything I'd done during the two days we'd spent on those hellacious acres, but finally I heard the sound of a small motorcade coming slowly along the winding path, lights flashing. All told, there were three sheriff's cruisers, two rescue squads, and two teams of fire fighters from the Department of Natural Resources. As soon as law enforcement saw the extent of the drug operation, two more units were called in.

Steve Manticore and Carter Warren were taken to the Walnut Creek Hospital in the first Rescue Squad with a deputy attending. An extra ambulance was called to transport the corpse of Mitchell Manticore to the County Coroner's Office for an autopsy. The guard and I were taken in the second Rescue, also under guard. Even though Diane had no external injuries, she was transported, under protest, by one of the sheriff's cruisers to the emergency department for evaluation.

At the hospital, the guard and Carter Warren got immediate attention. The guard was admitted to the ICU for shock, from what I could tell. Carter had a full set of x-rays and blood work. He strenuously objected to a chest x-ray for reasons I couldn't understand at the time. Only Ethyl and Ben's presence and insistence made him relent. Steve's bullet wound required the expertise of a hand specialist, so he was stabilized at Walnut Creek Hospital and then transported by ambulance to Green Bay for consultation. I remember thinking at the time, *if I never see that bastard again it'll be too soon.* But, of course, I knew I would.

Diane and I asked the nurse to put us in adjoining beds. There was a privacy curtain between us which we pulled away as soon as we could. At that point we were in hospital gowns, our stories were almost identical, and we had nothing to hide from the police. My parents were there to see me, had arrived at the hospital before I did. My mother was in tears the second she saw me, which made me tear up too. My bloodied shirt had been removed by then, thank God. I can't imagine what her response would have been had she seen that.

Mom did a quick check, as mothers always do, to make sure I

was still whole. Then she hugged me and said, "No more adventures for you, Sam." I cringed from the chest pain, but didn't tell her why just then.

"That's right, son," Dad said. "Find another line of work. One your mother and I can survive."

"You can survive? What about me?" I asked sarcastically.

Dad was not amused. "You don't seem to understand how your life affects the rest of us. You fall backasswards into shit and come out smelling like a rose. What's to worry for you? It's us sitting back home and waiting, that's the hard part."

Diane rescued me from the next cubicle. "You're right. But he smells like pond scum right now."

"That's enough out of you, Dee Dee," I said.

She *tisked* her tongue. "So, come over and stop me." She knew well I was hooked up to an IV, my arm wrapped with an automatic blood pressure cuff, lying on a gurney with the rails up. We both were.

The doctor came by and told me the chest x-ray was normal. The bullet hadn't hit anything vital, just a flesh wound. How lucky was that? I was dehydrated but my blood work was otherwise good. I'd be able to go home after the fluids and antibiotics were done. The black and blue area on the side of my face would take a week to fade away. X-rays of my face didn't show any broken bones. The skin on my arms and legs had suffered and so had my feet but with rest and time, they'd be fine.

Diane was "dry" too, as the doctor said, so she had to sit still for a few hours while she "filled up her tank" with IV fluids. The multiple cuts, scrapes, and gashes on her arms and legs would heal. They'd been washed up by the nursing staff. A few required a bandage and some attention in the days ahead, but again, all would heal, she said.

After half an hour, Mom and Dad left for a while. The nurse pulled the screen away so Diane and I could talk while we ate the meal brought from the cafeteria. I had roast beef and some kind of potato dish. She had a burger and fries. I didn't know what all the complaints regarding hospital food were about. Everything we had tasted delicious.

While we were talking, Ethyl and Ben came by and told Diane that Carter was being admitted to the hospital. Obviously, his leg needed more treatment, but there were also some shadows on his chest x-ray that were not normal. They thought he might have pneumonia.

"Maybe that's why he's coughing all the time," Ben said.

"Mom," Diane said. "Did you know Dad is working for Manticore hauling marijuana?"

"I didn't. He told me just now," Ethyl said. "I guess that's why he went out there, to work a shift."

Diane shook her head.

"They were the only people would hire him," Ben said. "Ex-cons don't get a lot of job offers."

I said, "I'm glad they did or I wouldn't be sitting here. He saved my life. Diane's too."

Ben looked quizzically at me. Ethyl said, "Really? He didn't say anything about—"

"Yeah, Mom. Steve and Mitchell were about to put us… six feet under and Dad stopped them. He had a gun."

Because of his parole, Carter didn't have any guns at home. Ben wondered where he would've found one.

I told him, "The office at the plantation. He and Mitchell drove out there in the same truck. When Mitchell saw what was going down, he walked right toward us. Carter figured it out too, so he went to the office and got a gun. He'd a got to us sooner, he told me, but his breathing was so bad."

"When did he tell you this?" Diane asked.

"When you went on the four-wheeler."

"My Carter," Ethyl said in wonder. "My Carter saved a life."

"Two lives, Mom," Diane said.

Ethyl sucked on her lips and blinked away the moisture in her eyes. Ben put his arm around her shoulders and said, "Let's go up to his room, Mom."

The two turned slowly and left.

After they were gone, I turned to Diane and smiled.

"What are you grinning at?" she asked.

"I've lived to *see* the day."

"The day of what?"

I said, "You called Carter 'Dad' and Ethyl 'Mom,' and on the same day no less."

She rolled her eyes and went back to her meal. "Did not."

"Did so."

"Okay, Mom, just now. But Dad, when?"

"When he surprised the cook, you yelled 'Dad!', not Carter. I remember, because for a second, it threw me off. I thought it was my dad."

She threw a French fry at me.

"Hey! Nurse! Over here." Arm extended, I pointed at Diane. "She's throwing food."

The nurse didn't get up from her station, but said, "Children, behave. And if you pull out that IV, I'm going to restart it with a needle twice the size and half as sharp."

Very carefully, I retracted my arm. I stabbed a potato and popped it in my mouth. "Oh, I gotta ask. Who taught you how to shoot?"

"Are you sure you wanna know?" She looked at me sideways. I dropped my fork. "All right," she said. "I warned you." She dipped a fry in ketchup. "Had a boyfriend couple years ago. He taught me."

"Get the fuck outta here."

Diane extended her arm and pointed at me. "Nurse, he's using foul language."

Again, from her seat. "One more time and I'm gonna separate you two."

I cut aggressively into my beef. "I should've known."

"Don't be bummed."

I shrugged. "I haven't taught you anything. All these guys with the dogs and the guns and the god-knows-what-else." I raised my knife. "I got nuthin.'"

She drained a can of soda. "You taught me the best thing."

"Oh yeah, what's that?"

"Family. You taught me family."

A couple of deputies entered the Emergency Department. One approached me, the other Diane. The screen between us was pulled. They had arrived to take our statements.

---

Diane and I were discharged from the Emergency Department at about the same time so my folks gave her a ride home. Ethyl and Ben stayed at the hospital a while longer to be with Carter until he was ready to sleep. I found out later he'd never been overnight in a hospital, and even though he'd spent ten years in a penitentiary, somehow the prospect of sleeping in a room where people could come and go at will gave him the creeps.

I slept long and hard that night, waking but once when I rolled too fast onto my left side and I was strummed awake by pain. By the next day, the hundreds of cuts and bruises were sorer than a bad sunburn. Even putting on shorts and a short-sleeve shirt was tricky. I walked into the kitchen. Mom and Dad were waiting for me at the breakfast table. Even though she'd seen me the day before, Mom cringed when she saw my swollen face, black and blue on the cheek where Steve had planted the butt of the gun. I told her not to worry, even though it was throbbing like a toothache.

They wanted to know every detail of the two-day ordeal. The gunshot, especially. Who pulled the trigger and why? Where was I when it happened? Was Diane in danger as well? How many shots were fired? There was much forehead rubbing, many stern looks, and more than a few times "how could you?" Mom dabbed her eyes, and then I realized the full extent of what I'd put them through.

Without saying his name, they reminded me of what happened to my older brother, James Jr., who's death had been at the hands of a shooter. Dad said, "We can't go through this again. It's too hard. It's too hard, Sam. We can't lose you, any one of you."

How could I have been so dense? I hadn't considered that parallel between my brother and myself, and now the recollection stunned me. I flushed. My eyes burned. Then I saw the pain and sorrow on the faces of my parents, as I'd seen it so many times before. But in the past, there'd always been James to blame. He was the one who'd run off. He was the one who'd gotten himself killed. And for what?

Now, it was on me. All of it.

We'd moved to Red Wolf Lake and bought Noquebay Resort to escape James Jr's death and now I was bringing it all right back home again. Had I thought of my folks or my brothers and sister for even a minute during any part of this miserable escapade?

No, not even for a second.

"Oh my God, I'm so sorry." Elbows on the table, I covered my face with my hands. "I never thought…" I couldn't say anything more.

Mom put her hand on my shoulder. "It's okay, Sam. That's not why we wanted to talk to you today."

Dad said, "We only want you to be careful. You're not made of steel and barbwire. And neither are we."

I rubbed my face, took a napkin from the holder, and blotted my eyes. "Yeah, I know." I took a breath. "I have to go to the doctor today at ten thirty."

"Yes, we know," Mom said. "Joe and Kevin rode with Terry Marz to football practice so you could have the car."

I asked if I could leave a little early. I'd promised Diane I would give her a lift into town to see her father. Her mother was already at the hospital. When I picked up Diane, she was anxious about seeing Carter again. His doctor had called a family meeting for that morning and she was worried about what he was going to say. She asked if I would come along.

"Sure. My appointment isn't until ten thirty and you know doctors; they're never on time."

Carter's room was on the second floor in the medical wing. As we approached her father's room we saw Ben standing outside the door, hands in his pockets. He started when he saw my face, more swollen than it had been in the Emergency Department.

Diane asked, "How is he this morning?"

Ben shrugged with his hands. "The same, far as I can see, but the cough and the breathing and the leg are still…" He shook his head.

"Do you know what the meeting's about?" I asked.

Ben looked both ways down the hall. "I don't know but the doctor's not here. Dad says he was here earlier and got called away. Some kind of emergency."

Diane waved us in the door.

There were two beds in the room but only the one next to the window, Carter's, was occupied. Ethyl sat in a chair next to her husband. Ben stood at the foot of the bed, Diane next to him. I stood behind her.

Carter wasn't lying flat. The nurses had raised his head and torso to about forty-five degrees. He had oxygen flowing through a couple of prongs in his nose, and an IV in his arm. He looked fairly comfortable until he went into a coughing spasm, which seemed to follow whenever he spoke. His color had never been good, and that morning he was sallower than ever.

"Hi, Dad," Diane said. "How are you doing? Does your leg hurt?"

"Only when I sing." Carter's little joke, and we all smiled.

"How did you sleep?" I asked.

"On my back." He was pretty devil-may-care, more than I'd ever seen him. "No, really, not worth a shit. Hell, there was someone in here every ten minutes checkin' this and doin' that. How's a guy supposed to get some shuteye with that goin' on?"

"You were sleeping real good when we came in," Ben said.

"That's the only time," Carter replied.

Diane asked about the doctor and when he was coming back. Carter did all the talking. Ethyl sat quietly, her eyes straight ahead, focused on nothing that I could see. Her hands were settled on her lap and held a tissue. She didn't challenge anything that Carter said. He'd gotten the full story from the doctor earlier, who'd offered to return later that day but Carter declined. He'd tell his family everything they needed to know.

Diane looked at me, then Ben. "Okay, then, we'll talk with the doctor tomorrow."

"Maybe," Carter said. "Can't never tell when he'll be here. His schedule is all over the place."

I couldn't see how Carter would know his doctor's daily habits after just one night in the hospital, but I didn't say anything.

"Save that for later." Diane moved a little closer to her father. "Okay, what's the news? How are the blood tests?"

Carter tilted his head. "They think they can avoid surgery with medical stuff, you know, antibiotics, bandages, stay off the leg. That sort of business." He put his hands on the injured thigh.

"The blood tests?" Diane asked.

Carter waved a hand. "Oh, they're fine."

Ethyl breathed in. "You have a low blood count. You're anemic."

Carter frowned at his wife. I was astonished. Ethyl had not only spoken up, she'd contradicted someone, her husband no less.

"Well, okay. Of course. I lost some blood," Carter agreed. "I was shot, for chrissakes. But Doc said that'll come around."

"Maybe," Ethyl added. "If your kidneys get better. They're only going at thirty-three percent."

"Thirty-three percent!" Ben exclaimed. "That's awful."

"Ethyl, knock it off. It's not as bad as it sounds. Doc said with the IV, it could be up to forty percent before I go home. And it has to go below fifteen before you think about dialysis."

"Dialysis!" Diane exclaimed. "What else are you *not* telling us?"

"Now wait a doggone minute. Are you callin' me a liar?" Carter pointed at the ceiling. "I won't have that. Not from anyone, 'specially my family." The outburst led to a coughing spasm during which he lost control of his breathing. It was hard to watch. He finally hawked up a gob of bloody mucous and spit it in a tissue.

"Oh my god, that's blood," Diane cried. "Does the doctor know about that?"

Slowly, Carter was able to settle down, then he nodded, "Yah, yah."

Diane watched him for a moment, then asked about the x-rays. Carter said the leg pictures were fine and showed no sign of any bone damage and no left-over pieces of the bullet still in his leg.

"What about the chest x-ray?" she asked.

Carter repositioned himself. "The what?"

Diane bent forward a bit. "The chest x-ray. In the ER they said it showed a pretty bad lung infection."

Carter cleared his throat. "Oh yeah. Pneumonia. That's what

the antibiotics are for."

"I thought they were for your leg," Diane said.

Carter's eyes shot bullets at Diane. "It's for both, okay? What is this? Am I on trial or something."

"Okay. Okay, I'm sorry. I'm worried, that's all." Diane gripped the side rails of the bed. "The doctor's not here so I have to ask you."

"Never mind. If you need to worry, I'll let you know." Carter's lips stretched into a thin, horizontal line. Ethyl looked at him briefly, then looked out the window, tearing at her tissue.

"Pneumonia's pretty nasty stuff," I said. "Gotta be careful."

Carter shook his head. "Yeah, Doc balled me out for the smoking. Said I have some kind of lung disease, and I better quit right now."

"All right, then," Diane said. "We'll get them out of the house. Right, Mom?" Ethyl didn't respond. "Mom? Right?"

Ethyl seemed to come out of a trance. "Oh, yes, of course."

"I quit," Diane said. "You can too."

"That driving job is down the drain, Dad," Ben said. "What you gonna do when your leg heals up?"

"And the lungs and kidneys and blood counts are better," Diane added.

"Yeah, that too," Ben said.

"Find another one," Carter said.

"Do you think you should be driving a truck, especially on a farm, with your lung condition?" Diane asked. "An inside job maybe, in air conditioning, no dust, no pollen, no fumes, that kind of thing."

"You find that job and I'll spin on my head," Carter said. "But I won't be fussy. Can't be. We can't live on Ethyl's disability forever."

"You seem pretty anxious to get back to work," I said.

Carter repositioned the nasal prongs, and again, hawked up some blood-tinged phlegm. "The one thing I'd been thinkin' on, 'specially these last few years in prison, all I wanted was an or-dinary life. Always thought there'd be time for that when I was old. Well, I don't know what old feels like, but it's gotta be pretty

183

close to what I got goin' now." He paused for a couple breaths. "I got a job 'cuz I wanted a shot at something like that. What I said, ordinary; just so I see what's it like." His chest rattled again, then he coughed.

Maybe I was ready to hear this from Carter, with Diane standing next to me, my chest and face throbbing, and the result of a life of misadventure lying in the bed in front of me. Yes, lying there because he'd taken a bullet for Diane and me, but also because he was spitting up blood and had lung disease. He wasn't the embodiment of the Summer of 2013, but his line about an ordinary life hit home. The excesses and successes of what had gone down over the last three months were put into focus by that one line. Diane and I had started out with a goal we hadn't yet attained, and already we'd paid a heavy price. When Max left town, Diane and I had lost a good friend. And Max had lost a lot more than that. For a second or two, as I was standing there, I even had a sympathetic thought for Steve Manticore. Maybe he'd played the hand he'd been dealt in the only way he knew how. So yeah, I could dig an ordinary life, one hundred percent.

Ben stood up. "Is there anything you wanna do, Dad, you know, when your leg gets better?"

Looking down, he said, "No, not really. Not much I can do." Then he gazed up at Diane. "I'd like to see Jean one more time… if I could."

# CHAPTER TWENTY-SIX
# A Mother's Intuition

Labor Day Monday was six days later. I still wasn't to full strength, but every day was better than the one before. The bruise on my chest had faded by about seventy percent, the pain by about the same amount. Many of the cuts and scrapes on my arms and legs were nearly healed or well on their way. I could roll over in bed and not wake myself from a sound sleep. The "raccoon eyes" I'd developed two days after the blow to my face were fading too.

The resort was busy, the last gasp of summer, the bookend twin to Memorial Day but without the optimism. Rather than talking of fishing and swimming, the conversations on Labor Day were about when to have the boats out so the piers could be pulled for the season. My wish for an ordinary life was coming back to bite me. School was to begin the next day. A much bigger worry was Diane and her job search. She had decided to go to Green Bay and work for her aunt and uncle at Van Zandt Construction weeks ago. The situation in the Warren house, however, had transformed dramatically since then. Would that be enough to bring about a change of heart in Diane and keep her in Walnut Creek? You can bet I was putting all my money on that horse. But there were still no comparable job offers in the Walnut Creek area. The drive to Green Bay was well over an hour. I was in no mood to give her up for five days a week.

During the week leading up to Labor Day, we'd talked about Green Bay some, but mostly about Memphis and going back one more time. The how and when were the problem. Our financial situation was on life support, and we had no transportation. We could ask Betty for the Volkswagen Golf again, but neither of us wanted to impose upon her a second time. The other issue was that if Bethany Jean decided to come back to Walnut Creek, the Volkswagen was too small to carry anything more than a couple suitcases and whatever else she could fit in a few garbage bags.

After supper on Monday night, the resort was already pretty quiet. The big night on Labor Day weekend was Saturday. Sunday was for rest. Monday for travel. The cell rang. It was Diane calling with a surprise. Deborah Manticore had called Diane and asked if she could talk with the Warren family and me in about an hour. I got the okay for using the car and hung up. On the six-mile drive over to Diane's home, it occurred to me the last time we met with Mrs. Manticore, it was done in a secret location, behind closed doors. That precaution had obviously gone out the window. From what I knew, Deborah was the only family member left on the farm. Mitchell was dead. Willard Sr. had been on house arrest, but had been implicated in the drug operation, and was taken back into custody. Steve was held without bond on six different charges ranging from attempted first-degree murder to the production and trafficking of methamphetamine. The middle son, Willard Scott Manticore Jr., was still off to parts unknown.

I drove down the gravel drive and parked next to a red Jeep Cherokee Grand that I'd never seen before. It looked almost new and had a Manticore Farms license plate frame on the back. Diane had told me Carter was home from the hospital. Surgery for the gunshot wound had not been necessary, had been avoided at all costs because of his bad lungs. He'd been told by his parole officer that technically he was in violation of the terms of his release. However, because of the extenuating circumstances, and they were numerous, he doubted the transgression would result in reincarceration. Nevertheless, a judicial hearing was necessary and scheduled for the next week.

I walked in the back porch and called Diane's name. She answered from the kitchen. I walked into a rather warm room. The house had no central air conditioning, but the window over the sink was trading outside air with the kitchen door and the breeze was cooling with the evening. The small kitchen table had an empty chair on the far end. I said hello to Ben, Ethyl, and Carter, then walked by Diane, bent, gave her a kiss, and sat down. I then nodded toward Mrs. Manticore, who was sitting in the middle of the table, and said hi. There was a pair of crutches propped against the kitchen counter behind Carter, and a tank of oxygen next to the refrigerator. A long, green-plastic hose ran from the tank to Carter's nose.

I asked Carter how his leg was doing. He'd be needing therapy for it, he said, and when he woke up in the mornings, it was awful stiff.

"And he's on antibiotics and pain pills, so he can't drink," Diane said. "Can't drink, even if he wanted to."

"Now, Diane, I gave up the beer for most of ten years." He raised his glass of tea. "And this is what I'll be drinkin' from now on."

Diane's eyes lit a little, as if she were ready to believe. "Okay, Dad. Just don't make me shoot you in the other leg to keep you out of the tavern." She smiled.

I laughed right away, but was the only one at first. Then the others did too. I realized then that I knew her humor better than anyone else at the table.

Carter tried to laugh but was wracked by another coughing spasm. The tea spilled. While others scrambled to clean up, he grabbed more tissues from a box, put them over his mouth, and hawked out the phlegm. "I'm sorry." He gasped. "Sorry, I'll leave."

"Don't get up on my account," Deborah said.

Half out of his chair, Carter sat again and nodded thank you in her direction.

"We're all here then," Deborah said. "Thank you, Carter and Ethyl, for the use of your home. I'll get right to the point. Both of you, and Diane too, understand what it's like to lose contact with a loved one. And now, so do I. It's not the same, I know, but you may have heard about my son, Scotty. Well, I haven't seen nor heard from him for over six weeks. He's run off." She had a handkerchief in her hand. "Anyway, I want to help you with

Jean, help bring her back home if I can. Scotty is gone, and if it's in any way related—" She stopped herself. "No need to get into any of that."

"Jean don't want to come home," Ethyl said. "She already told us that."

"Yes, that's right." Diane drummed her nails on the table. "But things have changed a lot since then. We, Sam and I, we think the drug operation was scaring her off. That's gone now." She looked at me. I agreed. Bringing her home was worth another try.

"I'd like to go," Carter said. "I want to go. But not with these lungs, or this leg. And I've got a court date." Another coughing spasm. This time he spit up blood.

Diane's mouth dropped open. "Oh Dad, blood again. Are you sure it's just an infection?"

Ethyl put her hand on Carter's arm. "The doctor said the antibiotics might clear it up."

"Our biggest problem," I said, "is getting there. We don't have a car."

"Yes, you do," said Deborah. "That Jeep outside is at your disposal. It used to belong to my husband. He won't need it where he's going. And it'll hold much more than that little car you took the first time. In case Jean agrees to come back. You'll need the hauling space, right?"

The offer surprised me, even with Big Daddy Willard Sr. in jail. "You're sure he won't be… upset?"

"I don't give a damn one way or the other. Glad or mad at this point, that's his problem." Deborah pulled an envelope from her purse and slid it across the table to Diane.

"What's this?" Diane asked.

"Expense money," Deborah said. "Same as last time."

## Chapter Twenty-Seven
# Memphis II

The following Friday I was absent from school. As before, Diane and I drove the entire day, but this time in the relative luxury of the Jeep Cherokee Grand. The vehicle had less than 3,000 miles on it, and was almost new inside and out. The trip down was remarkable for long periods of silence punctuated by fairly intense sessions during which we relived some of the more harrowing portions of the two days we spent on and around Crabalocker Creek. The talk was often morbid, the humor particularly so. I lost count of how often we ended a conversation with a shake of our heads, amazed at the fact we were both alive, here, and whole.

Carter's heroism was the strangest turn of all. I wondered how a guy capable of taking a bullet for his daughter could end up in prison.

"Very easily," Diane said. "I'll tell you how." She said that, when he was young, her father was restless and seldom satisfied with anything. Whether it be where he grew up, what his parents provided, the education he got at school, or the wages his employer was paying, nothing was ever good enough for him. We were still in northern Illinois, so the sun was on us as we drove and we felt it, even with the air conditioning.

Diane heard most of her father's early history from Jean. "Remember, I was only nine when he went to prison. Jean was twenty-one." She took a drink of water. "Anyway, Carter, impatient man that he is, decided to do a little cash hustle, you know, off the books."

"Like what?"

"Breaking and entering. Petty larceny. He'd break in to the nice homes around Red Wolf Lake when the owners were gone, rip them off, then fence the stuff for cash."

"Yeah, but negligent homicide?"

"I'm getting to that. So one fine day, he's got his eye on a place. No cars. No one around. Looks good, right? He stops the truck, looks in the backyard of the place, and there it is." She holds her hands up to size. "A big, eight-point buck, grazing below a bird feeder. Carter grabs his rifle—"

"Oh, no."

"Oh, yes. Shoots. Misses the damn deer, which just runs off. But now he can't rip the place off 'cuz he's worried the shot'll draw attention."

"There was someone in the house," I said.

She shook her head. "Napping on the back porch. Dead. Shot in the chest. That poor family. And of course, they had security cameras."

"Game. Set. Match," I said.

The road seemed longer this second trip south, but we didn't care. Time was still on our side, and we ignored it like so much asphalt passing weightlessly under our wheels. Did we talk about it then, on our second trip to Memphis? Of course not. We were still looking for ways to misbehave. The curves in the road were more exciting than the straightaways, there were always more things to see in hills and valleys. We were driving at the speed of time, and it wasn't catching up with us. Not yet.

Even with the larger gas tank, the Jeep required more frequent stops, but our cruising speed was faster, so our overall time to Memphis was about the same. We checked into the same hotel as before. The plan for the next morning was no more than an outline. We still had no phone number for Bethany Jean Warren Brooks, so we'd have to drive to her last known address and hope she hadn't moved yet again and that, on a Saturday morning, she wouldn't be away at work or, even worse, "working" at home.

The first time Diane and I had driven to Memphis, our

relationship was shaky; we were unsure of each other. The first night in the hotel room was a strange and somewhat lonely trek, even though we'd spent it in the same bed. On the second go round, the path was familiar, the surface paved, and the sky aglow. I don't know if anyone has ever coined a phrase for sex following a shared near-death experience, but somebody should, because it was incredible.

---

The next morning, we awoke tangled in the sheets, sleep deprived, not tired but in need of showers, both of us. I let Diane go first while I removed the bandages on my chest, the last vestiges of the Crabalocker affair. The bruising was all but gone, and the open areas were both healed over. I decided to ditch the white tape and gauze for good. Fully dressed, we caught a breakfast at the hotel then headed for the trailer park. We had the address in the GPS, but I knew the way well enough by then so really, I didn't need it. We got off the interstate, took a couple of turns, and found the Cedar Point Trailer Park sign.

We made our way to Bethany Jean's address. I don't know why it surprised me, but the park had changed very little since our last visit. Some of the toys sitting out front of the places had changed, but many of the major items, such as discarded furniture, had not, and seemed to be destined to bake in the Tennessee sun until winter came. I stopped the Cherokee in front of Bethany's trailer. We walked to the side door and noticed that a small, wooden platform with a rail had replaced the cement block that used to be the step up. There was also an operating door bell, which was new. I pushed the button. We waited. I pushed again. There was no car parked nearby; that was discouraging. Bethany had talked about the need for transportation the last time we were here, and that a used car was at the top of her buy list.

Still no response. The door was locked and there was no sign of anyone home. What to do? Our options were few. We couldn't very well search Memphis. Except for her last address in the inner city, her personal life was a mystery to us. We didn't even know the name of her church, and there were plenty to choose from. Ben and Toy were out of bounds as far as I was concerned. They scared the hell out of me. I wasn't going to approach them, even if they were having a friendly cup of coffee at a McDonalds. We decided to wait for Bethany Jean's return. The time was a little after ten a.m. She could be out on an errand or at a church function of some kind.

After the long ride yesterday, neither one of us wanted to sit, so we walked around Cedar Point, never wandering more than a block from Bethany's place. No one bothered us. We were strangers in the neighborhood but so far as I could tell, no one took notice except for a couple kids out riding tricycles in front of their homes. A couple cars drove past without a second look.

An hour passed. The sun was hot, making our recreational walking uncomfortable. We went back to the trailer and sat in a slice of shade thrown off by the trailer. Ironically, trees in Cedar Point were rare. There were no chairs on which to sit so we turned over a couple of five-gallon pails and used them instead. Twenty minutes later, a white Lexus SUV, washed and bright in the noonday sun, came around the loop. The mere presence of a Lexus in that setting was stunning, even more so when it pulled in next to the Cherokee. The darkened windows made it hard to make out the passengers. In fact, only after the door opened, did I see the man at the wheel, and then I had to look again.

"Hello, Sam," he said. The driver was Willard Scott Manticore Jr.

Still working on the assumption that Scott had been an abusive husband and had been part of the reason Bethany had left town, my eyes went quickly to the woman seated in the passenger seat. It was Bethany Jean. But, as she got out of the Lexus, she looked fine. Hardly knowing what to think, and forgetting Bethany's request about the use of his name, I said, "Junior, what? How did you get here?"

Diane must have been thinking the same thing, because she went directly to her sister. "What's going on. How did this happen?"

"*Scott* is my husband, Diane." Bethany smiled, I think.

Scott closed the driver's side door and dropped his head for a moment. I took half a step forward and asked, "How did you find her? I mean, I thought she was hiding from everyone."

Scott stuck the toe of his shoe into the brown grass. This was the first time I'd ever seen him in blue jeans and a t-shirt. In the past, it was always business wear with him: dark slacks, white shirt, and on all but the hottest days, a tie. "I was about to ask you the same thing."

I ignored the question and thought about the connection between the Manticore family and the Chicago mob, and wondered if they had found her for him. Called in one last favor before bolting out of the family business for good. If that was true, we'd had different sources, but the result was the same.

Bethany and Diane embraced. We were invited inside for coffee. Bethany was anxious for us to see all the work they'd done since we'd been there.

As we entered the trailer, the first thing that hit me square in the face was air conditioning, notably absent on our last visit. Scott brought up the rear, a couple of bags of groceries in his arms. We were directed to a small but better-than-before dining set. We sat. There was a large area rug in the living room and three pieces of furniture that were, if not new, then upgrades to the previous. The kitchen was well-kept and clean. The last time I wouldn't have taken a drink of water from the tap. This time, a cooked meal made right there would have been no problem. I looked at Diane with raised eyebrows. She mouthed back, "I know."

Bethany offered us drinks. We both took a soda over ice (ice cubes!). After the food was put away, they both got ice water and sat down at the table with us.

"Well?" Bethany said. I finally got a chance to look at her. She was wearing a clean blouse and slacks, good shoes, and her hair was washed and pulled back—the most notable change from our first visit. She might have gained a few pounds, but that could have been wishful thinking on my part. Her color was a shade better, as if she'd gotten a little sun.

"Well what?" Diane replied.

"You must have a hundred questions," Bethany said. "And I have a few of my own. Guests first."

Diane took a sip. "I'll start with the obvious one. Are you two back together?"

Bethany laughed. "Dee Dee, you haven't changed a bit. Why dance around the mulberry bush? Just pop Jack in the Box and get it over with." Diane shrugged. Bethany looked at Scott. "We're in a 'let's give it a try' phase. A definite maybe. We were together once, happily for a while. Maybe we can be again. We're different people now, shooting for a different ending."

Bethany wore short sleeves, so she wasn't trying to hide any bruises; there were none on her face and neck either. No scratches or abrasions anywhere and no needle tracks on the arms, for that matter. Nevertheless, I still didn't trust Scott, he was a Manticore, after all. And by the look on her face, Diane felt the same way. I think Scott noticed it too because he said:

"Bethany, maybe you should explain a little more about why you left six years ago."

Bethany took a napkin and used it as a coaster. "I already told them about overhearing your father, you know, talking to that guy from Chicago, and how Mitchell caught me."

"But you never told us what he said." Diane waved her finger back and forth between me and herself. "We figured it out. That's why we're here. One reason why, anyway."

Bethany's face went pale. "Figured out what?"

"The drugs," Diane said. "We know about them."

Bethany put her hand to her throat. "Dee Dee, please, leave those guys alone. They're crazy, homicidal. If you go back there, they'll kill you. If they find out you narc'ed on them, they'll kill you."

"Too late," I said. "The whole operation's been blown up. The meth trailer, the pot farm. All of it. They even got the distributor in Green Bay and one in Milwaukee. By the way, have you heard? Mitchell's dead."

Scott looked at Bethany and said, "We know. I found out and I told Bethany the details. Just so you know, neither one of us shed a tear."

That was a relief. You never know about families and how they'll react to the death of one of their own.

Diane tapped a Morse code on the side of her glass. "That's why we're here. To give you the all clear. You can come home."

Bethany Jean sat back in her chair, pulled in a deep breath then slowly exhaled. Scott's expression was still subdued. He tugged on an earlobe then uttered, "Hmmm," deep in his throat. The was a worrisome quiet that followed, during which I looked at Diane, then at Bethany. I sensed a confusion creeping over us. Bethany finally said:

"Well, I guess that's good, isn't it? You're sure you got them all?"

"Sheriff and the FBI and the DEA were all in on it." Diane pushed her darks curls behind an ear. "That's as sure as we can be, as anyone can be. You *do* want to come home, don't you?"

Scott said, "We were talking about the other reason you left, honey. About the bruises back then." He was sheepish as he spoke, and I thought he should be. Any man who would beat his wife was no man at all.

Bethany's voice weakened, her spine bent, as if she were embarrassed for him. "Are you sure?"

Scott nodded.

Bethany straightened a bit. "I know… we know, that back then, right after we were married, the rumor around town was that Scott"—she nodded bashfully in his direction—"was beating me. Well, he wasn't. And I wanted to say so, but he wouldn't let me."

Leaning forward, Diane had grabbed the table's edge with both hands, wondering, I'm sure, who the guilty bastard was?

Bethany looked to Scott, as if for permission to go on. He blinked. She clasped her hands together on the tabletop. "It was the old man. We'd get in arguments about a lot of things but if it was about the drugs, that really triggered him. Back then he could still get around without a wheelchair. But he had that bloody cane, the son of a bitch. And whether he used that crooked piece of hickory or his fists, it didn't much matter, the result was the same."

I looked at Scott. His expression remained a blank, but there was now a tremor in both of his hands, which he had been resting near the glass of water. He noticed the shaking too and moved his hands onto his lap. How could he let that happen to his wife? But of course, that's where his embarrassment and Bethany's hesitation at getting back together came from. Second, third, and fourth thoughts, if I was her. I didn't know then, but I know now what Bethany was looking for, at least I think I do. She needed to see if Scott had regained his self-respect before she could respect him again.

Finally, Scott took the hunch out of his shoulders. "I know what you're thinking. How could I sit back and let my father do that? Believe me, I've beaten myself up about it hundreds of times. And, for what it's worth, apologized. There's no excuse. My mind back then was different than it is now. The Scott of seven years ago was too afraid of authority, to ingrained with that 'honor thy father' b.s., and, frankly, frightened by the old man from as early as I can remember. Even when I grew stronger and quicker and smarter than him, I couldn't challenge him in any way. Never entered my mind. Couldn't do it.

"So, when I got married and brought Jean, Bethany, into the house, and it was *his* house, make no mistake about it, she had to live by *his* rules, just like the rest of us. Us Manticore kids, we all learned years ago, you don't cross the old man. Bethany didn't know.

"The day finally came when he really crossed the line, said some nasty things, used the cane and knocked Bethany down, the whole nine yards. I was ready to punch him into next week. He looked at me; I had a fistful of his shirt in one hand, my other arm cocked. He lowered his cane and laughed in that snide, mocking way of his. 'What you gonna do, Mr. Joe College?' he said. 'Go ahead, big man on campus. Beat up an old man that can barely walk.' I let go of his shirt and dropped my fist. 'Didn't think so.' It was like he'd screwed another bankrupt farmer out of a piece of land. He limped away and said, 'If guts were gunpowder, you wouldn't have enough to blow your nose.'

"I've told Bethany, that's not who I am now." Scott took a drink of water and paused a moment. "I don't think I ever loved my father. Looking back, I don't think I even respected him. What I thought was respect was actually fear. And now loathing. That's why I left. When the irrigation fiasco and the interstate scam blew up, I told the old man and Mitchell too, it was time to clean house and go legitimate, one hundred percent. They blew me off. Called me weak, a panty waist, and if I didn't like what they were doing, I should pound sand. So, I did.

"But before I left, I transferred some of the family cash, or what was left of it, to a numbered offshore account. I was the treasurer and bookkeeper for the farm and the ranch, so the purse strings were in my hands. The beauty of it, I made it look as if the old man made the transfers, so when the forensic accountants come looking at the books, his ass will be on the line for that, not me."

I didn't fully appreciate it then, but he was talking of a world with which I was not familiar, of places too dangerous for me to understand, and people too immoral for me to really know.

"Wow, that's a hell of a story," I said. "There's been a lot of crap in your life. But I gotta tell you, your mom is worried sick about you. I think she sent us down here for more than Bethany Jean. I think she had a hunch. She knows you better than anyone, except maybe Bethany." I tipped my head toward the front door. "Did you recognize the Jeep?"

"Right away," Scott said. "And I figured it was Mom who gave it to you."

"That brings us back to Walnut Creek." Bethany put her elbows on the table, leaned forward, and rubbed her temples with her fingertips. She said, "How do I put this? I see Walnut Creek different than you do. To me, Walnut Creek was just a place to grow up. It's in the rear view now, and it's so far back I can hardly see it. And that's all right. What happens there now, it's nothing to do with me. And I've told Scott, as far as the Manticores are concerned, I could care less, and as long as you two don't spill, they'll never know where I am."

Diane put on her bravest face. "Okay. All right. I don't understand it, but if it's what you want, I can respect it. But there is one other thing we haven't mentioned, it's about Ethyl and Carter, Mom and Dad."

"Mom and Dad?" Bethany's face went from surprised to bemused. She knocked the side of her head with her palm, as if she had a screw loose. "I'm sorry, girl. Who are you and what have you done with my sister?"

It was kind of funny, very much in the vein of something Diane would say.

When the smiles faded, Diane said she owed her life to her dad, and so did I. Bethany was very surprised by this, so Diane described the final twenty minutes of the skirmish of Crabalocker Creek, including Carter's bravery and courage. She also mentioned his ongoing struggles with pneumonia, lung and kidney disease, and the leg wound which lent a serious tone to the discussion. "He's back home now," Diane said. "His condition is touch and go. He's on oxygen and breathing treatments. Spitting up blood. Anyway, he wanted to come along with us, but he was too sick to do it." Diane let that sink in for a moment, then she looked Bethany Jean in the eye and added:

"He asked to see you."

# CHAPTER TWENTY-EIGHT
# Coming Home

The next morning, we met at seven a.m. to get an early start on what would be another long trek back to Walnut Creek. Bethany didn't intend to stay more than a week, so there wasn't a lot to pack for either her or Scott. They met us at our hotel. Naturally, Diane and Bethany wanted to ride together, and Scott had to bring his Lexus for the return trip, so we set up a rotating schedule. They'd ride with me on the first leg out of Memphis, then with Scott and so on. We were about to load into the SUVs when Diane got a call from Ben. Watching her reaction, we could see it was urgent, so we all sat down in the Jeep. She put the call on speaker.

Ben's voice sounded tired. "He's in bad shape. You better come ASAP."

Diane sat sideways in the front passenger's seat. "Where is he?"

Ben said, "In the hospital. They brought him in early this morning. He fell at home and broke his hip. They think the infection got into his blood, and Diane…"

Diane said, "Yeah, what? We're here."

Ben sighed. "He's been holding out on us. The lungs aren't full of pneumonia. It's cancer."

We all startled at that. My heart fell.

Diane about crushed the phone with her voice. "Cancer! Why didn't the doctors tell him that the last time he was there?"

"They did," Ben said. "Dad told them not to tell us. Only Mom knew."

I tapped Diane on the arm. "We better get going."

Diane put up her hand. "Is he there? Can I talk to him?"

Ben's voice went soft then louder, as if he was turning away from the phone. "He's going in and out. They got him doped up on morphine or somethin'. Just a second." In the background, we could hear Ben trying to rouse Carter. He told him that Diane was on the phone and wanted to talk to him. At first, it was obvious, even from hundreds of miles away, that Carter was both in a lot of pain and confused. Ben explained again who was on the phone. Suddenly, a raspy, weak, nearly unrecognizable voice came through the cellphone:

"Yeah. Who's there? Diane? I can't hear nuthin'."

Diane replied, "Yes! Dad, it's me, Diane. I'm with Jean. We're coming home to see you."

Carter wheezed and coughed. "What? No. I'm not home. I'm in the… Where am I? Ben, tell them." Ben, in the background, told Carter that Diane knew he was in the hospital.

Diane looked at me, her eyes worried and afraid. "Yeah, we're coming there, to the hospital, to see you. Jean and me."

Labored breathing and a heavy cough wracked Carter's body. The spasm must have given him another jolt of pain. He cried out.

Jean said, "Oh shit. Just tell Ben we're coming."

Diane said, "Listen, Ben, we're getting on the road right now. I'll call you back in a little while, okay?"

We could hear Ben trying to settle Carter down, then he said, "Yeah, right."

Diane hung up and said, "Shit! Cancer? That son of a bitch. Why didn't he tell us?" She started to cry.

"Let's get going," I said. "It's the only thing we can do. Once we're on the road awhile, you can call Ben again. Maybe he'll know more by then."

Diane nodded, got out of the passenger seat, and moved to the back seat next to Bethany. Scott got into his Lexus. Soon, we were on the expressway out of Memphis.

About a half hour later, Diane dialed Ben. Doctor O'Neil was in the room making morning rounds. He agreed to talk to Diane on the phone. She put it on speaker.

Diane asked, "What's happening with Dad?"

Dr. O'Neil's voice sounded younger than I expected. He had a slight East Coast accent, but whether it was Boston or New York, I didn't know. "Well, in addition to the lung and kidney problems you know about, and the leg; he's fractured his left hip."

"Did he fall?" Diane asked, "Wasn't he using his cane?"

Dr. O'Neil said, "According to your mother, he was. The hip fractured because it couldn't hold his weight anymore. The lung cancer has spread to the hip bone and weakened it. The bone probably broke while he was still standing, then he fell."

Diane had covered her mouth with her hand, and had to talk through her fingers. "Oh my god. Lung cancer. How bad is it?"

"Pretty bad. Stage 4, which means it's spread to a lot of places, even his brain," Dr. O'Neil said.

Diane said, "Oh shit, his brain. How do you know that? Did you scan him with the... the..."

Dr. O'Neil interrupted. "CAT scan. No, we didn't have to. All those tests were done when Carter was at the penitentiary. They did the CAT scans, even the biopsy while he was still in Waupun. I had all the records sent to me the first time he was here. His condition was incurable even then, and I recommended we talk about it with the family. He refused."

I looked in the rearview mirror and saw Diane, her cheeks moist and her eyes red. She dropped her head and sniffled into a tissue.

Bethany said, "Hello doctor, this is Jean, his other daughter. What's his condition right now?"

"He's pretty sedated." Dr. O'Neil said. "The hip is very painful and I'm worried the other leg, with the gunshot wound, may be infected. The pneumonia, the lung infection, may have gotten into his blood stream. If so, that's a very bad sign."

Bethany clucked her tongue. "I thought Ben said it was cancer in his lungs, not pneumonia."

"It's both, and he has emphysema," Dr. O'Neil said.

Bethany and Diane groaned.

Diane said, "Doctor O'Neil, this is Diane again. What's the outlook?"

Dr. O'Neil said, "Let me take a second to step out of the room. Your father is in a deep sleep from the morphine but you never know what he might hear. Okay. The prognosis is very poor. He may well die today. In fact, I've recommended Hospice care to your mother and brother."

Diane asked, "What did they say?"

"They weren't ready to make a decision." Dr. O'Neil took a deep breath. "I think it would be easier if you were here. She might be waiting for you. Has anyone talked to you about the 'Do Not Resuscitate' order?"

"No. What's that?" Diane asked.

Dr. O'Neil said, "Your brother and mother have decided to do whatever we can to keep him comfortable. Oxygen, pain medication, all of that. But if his breathing stops, or his heart stops, they don't want him put on a breathing machine. And they don't want resuscitation done, with the CPR compressions on the chest or the shock paddles."

Diane's voice was getting weaker with every question. "Do you think he's that bad?"

"He's in very bad shape, yes." Dr. O'Neil's voice was firm and clear. "And if his breathing or his heart stopped he'd be that much worse. To be honest, Ms. Warren, even if we did try and bring your father back in that situation, it wouldn't work."

Diane, in a half whisper, "He'd die anyway."

Dr. O'Neil said, "Yes."

A long silence.

Diane cleared her throat. "Okay, thank you. Just make sure he's not in any pain. That's what I want."

Dr. O'Neil replied, "I'll make sure." He handed the phone to Ben.

Ben's voice came on the phone. "Any idea when you'll be back?"

Diane slapped the armrest. "Hell, I don't know, Ben. We're still in Fuckton, Arkansas. Call me back if anything changes. I'll let you know when we get closer."

Bethany asked Diane for the phone so she could call Scott and give him an update. He was just ahead of me, cruising along somewhere north of eighty miles-per-hour.

A couple of hours later, Diane called Ben again. Carter's condition had not changed, though he had woken up for a few minutes. The pain in his hip became intolerable, however, and it was very hard for him to breathe. An oxygen mask was ordered and more intravenous morphine was given. He was resting again when Ben and Diane talked. Ben said that a cancer specialist had come by to talk to him and his mother. The specialist said the discharge from prison was *not* for good behavior, but because Carter had a terminal disease. The lung cancer had been discovered well over a month ago and further testing showed spread to his liver, brain, and bones. Even worse, he had the kind of lung cancer that could be cured only by surgery, and only then, if caught very early, stage 1. Chemotherapy would not work for him, and would only make him sicker. Radiation might have shrunk the tumors in his brain and helped with the headaches, but he refused that treatment while still in prison.

Mid-morning, Southern Illinois. We stopped for gas and to pick up water and a few snacks, stretch our legs, that kind of thing, but it was quick. The girls switched to Scott's SUV and we were back on the road. I took the lead this time. Naturally, I heard very little until we stopped for a late lunch a few hours later. We pulled into a hamburger place where we could eat and get back on the road as quickly as possible. I watched Diane as she climbed out of the Lexus. I could see that traveling was wearing her down.

I walked alongside her. "Any news?"

"I don't think we're going to win this one, Sam. We're not going to make it." She stopped. I did too, and faced her. She looked past my shoulder. "His blood pressure is going down. They're calling it a coma now. His kidneys aren't working." She bit on her lower lip. "Sam, I didn't say... I never forgave him, I never said it to him. Now I'll never get the chance."

Scott and Bethany were poised at the door to the restaurant. Scott said, "Hey, you guys coming?"

"Go ahead," I said. "We'll be right there."

I took Diane's shoulders in my hands. "But you did forgive him, that's what counts. I'm sure he knows. And anyway, you'll be able to tell him. Today."

"You think so?"

I pulled her close and nodded. It was the most confident thing I could do.

We went inside, ordered, and brought our food to the table that Scott and Bethany had selected. They told me a few more of the details they'd learned since the last call.

I ate my flame-broiled burger too fast and was burping it up for the next two hours. The girls were in the back seat, but the chatter from earlier in the day had faded into a somber, post-meal lethargy with an emotional burn-out chaser. For two hours there was little to talk about. No phone calls, and they supposed that was good. Nothing to see out the windows. No interest in listening to the radio, music or otherwise. It was almost time to gas up when Ben's name showed up on Diane's cell. He was calling from a family waiting room at the hospital. He had the speaker on. Ethyl was there along with a Hospice nurse, who'd been speaking with both of them on and off all day. Diane put her phone on speaker too.

Ben's voice echoed in the room. "It's time to make a decision. We can't wait."

Diane and Bethany looked at each other. Diane said, "Tell us how Dad is doing first. What's going on?"

"They keep giving him morphine more and more," Ben said. "I don't know the medical stuff—"

Then, a new voice spoke up. "Hello, I'm Linda Owens, I'm the Hospice nurse. Maybe I can help with some of those questions." She had an accent, Norwegian or German, that was immediately noticeable but was not hard to understand.

Ben said, "Yeah, go ahead."

Ms. Owens said, "Ben is right, your father has required higher doses of morphine to control his pain. From our point of view, there's no problem giving him the medication as long as the family knows that morphine has a bad effect on his breathing."

Bethany spoke up. "What does that mean?"

"In other words, morphine makes his breathing weaker and, at some point, he could stop breathing all together." Ms. Owens paused. "On the other hand, if we're worried about his breathing and give him less morphine, his pain will become worse. Ethyl and Ben have seen what that can be like."

Bethany, under her breath, said, "Oh my god."

Diane asked, "What about his blood pressure and his kidneys?"

"His blood pressure is so low we've had to lower the head of his bed, which is another problem for his breathing, but we don't have any choice," Ms. Owens said. "If we don't lower his head, the brain won't get enough blood, and that could cause a stroke."

In the rearview, I saw Diane lower her head and purse her lips.

Ms. Owens went on. "As far as the kidneys are concerned, they're probably shutting down. He hasn't made any urine since this morning."

"Mom, how are you doing?" asked Diane.

Ethyl's voice sounded far away and weak. "I'm all right. When can you get here?"

Diane said, "I don't know, Mom. Sam?"

I looked at Diane in the rearview. "We're almost to Wisconsin."

"Did you hear that, Mom?" Diane asked. "Almost...almost to Wisconsin. Ben, you said we have to decide something. What is that?"

It was Ms. Owens voice that answered. "Your mother, brother, and I have talked it over quite a bit, and we agree it's time for your father, Carter, to go on Hospice."

There was a silence, then Diane said, "What does that mean?"

Ms. Owens said, "First of all, it acknowledges that we understand that your father is not going to recover from this illness, so further attempts at curing him are futile and not worthwhile. Therefore, the antibiotics for instance, would be stopped. On the other hand, we would take every and all steps to make sure your father is comfortable. That includes oxygen, morphine, medication for anxiety and agitation, which can occur in patients who struggle to breathe. As a Hospice organization we specialize in knowing what a patient needs at this time in their life."

Ben added, his voice distant, "Because he's so sick. They think it could be done here, in the hospital, right?"

Ms. Owens said, "Yes. We have a Hospice room designated for this purpose. Ben and Ethyl have given their okay, but they wanted your input, Diane, before going ahead."

Diane sat back in her seat and placed her head on the headrest. "Sam, what do you think?"

I was surprised by the question. It took me a second to find my voice, but I knew my answer right away. "I don't see any other way. Sorry, babe."

Diane closed her eyes for a couple seconds, then opened them and said, "Yes, all right. Hospice, yes."

Ms. Owens said, "Thank you, Diane. Do you have any questions?"

"Just one. I think we're still maybe four hours away. Do you think he'll still…" I looked in the rearview again. Diane's lips were stretched into a parched line. "be there when we arrive?"

"I don't know, Diane," Ms. Owens said. "I'm sorry, but there's no way to predict that. Just don't turn it into a race. Get here in one piece."

Diane, Bethany, Ben, and Ethyl said goodbye and the call ended. Both of the girls blotted tears from their eyes. We didn't call Scott because we were about to stop for gasoline in a few minutes, and they would fill him in then.

The girls, Diane especially, were getting more anxious with every stop, and I couldn't blame them. Even though we were moving along well above the speed limit, the miles seemed to be crawling by. We stopped near the state border for a quick bathroom break and went right back on the road. The girls decided to split up at this point, to make sure both Scott and I had someone to keep us alert over the final leg of the trip. I thought it was a good idea. Even though Diane was understandably quiet for the next couple of hours, having her back next to me felt good. There'd been no calls from the hospital since the one from the Hospice nurse, and of course that had everyone on edge. Did we want a call or not? Any news at that point was bound to be bad.

We were only about two hours away, still on the interstate north. The sun was approaching the western horizon. Diane was getting restless.

"Why not give Ben a call," I said.

She snapped a look in my direction. I knew she'd been thinking about it, probably for hours. "Do you think so. You think I should."

"Sure. Not knowing is killing you."

"God, you got that right." She dialed up the cell. "Ben, it's Diane. Are you there, with him?" He must have said yes. I waved at her to put it on the speaker. She did.

Diane said, "We're going to be there in less than two hours. Anything new? Is he still in a coma?"

Ben's voice was raspy and lacked its usual depth. "Yeah, no change, that's what the nurse said last time she was here. But they keep giving him the drugs so how do I know. He coughs once in a while."

"Has he said anything?" Diane asked. "Does he wake up at all?"

"Nah. He's out. No words. Nothing." Ben sighed audibly. "Moves a hand once in a while. That's it."

Diane asked, "Is Mom there?"

Ben said, "Yeah. She's sittin' right here."

Diane said, "Put her on."

From what I could tell, Ethyl's voice had changed very little. "Hello?"

"Hi Mom. It's Diane. How are you? Did you eat anything today?"

Ethyl answered, "I guess so. They bought in a nice tray for me and Ben. He ate everything. I ate a little, the potatoes and some of the chicken."

Diane nodded her head. "Okay, good. We'll be there as soon as we can. Bye, Mom."

Ethyl interjected, "Diane?"

"Yeah, Mom, I'm here."

Ethyl said, "Get here right away. You better…" She started crying. At that point, it sounded as if Ben took the phone.

Ben's voice came across as if he were shouting. "We'll talk when you get here." He hung up.

Diane dropped her phone in the center console and stared out the windshield. "For chrissakes, this trip is taking for fuckin' ever. Can't you go any faster?"

"We're already going too fast. And it's dusk, the time when the deer come out. One a them crosses the road and we won't get there tonight." I softened my voice. "You know that."

She stomped her foot into the floor. "I know. I know."

---

We arrived at the Hospice room on the second floor of Walnut Creek Memorial Hospital out of breath, emotionally drained, and thirty minutes too late. Carter Warren had died that long before our appearance at the door. The nurse, Linda Owens, was still there with Ethyl and Ben. Dressed in street attire with blond hair and a light complexion, Linda appeared to be in her late forties. Ethyl, Ben, and Linda sat in chairs near Carter. We followed Diane into the room. I had Bethany Jean go in ahead of Scott and me, though I think she was probably hesitant about making her first appearance with her family in over six years at the side of her father's death bed. As difficult as that must have been, there was no other way it was going to work.

Everyone stood when they saw us at the door. Ethyl uttered something when she saw Diane and rushed to embrace her. Looking over Dee's shoulder, Ethyl saw Bethany Jean, and broke the embrace with Diane. Ethyl put the tissue she had in her hand over her mouth and uttered:

"Oh my God, Jean, is that you?"

"Yeah, Mom. It's me."

Diane went to the bedside and rested her hands on the handrail, her eyes cast down at her father. I stood next to her, rubbed her back for a couple seconds, then dropped my hand.

"I'm sorry, Dad. We came as fast as we could," Diane whispered, her eyes glassy. She grabbed my arm with her right hand.

"Go ahead, tell him," I said.

She shifted her weight, then cleared her throat and whispered, "All is forgiven, Dad." She kissed two fingertips then touched his forehead. "Goodbye."

Ethyl had stepped aside from Diane and looked at Jean, her eyes rounded. "But you're so thin, and, and, well… are you all right?"

"Yes, I'm…" Bethany Jean nodded. "I'm fine." She took the two steps that separated her from her mother and gave her a hug; it seemed to me as much to stop her mother's scrutiny as to show affection. "I missed you, Mom."

Ethyl said, "We have so much to talk about, but first, come say hello…" she put the tissue over her mouth to control her sobbing. "And goodbye… to your father."

———————

The funeral service and burial were lightly attended. The urn holding half of Carter's ashes was buried next to his parents in the Walnut Creek Cemetery, the other half spread behind the barn on the twenty acres of land that remained of the family farm to which he was born. Knowing well the financial straits the family was in, and that he was, in large part, responsible for the problem, Carter had left instructions that no wake or reception be held on his behalf. A surprisingly wise, forward-looking decision for a man who had so tragically lacked both of these virtues as a younger man. I've wondered, in the intervening years, what made the difference. Was it incarceration and the absence of family that finally turned him, or matured him? Or was it the cancer that showed him his mortality and changed his point of view? My money has always been on the latter, but then again maybe it was something else altogether.

During the three days between Carter's death and the funeral, much transpired in the lives of Bethany Jean Warren Manticore Brooks and Willard Scott Manticore Jr. To a large degree, this had to do with the reunion of Scott with his mother, Deborah, and the quickly deteriorating state of the Manticore operations: both Square M Construction and Manticore Farms. Quite simply, there was no one left to run them. Deborah was not trained nor inclined to do it. Upper level managers were doing their best, but without a guiding presence at the top, the Manticore empire was a rudderless ship in a hurricane. Square M was on the brink of bankruptcy. At Manticore Farms, crops were going to rot in the fields if someone didn't take the reins and make some decisions.

Deborah offered unfettered control over the entire operation to her last remaining, unindicted son, Scott. He could do with either operation what he would, from hiring and firing to changing the business to complete liquidation. Whatever he saw fit. She, in fact, regarded him as the only Manticore fit for running the company: possessing the right combination of judgement and conscience, training and experience to do the job properly.

Scott had to admit the offer was tempting. He explained everything to Bethany Jean on a Friday evening when I was visiting Diane. Scott and Bethany Jean now had to decide. She had originally intended to go back to Memphis and continue her life there. Now, they weren't so sure. The new offer was enough to make Bethany Jean reconsider, especially since the old man and Steve were most certainly gone for a long time to come, probably for life.

While Scott, Bethany Jean, and Ethyl debated the offer from Deborah Manticore in the kitchen, Diane and I sat out on the back porch, eavesdropping half the time, but talking too. They went back and forth for over an hour, but the tone of the discussion was a tide rolling in to shore: Bethany Brooks was no longer. Jean Warren Manticore was reborn and back in Walnut Creek. When the realization hit me, I was ecstatic. I held Diane's face in my hands and kissed her like never before. I hoarse whispered, "It's over! You did it. We did it. She's home."

Her smile was wide, but her eyes weren't sparkling the way I expected, the way I'd seen in the past, and it was telling. I made no mention of it, supposing I was overreacting somehow. We kissed again. She said, "Ethyl will be a new woman."

"Not an easy thing at her age," I said.

Then Diane dropped an unvarnished truth of her own. Now that Jean was found and likely to stay home, Diane didn't have to worry about Ethyl living in Walnut Creek with only Ben to watch after her. Diane was free to take the job with Van Zandt Construction in Green Bay. Inside of a week, she'd be gone.

# CHAPTER TWENTY-NINE

# Crossroads

On the last day on summer, 2013, Diane left for Green Bay. I'd volunteered to drive her down, but she insisted on taking Fanny and Wes' offer instead—bigger vehicle, less bother, less mileage. Our painted-corn, iron-arm, bears-den relationship had fallen victim to practicality. With a kiss and a hug, we said goodbye. She said she'd call and text and I'd visit, but I didn't have a phone nor a car of my own, so it all had a hollow ring that became problematic as the school year went on. I think she felt it. I know I did. The tides were pulling us in opposite directions. Then she said, "Come look for me next summer, after you graduate." I watched them drive away with a strong sense of déjà vu, almost a flashback to the night I said goodbye to Erin. That same hollowness in the pit of my stomach, the smooth pebble lodged in my throat that wouldn't be swallowed, the longing to turn back the clock.

Right then and there, I should have told her what was on my mind. But the voice was so small that I could barely hear it over the din of daily life. And at the age of seventeen, who listens to those premonitions anyway? Certainly not me. Even if I'd taken the time to hear the message, I didn't have the fortitude to be its messenger. I'd stated my case to her already. She had made up her mind. It was her life, her decision. Who was I to tell her otherwise?

The voice remains to this day and will not be silenced, saying words I'd never said with a confidence I didn't have. *You should stay here with me. I'm good for you. We're good for each other. You won't find anyone better in Green Bay.* These are not the words of a high school senior. They are the words of corpulent regret.

Just as in August, we hadn't said it in so many words, but we had broken up. Oh sure, we did the obligatory texting with a call here and there, mostly during the first several weeks after she moved. I never asked her about any guys she might have met and she never asked me about other girls. But after a couple of months there was an unmistakable distance between us that couldn't be measured by the miles on a map. Everyone knew the drill: she hadn't been home, and I was too busy with school. She'd lived with the Van Zandt's at the beginning, but soon was able to afford her own apartment. The job was great. Her Uncle Wes was an affable boss and not much different at work than he was when drinking Pabst in the Noquebay Tavern. The money was good. We didn't talk about her weekends, I was afraid to know. She didn't say to come down at Christmas, or that she'd be home for Thanksgiving.

After that, my existence went from one step to the next, guided, it seems to me, by no more than its own volition. My life became a connect-the-numbers drawing that someone else had put to paper, and I just happened to be the one holding the pencil. Everything done by rote. When high school ended, I went to college. Another series of numbers connected. In small and restless steps college passed, and another crossroads loomed.

Diane had stayed in her job at Van Zandt Construction for less than a year. On a day trip down to Green Bay the week after I graduated from high school, I visited Fanny and Wes. I hadn't seen much of them. In the year since Diane left, their trips to Noquebay Resort had become infrequent, so I couldn't very well use them as a way to track Diane's whereabouts. Besides, summertime was always their time to party at the lake, so I didn't expect to see much of them during the school year. As it turned out, the summer of 2014 would be their last at Red Wolf Lake. Whether that was connected to Diane's absence or not, I don't know. For all of that, the Van Zandts, and Fanny in particular, still represented my best and closest connection to Diane.

They lived in an older part of town, in a modest home well

below their means, or so I guessed. The single-story ranch didn't appear to be more than three bedrooms but was beautifully land-scaped, the lawns trimmed like a French poodle. I never asked but it was clear this was the one place where their money showed, the green groomed yard, a pool in back with a small pond and stone waterfall. The inside of the house was not so fussy. When I knocked on the door and Fanny showed me in, the front room was inviting, lived-in, the décor thought-out and coordinated but functional.

I got a big hug from Fanny. She'd not lived in the South for decades but still oozed a hospitality that reminded me of Elvis singing Gospel on the front porch. As was her want, she had a small flower perched above her left ear and a smile to match. Standing behind her was Wes, a big bear of a man with a face wizened by age and hard work. The roughened skin of his hand swallowed mine in a firm handshake. I paused in the foyer to remove my shoes.

"Oh, don't bother 'bout that, honey," Fanny said. "Keep 'em on. We do."

They gave me a brief tour of the house, which Wes kept short. "He's seen enough, Fanny. Let's sit out back and I'll bring some-thing to drink." He correctly guessed mine as a cola.

I followed Fanny to the patio. It was a pleasant afternoon, warm enough for May. We sat under an umbrella at a table. They asked me about my graduation, the family, my upcoming plans for college, small topics like that knowing full well I was there for one reason—to find out about Diane. They were too nice to watch me founder about, looking for a way to break the ice, so Fanny did:

"Have you heard anything from Diane?"

I sat up in my chair. "Well, no. Not a word for the last four or five months." That was a dishonest answer. I knew exactly how long it had been, 127 days in fact since the last text. I'd asked how she was and she answered with a cold-shouldered "All right."

I looked at Fanny. "I was going to ask you the same thing."

Wes took a sip of his brandy old fashion. "Same here. Damn shame."

"Well, hold on, Wes," Fanny said. "She called and told us. When she moved."

"Moved?" I said. "But she's still in town."

Wes sighed heavily. "We don't know where she is."

"Not exactly," Fanny added. "We're pretty sure she's in Milwaukee."

"Milwaukee!" I said.

Wes's eyebrows raised. "Tell him the rest."

"I was getting to that." Fanny took a drink of her beer, then set the bottle down carefully on the table. "She met a fella, Sam, while working. A concrete finish guy, bad-boy type. I tried to warn her off him but…"

This was starting out badly and at the same time, had a familiar ring.

"Okay. But how did she end up in Milwaukee?" I asked.

"I fired him for drinking on the job." The gravel in Wes's voice was rougher than usual. "Too bad. He knew his craft, when he was sober."

Fanny pointed her bottle at Wes. "Tell him the rest."

Wes glanced side-eyed at his wife for a second, then said, "I think he was selling, too."

"Drugs?" I asked. "At work."

"Right on the job site. Never caught him straight up, but when he showed up drunk the second time, adios."

I asked, "What is his name?"

"Devin Jelusick. Big boy, strong," Fanny said. "But not the sharpest knife in the drawer. He moved south when he lost his job. Diane followed."

Fanny reached over and gave my hand a squeeze. "I'm sorry, Sam."

I nodded and, for a few seconds, kept from falling to pieces by taking a sip of cola and pursing my lips. But then I looked at Wes, that tough, strong guy. Diane's uncle by marriage. He'd already diverted his gaze to the babbling waterfall, the coy swimming listlessly in the pond. A tear traced down the creases of his face. This I couldn't bear, and my eyes misted too. Fanny's response, the reddened eyes, the sniffling nose, was predictable, and I probably could have handled it. Wes was another story. If this block of granite was cracking, then how was I supposed to hold it together? Was there something about Devin and Diane that they weren't telling me, something so obvious they thought that words weren't necessary? Perhaps I didn't want to know, because I never asked the question.

Try as they might, the Van Zandts lost track of her after that, and so did I. I was never close enough to Ethyl to call her more than once to see if she'd been contacted by Diane. The one time I did was on the occasion of my graduation from college. By that time, I hadn't heard from Diane in over four years. Ethyl said it had been about that long for her as well, but she'd call if anything came up. That call never came. While I took a perverse consolation in the fact that Diane's family and I had been swept out of her life with the same broom, I couldn't ignore the pattern taking shape before me. The circumstances were different, but like her sister before, Diane had disappeared.

I called Jean too, several times. She'd heard from Diane on occasion through the years. The conversations I had with the now happily-married Mrs. Manticore were hard to gauge, rather strange in fact. So, the last time I showed up at the Manticore home unannounced, again toward the end of my college years. Scott Manticore had liquidated Square M Construction after it declared bankruptcy years ago. Manticore Farms was still a going concern and now legitimate. I'd been accepted to medical school and wanted to get word to Diane about it, even if only through a third party. Jean greeted me at the door. Looking back, I realize now how much bravery it took for her to attempt a happy face. But no matter how she tried, her smile was a sad one, and that told me more than all the phone calls combined. Something had gone awry with Diane, I could feel it as surely as the ground under my feet, and I needed Jean to tell me what it was.

In the end, she told me more than I wanted to hear, and less of what I wanted to know. She couldn't give me contact information because she didn't have any. She congratulated me on the medical school appointment, and found it a little ironic that once again, Diane and I would be living in the same city. Diane had no phone of her own. All calls between the two were started by Diane, usually on her husband's cell.

"Oh, she's married then," I said, trying to hide my disappointment.

"Yes, unfortunately," Jean replied. "And I get the feeling she's not always free to talk when she's on the phone."

There was no address either, because they "moved around a lot." Diane and I had heard the same about Jean when she was living her lost years in Memphis, but I didn't say that to her. The implications of drug use and all the baggage that went with it was not something I wanted to put on Jean, nor cast upon Diane. I congratulated her and her husband on their success with the farm, thanked her for her time, and said goodbye.

———————

I was in medical school and living in Milwaukee for over three years, my eyes and ears open the whole time, hoping for a glimpse of Diane in a shopping mall, or to hear her voice across a crowded dining room. There was nothing of the sort. Nothing.

It was during this time I remembered Professor Templar. During my undergrad years, I took a single class in Philosophy, but only because I needed the credits. I regarded most of the course as mental masturbation and, by the end of the semester, was ready to flush everything I'd learned down the toilet. Try as I might, there was one lecture that stayed with me, an hour-long monologue by Templar on random events and how they influence our lives. He contended that, "We, as humans, are handicapped by a paradox: our line of sight is a straight line, but life is not. It is a curve, much like Einstein's space-time, and the warp in the fabric of our lives becomes more conspicuous as the mass of our experience grows. Is it any wonder, therefore, that we humans, with our tunnel vision, are constantly flying off course, on tangents as the physicists would say." The professor came in for the big finish. "So that eventually, if our life traveler is not very, very careful, he or she ends up on some detour in the middle of space far from the place he started."

"We see, we plan in a straight line, but life is a curve." With some kind of metaphysical bullshit, he'd explained my life down to a T, and finally I understood.

I had dated a few times in college. Once had a steady that lasted a month or two. But then she transferred to another school and neither of us was up to a pursuit. In medical school, the pattern repeated itself though, due to the demands of the curriculum, with less frequency. Taken as a whole, I was happy, sharing a three-bedroom flat with two other med students, Clare and Brian, both from California, well-healed, and smarter than me. It was a good arrangement. There were days during certain weeks, and weeks during certain months when, depending on which rotations we were on, I'd see very little of one or both.

Some third-year rotations were more difficult than others. The month of Medicine at County General Hospital was among the most intense. The workload was heavy, rounding teams large, and the hours long. The team to which I was assigned had a third-year resident, a first-year resident (also called an intern), two fourth year med students, and finally me, the low man on the totem pole, the third-year med student. Our five-man team did most everything together: made rounds on our roster of patients, went to conferences, ate lunch, took bathroom breaks (only a slight exaggeration).

When a new patient was admitted to the hospital, a physical exam was performed and then dictated into the computer system. This last chore could not be entrusted to a lowly med student, so we sat by and listened while the intern dictated. She'd just finished dictating and was making some notes when the voice of another intern from a surgical team caught my ear. He'd mentioned a social history of IV drug use, alcohol abuse, and smoking. But it was the family history that turned my ear. "From northern Wisconsin. Mother on disability due to depression. Father died in his fifties. Metastatic lung cancer, pneumonia, gunshot wound to the leg. Sister history of drug abuse."

The similarities were too compelling for me to ignore. I was violating about half a dozen privacy regulations, but I did it anyway. I stole a look at the computer screen. The name burned a hole in my brain. Diane Jelusick. Such an odd last name. How many Diane Jelusicks could there be in Milwaukee? And why was she in the hospital in need of a consult from the cardiothoracic surgery team? I couldn't wait until the end of my shift to find out. I broke away from the medical team and shopped around the unit in search of a computer terminal that had been left open. I couldn't open one myself without being tracked by the security software. Finally, I found one unattended at a nurse's station. I opened D. Jelusick's chart and went to personal information. "Age 27. Maiden name: Warren." My vision crackled. A wave of vertigo crashed over me. Thankfully, I had hold of the station pedestal. The dizziness passed. I clicked the physician page and went to the diagnosis section.

My knees buckled.

Her room was on the other side of the unit, number 1122. The devil gripped my chest as I approached the door. I put out my hand, touched the wall, then leaned my butt against the cart guard. For a moment I didn't know if I could do it, if I could go in and see her in this condition. For years, she'd been tucked away in a carefully guarded place in my heart, in a world where her eyes and hair shined even in the dark, she walked in that same irresistible way; a place where no one aged, not even me. The second I walked through door 1122, that carefully crafted little hollow would be gone forever.

But, of course, I had to go in. There was no way I was leaving the building without seeing Diane, whatever the ramifications might be. Signs on the door warned that "Contact Isolation Precautions" were in effect. I put on gloves and a semi-transparent gown and entered the single room. The TV was off, the lights low, there were no visitors. Two IV pumps whirred at the head of her bed. I heard the sounds of her sleeping. I approached slowly, quietly, and stood next to the railing. I looked down at her, and felt a sudden sense of loss and anger.

What had they done to my girl? She'd once been the prettiest thing; the best of what female hormones could design. Now, her bones were easily seen, her flesh somehow wrong like a piece of driftwood tossed on the windward shore wrapped in a hospital gown. What had he done, that Devin bastard? This had to be his fault. My eyes burned. My neck flushed. I had a sudden urge to rip off my isolation gown. But I didn't want to get thrown out of the room by her nurse. There were oxygen prongs in her nose, a sight that bought back memories, unpleasant and sad, of her father. The in-room monitor showed an irregular heartbeat and a low blood pressure, but her oxygen level was holding.

I listened to her breathe, different and somehow the same as I'd remembered. She was covered to her midriff with a sheet and covers, her arms exposed for the IVs. Knowing the diagnosis, I looked from wrist to elbow and saw them, the track marks. For many seconds, I had to turn my eyes away. My teeth clenched.

When I looked back, her eyes fluttered and then opened. I don't think she recognized me at first. It was as if her eyes, still dark but now haunted, were looking right through me to some past she only vaguely remembered; a life she once lived. Her lips moved, "Sam?" but she made no sound.

"Hi, Dee. Yeah, it's me. How's my baby?"

Her eyes were not those I'd remembered, but sunken and dull. Then, at once they were wide and frightened, like those of a little girl. "Sam? Oh, Sam, I lost you." She tried to move her arms. The IVs tugged. I held her hands with mine to settle her down.

"No. No, it's all right. I'm here. Everything's all right, babe."

"Oh, Sam, what did I do?" She groaned. "What did I do. I'm so sorry." She was half crying, half talking at this point, and I didn't know how to comfort her.

"You can tell me all about it," I said. "Later. Later. It's been seven years; can you believe it?"

She looked at me again, the collar of my white coat in partic-ular. "Holy shit, Sam, you're a doctor?"

I flashed her the *Medical Student* scribed on my coat. "No. Not even close."

"You coulda fooled me."

I winked at her. "All I gotta do is keep up the act for another forty years and I got it made."

Finally, she smiled. "You're my first visitor."

"And I'm going to keep coming until they let you out of this place. What about…" I didn't know how to ask this. "Your family?" She didn't have a wedding ring on, but I knew about the marriage.

She looked out the window. "You mean Devin. I haven't seen him for months and I won't see him for ten to twelve."

"Months?"

"Years. He's up in Oshkosh on a drug charge. Don't ask me about it, okay?"

"Okay."

She was willing to tell me the rest of her medical history, which gave me sleepless nights for a week. She was in the hospital for an infected heart valve, and not for the first time. The diagnosis that had buckled my knees. On two other occasions she'd required IV antibiotics. She was also supposed to enter drug rehab both times. She gave a handful of half-assed reasons why the rehab didn't happen, all of them ones I'd heard before from other addicts who'd failed their programs. I didn't call her on it. The time for that would come later. She admitted to me the longest she'd been off heroin in the last three years, not counting time in the hospital, was less than twenty-four hours. My heart ached.

That was going to be past history. That was going to be before I arrived. If it was the last thing I would ever do, I was going to save her. And on a subsequent visit to her room, I told her so. Every night, after work was done, I stopped to see her. She gave her doctors permission to talk to me about her medical history and gave me access to her medical records with one condition, and it was absolute. I was not allowed to call home. No one in her family was to know she was in the hospital. This was true for Ethyl and Ben but especially for Jean. Given everything that had happened between the sisters, especially the effort made by Diane on Jean's behalf when she was alone and in trouble down in Memphis, it only seemed natural to call her, let her know of Diane's situation, and give her the chance to return the favor. For reasons I learned only later, Diane wouldn't allow this to happen. Some bridge had been burned. Neither could I tell my parents for fear they'd let something slip, and it would get back to the wrong ears. She knew my folks were the last to gossip about anything. They had always loved her and I thought, the more support the better. She would not be swayed. It was going to be her and me or just her alone, and that was it. I wasn't fine with it, not by a long shot, but us together was always a negotiation, a work in progress. Sitting in that room I remembered something else—since the day I lost her I'd been looking for my life; while I was with her, I'd been living it. That's what I would hang on to. I was going to start living again.

Her appetite improved a little, especially when I was there. Me with my sandwich-shop bagel and chips. Her with the tray from the kitchen, half of which she tried to pawn off on me so the nurse would think she'd eaten better than she had. Her appetite of old: where had that gone? Though she never weighed more than one hundred fifteen pounds, there was never any question about her getting enough to eat. Forget a meal once in a while, sure; but she'd make up for it on the very next one. Now her weight was hovering below one hundred pounds, and some of that was the water she carried in her puffy ankles, a sign of the heart failure she was battling, a frequent complication of heart valve infections. She hated the diet. No more cheese, crackers, beef jerky and beer, the very meal we shared on Nic's boat all those years ago. I heard about it every day.

The third time around with this valve infection wasn't going to be strike three. She still had youth on her side. After a week of antibiotics and rest, medication adjustments and rehab counseling, she was deemed stable, and ready to go home. But there was no one to go home to. I knew that and tried to be, wanted to be that someone to support her. She blew me off with extreme prejudice. When she said this to me, I was crushed. Luckily, I was sitting at the time, so I was able to hide my profound disappointment. I tried to respond, but the words shriveled in my throat. She had nothing, and I was, apparently, less than nothing. That's how I felt at the time. Someday, perhaps I'll see it a different way. She was embarrassed about her situation and didn't want me to see it. Maybe.

In any case, she refused to give me the address of her apartment. Yes, I could've looked it up in her medical record, but she gave me specific directions not to and, idiot that I am, I respected her wishes. Had I checked it and put it to memory, perhaps I would've been able to live to a comfortable old age before telling this story. Maybe I'd have never told it at all.

Her discharge date happened to be at the end of the month, which coincided with the end of my medicine rotation, and the midpoint of the third year of my medical education. She made a "sacred vow" (Diane, sacred? Really? The most irreverent person I ever knew) to see the cardiologist and make the rehab appointments. I told her I'd known her too long to take it on her word, and that I wanted to meet with her three times a week. She refused to meet at my apartment. At first, she said it was too far out of her way, and the bus service not reliable enough to get her there conveniently. I suspected there were other reasons, but I didn't press her on it. We agreed on a neutral site, a city park about a mile from where I lived. She said she could get there easily on the city bus, but gave me no further details.

"But how are you going to see me three times a week with your schedule?" she asked.

It was then I told her. I had taken a leave of absence from medical school.

## CHAPTER THIRTY

# Gap Year

The first couple of weeks following Diane's discharge were a struggle. We were able to agree on a meeting schedule of Monday, Wednesday, Friday, and a location. She refused to meet at either my place or hers, judging both to be too intimate, and for that reason, too dangerous. At first, we were to meet for an hour, her endurance being the (supposed) limiting factor. She remained during the first week as she'd been in the hospital, very careful not to get caught up with nostalgic topics or reminiscing, especially about the summer of 2013, our exploits, or Max. Now that I look back on it, she seemed willing to put her toe in the water on these topics, but somehow found the water too inviting or maybe beyond what she deserved. And therein lies one of my faults—psychoanalysis after-the-fact. I've still not found a cure for my own affliction.

That's not to say we weren't making progress. During the second week, she had an appointment with her cardiologist, and she agreed to let me come along. She was bright enough to understand what the doctor was saying to her, but she had the sense that this physician had a thinly veiled streak of misogyny. And after sitting in with her, I had to agree.

By then, we had each other's phone numbers, but had not exchanged addresses. I could wait for that and I told her so; I had become a patient man. "After all," I said, "what is a medical education if not an exercise in delayed gratification?"

"What the hell kind of b.s. is that?" she asked. "Are you bragging or complaining?"

"Oh, I'm not complaining." We were on our way back to my car after her doctor's appointment. "I feel lucky to be in med school. It'll be a privilege to be a doctor someday. But if you ask most people when did they have the most fun in their life? Most would say their twenties. We give up our twenties going to school."

"Oh, so that's how you're going to spin this so called 'leave of absence.' Is that what you called it?" She side-eyed me. "You're going to catch up to all your friends. And so on the seventh day, God said let there be a gap year. Is that it? I worry about you, I really do."

We stepped out of the medical building and headed toward the patient parking lot.

She went on. "And I got to tell you, I think you should have told me about this year off crap before you did it."

"Why?" I asked. "It's my career. My decision. It's nothing to do with you."

"It has a lot to do with me."

We crossed the road against the light. "You're not the one going to medical school," I said.

"Do you hear yourself? Are you on this planet?" I was glad to be outside the building because Diane's voice was getting an edge. "Come on, Sam. You never would have dropped out if it wasn't for me, and you know it. I've got enough to worry about. I don't want that kind of shit on my shoulders."

I tried to defuse the conversation by slowing my gait. She slowed with me. I said, "You're making too much of this. I didn't quit. Leave of absence, like I said. There's a big difference."

She stopped and said, "Sure. And what if you decide to make it a permanent vacation? That'll be all you too?"

"Now you've got it."

"Ah huh. Sure."

———————

There came a day in early April when she let me take her to lunch in celebration of my birthday. I couldn't afford anything fancy, so we went to a place a grade or two above a chicken shack where I could order a piece of pie if I wanted, and settled into a booth.

As always, Diane remained emotionally distant, wouldn't even let me sit next to her for the meal. She became easily exasperated when I made this kind of request.

"What are you looking for, 2013?" she asked. "You're living in the past. I'm married, remember?" She flashed a cheap wedding ring, the first time I'd seen it. I think now it wasn't real, but a decoy. A bauble to put me off. "Come on, Sam. I've burned too many bridges. You haven't, okay, fine. But you can't go back either." We had already finished half of our food by this time. I had enchiladas and she had a burger and fries. "And do you know why?"

"Why?"

"Because you don't want to; you just don't know it yet. With everything that's gone down, college, med school, even if I'm not sitting here, Sam, 2013? You can't get there from here. Why would you? You'd be throwing away eight years of work."

"I'm not trying to throw away anything." I put down my knife and fork. "I'm trying to get something back." Why was this so hard? We'd been lovers once. Could time and experience and distance really make such a difference? Couldn't we, in just the time it took to drink a cup of coffee, find the rhythm of two hearts beating together again? I looked at her with as much intensity as I could, then cocked an eyebrow just a bit.

Something changed in her face, but I knew it wasn't what I wanted. She pointed a French fry at me. "Okay, tell me the truth. Why did you drop out of med school?"

"Drop out! I didn't drop out. I told you. Some people take it —"

"Yeah, yeah, yeah, that's not what I mean." She ate the fry. "Why *now*, Sam?"

My stomach was in my chest. "Because... I want to help you."

She threw down her napkin and sat back, her eyes darting about the booth, the restaurant, then back to me. I sensed something inside her was about to erupt, and she didn't know how to stop it. "You could have done that without dropping out. Helping me? You've done that. Why, Sam? Why did you drop out now?"

My neck flushed. My ears burned. "Because... Because I'm still in love with you."

Her eyes darkened, then glistened. "No." She dabbed her eyes with her napkin. "No. Don't say that. Don't you dare say that." She put her hands on the table. Her voice was raspy. "How can you say that? It's not fair. Are you deaf? Do you have eyes? Look. For once in your life look and see what's really... what's in front of you." She banged her fist on the table "You can't hang that on me, Sam. It's not fair."

Suddenly, lunch was over. She grabbed her coat, scrambled away from the table and headed for the front door. I threw thirty bucks on the table and went after her. By the time I got outside the restaurant, she was halfway down the block. I shrugged on my coat and jogged to catch up. When I was close enough to speak to her without yelling, I said:

"Where the hell are you going? I'll drive you back. It's too far to the bus."

She turned on me. "Back off. I can take care of myself."

"What did I say? That I want you and me to be together. Is that a crime?"

She turned and started walking again, though slower than before. I caught up to her, took her by the arm, and spun her around. "Diane! Tell me why you're doing this. I deserve to know."

Tears were in her eyes, but anger in her words. "One. I don't owe anyone anything. Two. I'm married to another man. Three. I've got a hole in my heart—"

"Valve."

"What?"

"The hole is in a valve. There's a difference," I said.

"Whatever the fuck are you talking about?" she asked. "You gonna fix it?"

"Yes."

"No! No, you can't, so shut up and let me finish." She held up four fingers. "Four. I have a place and friends and..." She looked away. "And they're helping..."

"They're helping you what?" I asked.

"They're... And I have..." Her voice softened. She tipped her forehead into my chest. For the first time in many years, I put my arms around what was now a frail, thin frame.

"I'm so afraid," she whispered.

I pulled her closer. "Afraid of what?"

"Everything."

"Afraid of what, Dee?"

She rubbed tears from her face onto my shirt. "Dying," she uttered.

I put my chin on her head. "You're tough. No one knows that more than me. If the devil comes calling, tell him to fuck off."

She turned her head, her cheek now on my chest. "He scares me. I have dreams."

"One step at a time, Dee." I put my hand on her head. "First, stay away from the needle. Your sister did it. You can too." She didn't respond, which worried me. I felt then an emptiness between us, and for the first time I wondered, if the chasm was one which I couldn't fill. In the last eight years, what had I forgotten?

"There's something else I have to tell you."

"All right."

She remained motionless in my arms. "Babe, you can't latch on to me. I'm not going to grow angel's wings. There's no halo to polish here. Never was." She looked up at me. "Are you hearing me?"

Nodding my lips into her thin, frayed hair was the best I could do. She'd called me babe for the first time in seven years, and I was choking up. I couldn't speak. It was a silence more dangerous than I knew.

Then she let go and put me at arm's length. "I'm serious. Don't screw up your life by hooking up to mine."

"You can't mess up—" She put two fingers across my lips to silence whatever objection I was going to make, and shook her head very slowly. She left her fingers there until she was sure the conversation had ended.

We drove back to the park in silence and sat down on the bench, waiting for her bus to arrive. For the first time, she allowed me to sit close to her.

I said, "Listen, forget about this gap year stuff. I'm starting right back in school next year. What difference does one year make? In ten years, none at all. But it means everything right now."

A very sad smile appeared on her face for a moment and then, she looked down and it was gone. "Sam, I'm not Jean. You don't understand that, do you."

I nodded. "No, I know."

She put her hand on my thigh, gave me a sad smile, kissed my cheek and said, "Goodbye, Sam."

"See you Monday."

She walked away, as she did every time we met, to the bus stop at the next corner. A drizzle put a sheen on everything as, once again, I was back in high school history class, and felt the pang of watching her leave, and wondering when I'd see her again. The bus doors opened, she stepped up, showed her pass, and found a seat. She was not one to look back. As the bus pulled away, the rain became a downpour, and I ran for my car.

That was a Friday afternoon. She called and cancelled our next get together the following Monday. She was tired she said, and wanted to rest. She thought she might be coming down with a bug of some kind. I asked if she had taken her temperature. For anyone with her heart history, fever would be a bad sign and reason enough to call the cardiologist or go to the Emergency Department. But she blew me off and said she "knew what that felt like" and was sure she'd be good in a day or two. I didn't agree, but it was for reasons I couldn't say to her. The words coming over the phone were too rounded on their edges, her words running out before the sentence was complete. I'd taken the real Diane to lunch. There was a different Diane on the phone.

Wednesday came. I decided not to call Diane ahead of time. She'd made her feelings known about such "helicopter friend" calls in the past. If she saw my name on her phone, she might not answer. It was an early spring day, one of the nicest we'd had for some time. The robins were back in force and making their welcome racket. Diane was a little late so I perused a couple daffodil beds that were starting to pop, all the while keeping my eye on the bus stop. The next bus came and went, and no Diane.

I sat down again, on the same spot on which I'd waited so many times, and dialed her number. She didn't answer. The call went to voicemail which was full. I redialed numerous times over the next thirty minutes. Two more buses came and went. I stopped dialing and went home.

——————

I still had my County General Hospital ID and my white coat. The stethoscope draped around my neck added a touch of authenticity to my disguise. Walking into the hospital and getting access to a computer terminal was not any different than it had been before I "dropped out" of medical school. I went up to the general medical department on the fourth floor, found an unattended, open terminal, and typed in Diane's name. Three seconds later I had her address on North 35th Street.

The neighborhood was strange to me—I'd never been anywhere near this part of town—and yet eerily familiar. The area had the same feel, the same look I'd seen many years ago in Memphis when we'd gone to pick up Bethany Jean's few remaining personal items from her former address. It was midday on a Wednesday. The day had turned breezy and wall-to-wall cloudy, but not threatening rain. The street was quiet so far as I could see. The address was for an upstairs flat in a broken-down, older home. Sections of the siding were missing or hanging by a nail or two. There used to be a full front porch, but it had fallen, literally, into disrepair and beyond use. Only the four-foot section leading to the two, side-by-side front doors looked safe for foot traffic. The house overfilled the lot, allowing for only a few feet of poorly-kept grass on all sides. I left the white coat in the car. A chain link fence surrounded the property at the outer edge of the lawn. The links were peppered with plastic shopping bags, mailbox fliers, and other fly-aways, plastered there by the wind. The gate was secured with a combination lock, so I jumped it.

The right, front door led to the second floor and was not locked. I opened the door and called, "Hello" up the stairwell, then called again, but there was no answer. The stairs were dusty with a few footprints, the single window illuminating the way cracked and grimy. Beer cans were scattered throughout. The railing was loose and useless, as if it'd been abused many times over. I scaled the steps.

Another door stopped me at the top of the stairs. I knocked and called Diane's name, but heard nothing inside. A mildly sour smell was noticeable, but I thought it was from the cans and stale beer. I knocked again and said, "Hello. Anyone home?"

Just then I heard the other front door open. A black woman about thirty years old stuck her head through the door I'd just come through, looked up at me and said, "You know her? You know Diane?"

"Yeah, I do. Do you know where she is?"

"No, I don'. I ain't seen her for days. No one been up there either. You bes' check on her." She was about to leave.

"Hold on. Do you have a key? The door's locked."

She smirked. "A course I ain't got no key. I don' live there." She almost closed the door.

"Wait! What about the landlord? Can I call him?"

She laughed hard enough to crack the stairwell glass clean away. "Landlord! Honey, you get the landlord a this sorry place, let me know. I got a list for him." And with that, she was gone.

If I left without seeing what was going on inside of Diane's apartment, I'd have been right back the next hour, I knew it. I took a step back and put my shoulder to the door. Then did it again. I was probably assaulting the only place in the whole structure that still had sound construction. Rubbing my shoulder, I took another step back and kicked the door. The molding gave a bit. I kicked again. Wood splintered. One more slam with my shoulder and I was in.

As soon as I stepped in the apartment it hit me; the stench was overwhelming. I opened the first serviceable window I could find, which was in the front room. It was quite cold, so I turned on the heat, a point I left out of my report to the police. I didn't want them or her family to get the "wrong" impression about what had happened. The living room and kitchen were a mess and obviously hadn't been cleaned for weeks. Cartons of various delivery and take-out foods were strewn about, as was the occasional syringe. A handheld propane torch sat on an end table next to a bong. I'd seen enough. I didn't look closely at the kitchen except to be sure Diane wasn't there.

I thought I heard something in the walls. Mice maybe. But no, they scratch and tick. This was louder and coming from a room down the hall. It was a tapping sound, random, like Morse code. Diane! It was Diane and her habit, her tapping fingernails. I'd found her.

I spun out of the kitchen, went down a short hallway, and followed my ears to a small bathroom. There was a sink and commode on the right, closet and bathtub on the left. The mirror over the sink was badly cracked, pieces of it scattered in the sink and on the floor. Dirty ceramic was everywhere, even the bar of soap looked unclean. But no Diane. I looked up. There was a small window high on the far wall. A tree branch waved in the wind and hit the glass in irregular bursts. Tapping. Tapping. Tapping.

At last, my eye caught the shower curtain, pulled shut, enshrouding the tub. My heart sank. There were towels, a hair brush, and a TV remote on the floor, blocking my path. I pushed them away with my foot. My hand was shaking as I raised it to grab the curtain and push it aside. There were three empty vodka bottles and a fresh twelve-pack of beer lying about, but otherwise the tub was empty.

There was only one room left. I turned left out of the bath, my heart in my throat, and went to the bedroom; the room farthest back. The door was half-open. I stepped in and found her there, lying on the bed. She'd been dead for some time, the offending syringe and tourniquet next to her. Then I dialed 911 and held myself together long enough to give the address and a few details. I dropped the phone and opened another window. I looked around the room for a note, checked the drawers in a flimsy chest in search of some clue as to what might have happened here besides the obvious, but found nothing.

Whoever they were sending would probably be only a few minutes, but I didn't know if I could wait in the same room with her or not. Then I saw one other item, a folded piece of paper cradled in her left hand. I reached across and took it from her. The instant I opened it I knew what it was, and it ruined me. My free hand found the wall and I steadied myself. There was no need to reread what I'd found. I refolded the paper and put it in my pocket. I cleared a place on the floor on which I could sit next to the bed. Forearms crossed over bended knees, I propped my chin there and saw a beam of sunlight streaming in the window. How dare it? How dare the sun, on this otherwise overcast afternoon, suddenly illuminate this mournful, lonely scene, mocking the fire that once glowed in her soul? But then, as tears filled my eyes, the rays became like flames consuming the room. She was there, dancing for me in one last goodbye. I blinked and they were gone, the sun and the tears. I was left sitting alone, still searching for a world I finally realized had long ago slipped from my grasp.

# CHAPTER THIRTY-ONE

# Love Letter

I made the call to the next of kin. Jean Warren Manticore answered the phone on the third ring. After the initial shock and grief, she admitted she'd been worried for a long time about the day when this call would arrive. Having been down the same road, she knew the signs, and said, "There but by the grace of God go I."

It was then Jean told me about the Interventions and the Inpatient Rehab stints—two each—all instigated and paid for by Jean. She'd called me to participate in the first intervention but I was on vacation. When reminded, I remembered. I didn't know what the call was about at the time, and finding out later that it was to help Diane get clean, made me sad beyond words. I'll regret that vacation forever, and that I wasn't able to be there for her. The second intervention was run by a professional mediator. It occurred right after the first hospitalization for a heart infection. Rehab followed and right on its heels another relapse. I understood then why Diane didn't want Jean notified of the last hospitalization. She couldn't face Jean again. Couldn't face another intervention, suffer through another rehab. At least that's how I see it now.

Jean made all of the arrangements to have Diane's body transported back home. The coroner had ruled her death an overdose due to fentanyl and heroin. There was no insurance money in play, so no further investigation was requested, and the ruling stood. I was and remain the only person to know the truth.

As regarded the burial, I asked for only one thing from Jean—a

4x4 pillar of pink granite four feet tall engraved with a stalk of corn to be put next to Diane's gravestone with the date July 12, 2013 at the top. I didn't have the money to pay for it then, but promised to reimburse her the minute I had an actual income. She knew it would be many years before that happened, but didn't flinch at the request. She asked about the significance of the corn and the color, and when I explained she was happy to forward me the money. She and Scott were doing well on the farm, and had the resources to do it.

No one knew the truth so no one asked about the true reason for Diane's death. I had to ask myself how could I have been so blind. The answer I told myself most often, because it allowed me to shed an ounce of the blame that burdened my soul since she died, was that my vision of who we were had raced beyond the curve of her life. But, of course, this and any other explanation amounted to rationalization, nothing more. And in the end, I was lost again.

I searched constantly for the right verb. She didn't want me, didn't need me or, perhaps, knew me too well. And for all my medical training, meager as it was, she understood her own diagnosis, felt it more deeply, than I ever could. Even in her drug-addled state, she was more clear-eyed than I was. The shadow of doubt this cast over me grew darker every day, and I wondered whether I was worthy to continue my medical training.

Jean decided on a cremation. I asked for a vial of the ashes, and on a clear day that following summer I took a boat out to the very spot over Finnegan's Hole on Red Wolf Lake where, eight years earlier, she'd help me put the memory of my dead brother finally to rest. It had been just the two of us, on our knees, in the very same fishing boat. This time, I was alone, except for the vial and the paper she'd been clutching in her hand. Eight years earlier I'd dropped my brother's dog tags into the water. Diane's ashes would follow the tags. I undid the cap and gently sprinkled them to the light breeze and depths below.

I whispered a final, lonely, "Goodbye, my love."

The paper was all-together different. It would not follow the tags or the ashes. It wasn't a suicide note. No, not in the usual sense. I did then, and always will, call it what it was: a love letter. It was, after all, primarily in her hand. Yes, two others had written on the page, which consisted mostly of numbers paired to letters, some of which had Mr. Anderson's red check marks next to them. He'd also written a red "D+" next to Diane's name at the top of the page.

The third writer was me. A single line at the bottom of the page, in my sophomoric scribble, "Sorry. I'll do better next time." A love letter from me to Diane, given in return on the last day of her life. She was saving me, I see that now. But then, she always was the tough one.

I wasn't strong enough to keep you, Diane, so you gave me what you could—an unforgettable flame.

She'd kept the note all this time.

Thank you, Diane, for giving it to me.

# Acknowledgments

My editor at Open Books is Kelly Huddleston. I want to thank her for the insight and guidance, suggestions and corrections that this manuscript needed to make it into its final form. Any mistakes or omissions that remain, however, are my own. A shout out too for my friends at Author's Echo. For over twenty years my reading group has kept me inspired and, most important of all, writing. Thanks also to David Ross and Open Books for publishing my work.

And, as always, much love to my family. Indispensable. Priceless. They know who they are.